Dream Girl Drama

Dream Girl Drama

a
novel

TESSA BAILEY

AVON

An Imprint of HarperCollins*Publishers*

DREAM GIRL DRAMA. Copyright © 2025 by Tessa Bailey. All rights reserved. Printed in Italy. No part of this book may be used or reproduced in any manner whatsoever without written permission except in the case of brief quotations embodied in critical articles and reviews. For information, address HarperCollins Publishers, 195 Broadway, New York, NY 10007.

HarperCollins books may be purchased for educational, business, or sales promotional use. For information, please email the Special Markets Department at SPsales@harpercollins.com.

FIRST EDITION

Interior text design by Diahann Sturge-Campbell

Hockey illustration © OSIPOVEV/Shutterstock

Library of Congress Cataloging-in-Publication Data has been applied for.

ISBN 978-0-06-338078-3
ISBN 978-0-06-338077-6 (library hardcover)

25 26 27 28 29 ROT 10 9 8 7 6 5 4 3 2 1

ACKNOWLEDGMENTS

There is a reason I thank the same people every time I write a book, and that is because I couldn't do this without a very special team cheering me on. Thank you to my editor, May Chen, for allowing me to write this *verging*-on-taboo story that neither one of us saw coming. Blame a certain defenseman on the Red Wings for making fleeting eye contact with me at an Islanders game and knocking this whole idea loose. Sending a huge blast of gratitude to independent bookstores for hosting me on various book tours throughout the last year. Meeting readers who are enjoying my books gives me the confidence and encouragement to keep writing. Thank you to Danielle Bartlett and DJ DeSmyter at Avon for all their constant hard work on my behalf. As always, thank you to my husband and daughter for being my motivation and joy. This series is going places I didn't anticipate and couldn't have imagined, so thank you especially to the readers who are down for anything . . . and are willing to suspend their disbelief enough to enjoy a hockey-baseball rivalry igniting at a dog park. I love you!

Dream Girl Drama

CHAPTER ONE

When good things happened to Sig Gauthier, it never failed to surprise him.

But "good" wasn't enough to describe the moment he met Chloe.

No word existed for that.

There was simply an understanding that his life would never be the same—and the life he'd led up to knowing Chloe became a collection of indistinct sounds and shapes, while the present became incredibly clear, like a window being defogged.

There she was.

Eight minutes earlier, he was on his way to the snobbiest goddamn section of Connecticut in existence. Darien held the title for wealthiest town in the state. Elite schools. Sprawling estates. Old money. In other words, not his vibe. Sig wasn't exactly sure why he'd agreed to this dinner with his father and his latest love interest—also known as his richest sucker to date. Normally, he turned down invitations from Harvey Lerner, but after Sig looked up the affluent address, he'd driven the three hours from Boston out of sheer curiosity.

Was Harvey going to swindle this rich woman, too?

If so, it would be a pattern. Sig's own mother claimed Harvey had drained the contents of their bank account and left while Sig was still a baby. Harvey claimed to have changed, that he wanted an authentic father-son relationship with Sig, but Sig never truly believed him. Every once in a while the deeply hidden need for a father-son bond reared its head and Sig agreed to meet with Harvey—and he regretted it every single time. Tonight would be no different.

A rattle in the engine of his 1998 Chevy pickup made Sig sit up straighter.

"Ah, fuck."

He'd heard that sound before. This wasn't going to end well.

In fact, he had about a minute before the old banger he'd been driving since his college days sputtered to a stop. *Damn.* And only three minutes from his destination?

With a quick check of his blind spot, he started to pull over onto the shoulder of the tree-lined road, but a sign caught his attention up ahead. Country Club of Darien.

Sig snorted.

His red, dented-up truck was going to be more out of place in that parking lot than a priest in the penalty box, but he didn't want to risk waiting for AAA on the side of the road. The sun was going down and there were too many blind curves. Someone could easily slam into him. Better to wait it out in a lot.

"Guess I'm going to miss caviar and gimlets in the conservatory," he muttered, taking a right at the sign heralding the country club since 1957. As he slowed to a stop in an available spot on the farthest edge of the lot, he whistled long and low, observing the club through his rearview. It was something out of a movie. Flickering lanterns and sparkling fountains and white pillars. Tennis courts, valet parking, a golf course. Probably an underground cigar room.

Even the air tasted expensive.

In fact, Sig would be shocked if a parking attendant didn't ask him to get his ratty ride away from these feats of German engineering asap. And they were welcome to try.

As a two-time NHL all-star, Sig wasn't easy to move.

Once the Bearcats offered him a new contract, he'd probably be able to afford the most expensive car in this lot, just like the corporate lawyers and trust fund babies drinking Macallan while overlooking the back nine—but he *still* wouldn't want one.

Sig unplugged his phone from the charger and looked down at the screen, cursing when he saw the dreaded empty battery icon. One percent? He'd had the damn thing plugged in the entire ride. Maybe he shouldn't be shocked that his frayed—and discontinued—cigarette lighter charger had finally stopped working, but it couldn't have picked a worse time.

The phone went ominously dark and Sig dropped his head back against the seat. "This is on you, man. You shouldn't have come." Without looking, he tossed his lifeless phone onto the passenger seat. "Should have stayed in Boston."

Didn't he know by now that bad shit happened near his father?

There was no choice but to walk into that mirage of wealth and ask to use the phone.

Or a charger. Just until he was able to put a call through to AAA.

Jesus, he couldn't think of anything worse than venturing into this playground for one percenters. Except maybe sniff testing everyone's gear after an overtime game. What other option did he have, though?

Blowing out a breath, Sig retrieved his phone and pushed open the driver's-side door, peeling his six-foot-two frame off the leather seat, stretching in the darkness while he considered the brightly lit club.

Just get it over with.

He kicked the door shut with a rusted shriek and started toward the valet, his bootsteps loud on the asphalt. The two dudes in royal blue jackets watched him approach warily, but he knew instantly when one of them recognized him.

A hockey fan—thank God. That would work in his favor.

"Gentlemen." Sig greeted them with a nod. "Having a little car trouble and my phone just gasped its last breath. Do either one of you have a charger? Or a phone I could use?"

"Sig. Gauthier, right?" One of the young men approached with his hand extended and they shook. "I'm Benny. Oh man. What are you doing in Darien?"

"Making a huge mistake, probably. About that charger . . ."

"There is a strict no phone policy while we're on the clock. Everything is in my locker." The poor kid looked sick about it. "Uh . . . crap. I don't know what to do." He took on a conspiratorial tone. "They won't even let you use the bathroom if you're not a member. Basically, you might as well be invisible."

"How cool," Sig deadpanned. "Maybe you could make the call for me?"

The guy visibly started to sweat. "I'm not supposed to leave my post, Mr. Gauthier—"

"Sig."

"Holy shit, Sig. That goal against the Red Wings last week? I fucking—"

The other valet hissed at him. "Dude. Language."

"Sorry." Benny shifted from left to right in his immaculate white tennis shoes. "Could I get an autograph?"

"Sure."

Sig rolled the stiffness out of his neck while the kid fumbled for a pen and an unused valet ticket, laughing in disbelief when Sig laid down a quick signature, before getting his mind back on the problem at hand. "Look, Benny. I'm just going to walk in. I'll tell them you tried to stop me."

"Badass," whispered the hockey fan. "Exactly what I'd expect."

"Nice meeting you, kid." Sig was already jogging up the steps. Before he'd even opened the door, he locked eyes with the suited employee behind the reception desk, the man's expression grow-ing progressively pinched as Sig drew closer. This was going to be fun. "Hey, man. I need a charger or a phone. Your choice."

The man gave a sudden broad smile. "I'll just need to see your member ID."

Sig grinned. "We both know I don't have one."

"Well, then I'm afraid I'll have to go with option C. Neither."

"Clever." Sig propped his elbow on one of many white pillars in the lobby. "Look, I didn't choose to break down outside your club, but here we are. One phone call and I'll be on my way."

"I'm afraid I can't—"

"Oh, *there* you are!"

That was the first time he heard Chloe's voice. Eight minutes after his truck started to shit the bed. His bones just knew it had been eight minutes—he made a living keeping track of the clock without shifting focus from the game—and everything within that parameter of time had led him there. To the right place.

He just fucking *knew*.

Before he even turned around.

But when he *did* turn around? He almost got down on his knees, right in the middle of that lavish lobby. She was that damn . . . enthralling.

Yeah, fine, she was a hot blonde dressed in a pleated, white tennis skirt, which was apparently his newest and deepest fetish. Somehow, though, her looks were the least of what stopped his breath. How about: she fucking floated? Had to be his imagina-tion, right? But that's how he registered her graceful movements. Even the way she blinked was elegant, those long eyelashes sweeping down to hide lively blue eyes, before gracing the world with them again. She had this magical fucking smile that made Sig feel like he'd been socked in the solar plexus.

Holy . . . holy shit.

Who is this?

"I've been looking everywhere for you." She laughed, laying a hand on Sig's arm and squeezing. "Play along," she mumbled out of the corner of her mouth.

Now, look. Sig was normally nimble enough to jump in on a gag without so much as a wink, but her touch made him drunk. Instantly. He couldn't have remembered his own address, much less play along, as she'd requested. Play along with what?

The blond goddess turned her amused smile on the front desk clerk who blushed bright red in response. "Hamish, you dear man! You found him. This is my childhood friend, Ivan. We were in diapers together. Can you believe it? He wandered off, but *you* found him. Oh, thank goodness. I can't wait to tell the management how helpful you continue to be, Hamish."

Dude's chest was inflating like a balloon. "You're very welcome, Ms. Clifford, but—"

"I'm just going to take him to the lounge, my dear. I'll keep a better eye on him going forward." A sudden twinkle in her eye said she had a delicious secret. "Your hair looks even fuller lately, Hamish. I've been meaning to tell you that for ages."

"All thanks to the leave-in conditioner you recommended, Ms. Clifford—"

She pouted at Hamish, and Sig heard static snaps in his brain. "How many times have I begged you to call me Chloe?"

"Oh, I couldn't," Hamish blustered.

Sig tuned out.

Chloe. Chloe Clifford.

Perfect fit. Sort of whimsical, but classy as hell.

Her hand was still on his arm. The man had called her "miss," but Sig still checked for a ring, because something inside of him needed to be doubly sure. The appropriate finger was bare. Not her wrist, though. It had a string of diamonds around it—and he had a feeling they were equally real as the heart going end over end like a boomerang in his rib cage.

Wake up.

This is important.

She'd asked him to play along. For some reason, this woman had decided to save him and he was standing there like a lobotomized ape. "Uh, yeah." He cleared his throat hard, hitting Hamish with a look of chagrin. "Sorry, I forgot to mention I was Chloe's guest."

"My *guest*," she echoed, patting his arm. "Yes. An esteemed one."

"Ah, no need to flatter me, Chlo."

Her eyes sparkled a little brighter. With humor. "Oh, *that* old pet name. No one has called me that since—"

Sig snapped his fingers. "That long weekend we spent on the Sound."

Chloe sighed dreamily. "You were just learning to sail."

"And you ate *way* too many oysters."

Their fake laughter was nearly identical.

Hamish had turned green. "Well." He folded his hands very precisely on the front desk. "You certainly know your way to the lounge. Please excuse me if I didn't treat your esteemed guest as I should have."

"You're excused, Hamish," Sig said, winking at the other man.

Murder flashed briefly in Hamish's eyes, but he hid it quickly. "Have an exceptional evening."

"We shall, but only thanks to you, dear man," Chloe said effusively, linking her arm through Sig's and guiding him across the immaculate lobby, Sig leaving boot prints in the gray carpeting, his pulse hammering in his ears. Was he going somewhere he would be *alone* with this person? Was she always so trusting of strangers? "Well, I, for one, think that performance calls for a bottle of stolen champagne," she whispered near his shoulder. "Don't you? We can toast to our fake memories of the Sound while we wait for your phone to charge."

"Make it a bottle of beer and I'm in."

She squinted thoughtfully. "I don't know where they keep the beer. I've only ever stolen champagne."

"I'll suffer through it, I guess." She was leading him into a room full of couches and a full bar, soft music playing. A pool table lit by a chandelier. Holy high rollers. "What made you help me out like that, Chlo?"

"Well." He already loved the way Chloe squared her shoulders, shimmying them up and down, as if settling in for story time. "I was leaving through the tennis courts, and I saw you being nice to the valet. Not enough people are nice to them, you know! And I knew Hamish was going to stonewall you, so I circled back and intervened." She tilted her head curiously. "Why did that valet want your autograph? I couldn't hear that part."

"I'm a hockey player."

She gasped. "A famous one?"

"Only to people who watch hockey, I suppose. To everyone else, I'm just crashing the country club."

"You *were* crashing it, too." She clucked her tongue in mock reproof. "Hamish has *never* been spoken to in such a manner."

"He'll live."

A smile spread across her gorgeous mouth to reveal a perfect row of pearly whites. "You're going to be fun to get drunk with, I think, Mister . . ."

"Gauthier. Sig Gauthier."

She reared back slightly, nose crinkling. "Oh. That name *does* sound weirdly familiar. I must have heard it while flipping past *SportsCenter*."

"Past it, huh? Not a sports fan?"

"Does tennis count?"

"Nah."

She laughed, and he smiled enough to notice his facial muscles shifting. Stretching. Damn. Damn. Beautiful *and* fun *and* quick. He suddenly couldn't care less if he made it to dinner tonight. He'd let his phone charge well past 100 percent, too. Just sitting there talking to this girl. Looking at her. There was something big and scary happening inside of his chest that he couldn't name or explain. Only that he wanted, needed, to let it happen.

Somehow, he knew that she wasn't a choice.

"We'll sit here, since it's the closest to an outlet." Chloe indicated that he should take a seat on a leather couch the color of whiskey when it's held up to the light. She rummaged in her purse a moment and took out a white phone charger, kneeling down to plug it into the wall and holding out her hand for his phone, giving him a riveting view of Chloe from behind. "You'll be back up and running in no time."

His gaze traveled up the backs of her thighs. "I don't seem to be in a rush anymore."

"Hmm. I bet." She leaned sideways and lifted her chin to look over his shoulder. "I need to wait for the bartender to turn his back so I can steal our drinks."

"Why don't I just buy us some drinks?"

"Money doesn't exchange hands here. That's considered garish," she explained matter-of-factly. "It's all included in the membership fee."

"Out of pure curiosity, about how much is that fee?"

"Oh. Huh." She blinked. Frowned. "I have no idea."

Okay, so she was *that* kind of rich. The kind where she didn't even feel the probable six-figure deduction from her bank account on a yearly basis. Sig had money, but his star had significantly risen since he'd signed his initial contract with the

Bearcats—and he'd definitely been undervalued on his way *into* the league. Hopefully soon, chances were that he could belong to this stuffy-ass club, if he so chose. But would he ever? Fuck no.

Right?

Sig had grown up dirt-poor, thanks to his father, but even now that he was financially comfortable, he still shunned the finer things. Didn't want them and *definitely* didn't need them. An hour ago, Sig wouldn't have believed there was a woman alive who could convince him that a membership card to this place was worth the cash. But hell if he wasn't considering the opposite now. Along with the bare legs that flashed as she sat down on the couch beside him, the hem skimming high, so blessedly high, before she tugged down the white pleats closer to her knees. Crossed her shiny thighs.

Sig swallowed a fist-sized knot. "All right, if drinks are included with a membership, why don't you just go ask for a bottle of champagne?"

"It tastes better when it's an ill-gotten gain."

"You fit right in with the bankers who probably belong to this place."

She flashed him a grin. "It's not that I enjoy ripping anyone off. It's just that . . ." She looked around the lounge and he could tell she'd seen it thousands of times before. "I just try and take some excitement wherever I can. My days are scheduled very meticulously. Early morning practice, followed by lunch with some acquaintance or another. More practice. Followed by tennis lessons—"

"You keep saying practice. Practice for what?"

"I play the harp. I'm a harpist." She fluttered her fingers for emphasis, then proceeded to look at them as if they were foreign objects. "Let me ask you something. What is the point of being labeled a prodigy if I have to practice all the time? Doesn't prodigy mean I just get to show up and be amazing?"

"Do you want me to call one of my harp prodigy friends and ask them for you?"

A laugh burst out of her, satisfying something very deep in his chest. "Are you a hockey prodigy?"

"God no, I had to work my ass off. *Now* I get to show up and be amazing."

She huffed her lips up into a half smile. Those blue eyes ran laps around his face, like she wanted to see inside of his head. Or maybe surprised to find that he was unexpected to her. And he liked that. He liked being something unknown for her, the way she seemed to be for him. "I think I might like to watch you play hockey sometime, Mister Gauthier."

"Come to Boston. I'll let you watch me do whatever you want."

For long moments, she simply stared at him, as if trying to categorize or figure him out but not being able to quite do so. Eventually, her gaze drifted down to his mouth and hung out there, slowly meandering back up to make eye contact. "Is it very forward and extremely soon if I say I'm attracted to you?" she whispered.

"I'm only pissed I didn't get to say it first." At some point, they'd gravitated closer together on the couch. Though it was hard to say who'd made the move, their thighs were now pressed together, bodies turned slightly, his head tipping down toward hers from above. "I think I might like to watch you play the harp, Miss Clifford."

"Well, we're just a couple of people wanting to watch each other do things, aren't we?"

"Looks that way."

"I have somewhere to be tonight."

His right eye twitched. "You got a boyfriend, Chlo?"

She pursed her lips. "Would you steal me away if I did?"

This was no time to lie. "In a heartbeat."

Her pupils dilated, lips parting on a quiet laugh.

Briefly, her attention ticked left. "The bartender just left to get ice. I'm going to make my move on that bottle of champagne, because I feel myself on the verge of making impulsive decisions."

Sig quirked a brow. "And the champagne is going to stop you?"

"No," she breathed, rising fluidly to her feet. "It's going to help me make excuses for my behavior."

Bemused and horny and frankly, in awe, he watched her butt twitch the whole damn way to the bar, his cock turning stiff as a mallet in his jeans. Sig wanted desperately for this to be a wild, cosmic attraction thing. A lightning strike of lust. Because these unknown feelings of kismet and possessiveness and fascination that she'd inspired in him so quickly were scary as shit.

But Chloe turned at the bar and gave him a look of conspiratorial mischief and winked. Then, slick as a cat burglar, she draped herself soundlessly over the bar, reached down, and landed on her feet again with a bottle in hand, sticking her tongue out and making the universal symbol for *rock on*. And his heart lodged permanently behind his jugular.

This was more than lust at first sight.

He didn't have a name for the alternative yet.

But the night was young, right?

CHAPTER TWO

Maybe I'm dreaming.

She'd taken a line drive tennis ball to the forehead and the paramedics were loading her onto a stretcher right now. She wasn't *really* sitting in the lounge with the most casually intense man she'd ever met in her life. It was all an illusion.

But when she sat back down beside him and the cool, ultra-smooth leather kissed the backs of her thighs and he draped his arm along the back of the couch behind her, the warm shiver that snaked all the way down to her toes was very real.

Who was this man?

He'd made it known that he was interested in her, like *really* interested—and he did it without making her uncomfortable, which was not easy. At all. Especially considering his size. And his *presence*. His rough-edged charisma took up the entire room, let alone the couch. When she'd watched him stride confidently toward the valet earlier and stop to acknowledge his fan, he'd literally frozen Chloe in her tracks. Sig had accepted those compliments from the valet without any false humility, just an air of security. In himself, his abilities, who he was.

This man had grown into himself.

Had only the tiniest speck of self-doubt. She'd glimpsed it in his eyes when he looked around at the lavish lounge. When he'd registered the luxury of the leather as he sat down. That touch of humility had been so small she almost missed it, but there was something extremely attractive about it. The fact that this self-assured person seemed to find her equally compelling . . . it made her feel awake. And secure.

Excited.

Also, *my goodness*, he was a smoke show.

Something about the way he wore a T-shirt suggested he took it off multiple times a day. In his bedroom, in the locker room, prior to collapsing into sleep at midnight. Clothed was not his natural state. A shirt was a formality. He was six feet, some odd inches of athletically honed muscle, thick in some places, trim in others, and there was a hint of cockiness about him that tended to turn her off in other men, but not this one.

Perhaps because, unlike the men of her acquaintance, he'd earned it himself?

Without removing his attention from her, Sig took the bottle from her hands, unwound the wire from the neck, and popped the cork. Barely a sound escaped because he muffled it with his, wow, gigantic hands. Then, tossing a casual look toward the bar, he tipped the bottle to her lips, his golden brown gaze fastened to her mouth while she took the first sip. Two sips, three. She kept going because she enjoyed him quenching her thirst, the way he swallowed hard while looking at her throat.

Seriously, what in the Connecticut heck was happening here?

Her toes were curled in her sneakers, her thighs flexing involuntarily.

A pulse tick-tick-ticked at the base of her neck, in her wrists, in her chest—and it accelerated the longer they stared at each other.

Finally, he took the bottle from her lips and brought it to his own, gulping deeply and wincing at the taste.

"Not a fan?" Chloe asked, laughing.

"There's no flavor," he grunted. "It's just a bunch of carbonation."

"The bubbles are what make it a celebration."

He reached forward, setting the bottle down on the low pink-quartz table in front of them, before leaning back into his manspread. "You let me know when you want more."

Chloe dug the fingers of her right hand into the leather couch cushion, hoping to distract the rest of her body from the sudden onslaught of giddy heat. *You let me know when you want more.* She had no right liking that so much—the assumption that he would oversee her consumption of the drink. She didn't need him to do that. But she . . . wanted him to?

Simply put, his honest brand of arrogance turned her on.

This was not the typical brand of trouble she looked for at the country club.

No, she specialized in . . . stolen liquor.

Playing harmless pranks.

Going topless in the spa.

Sig screamed Big Problem . . . and yet she continued to sit there, growing more and more fascinated as champagne bubbles zipped around her head and his heat surrounded her. "Do you like living in Boston? Is that where you grew up?"

"No, I'm from Minnesota. Just outside Minneapolis. Went to college in Michigan. But Boston has been home for six years. It's . . . yeah, I guess I consider it my home now."

"What is it like?"

"Depends on the neighborhood, but it's loud and busy. Congested. Kind of messy at times. But it's got a lot of heart. The *most* heart, actually." He thought for a second. "On a Sunday afternoon, when there's a game on, the whole place kind of hums. Everyone's got a little bit of a buzz on, and you can walk down the street and hear whistles and cheers going off on everyone's televisions. Laughter. It's a good town. I love it."

Chloe's heart raced, as it often did when she thought about

leaving home, fleeing the sheltered bubble of Darien, and experiencing an entirely new world. How scary it would be, but how rewarding at the same time. In fact, she'd been thinking of it to the point of distraction lately. "You make it sound magical."

Sig studied her face. "It is. You'd fit right in."

"Really?"

"Yeah," he said, like she was crazy to ask. Or doubt.

And his—perhaps premature—faith in the fact that she could make it in Boston, in a whole ass new city, made her want to confide in him. To reveal something about herself. Something she'd told her mother—on several occasions, only to be casually shut down. "There is a conservatory in Boston that I've dreamed of attending for so long. Berklee. They invited me once to play for the faculty and afterward, even after the tiniest glimpse, I couldn't stop thinking about the people, the place. The students who came and went as they pleased. And . . . I applied. Secretly. Almost a year ago now." She whispered the last part, as if her mother might overhear. "But . . . the dean said I have a standing invitation. At no cost."

"That's . . . incredible. Damn." Sig faced her a little more fully. "So you *have* been to Boston?"

Chloe shook her head. "I've been inside of a town car, a hotel room, and an auditorium in Boston. I didn't go walking or exploring."

"Did you want to?"

She nodded. And suddenly, she needed another draw of champagne.

A groove formed between his dark brows.

Before she could ask, he lifted the bottle from the table and tilted the chilled glass against her lips, her nipples slowly winding into stiff peaks over the possibility that he could read her needs so accurately.

And fill them.

"How old are you, Chlo?" he asked, searching her face.

"Twenty-five," she murmured.

He nodded. Wet his lips. Leaned in. "Then what's keeping you from Boston?"

"Nothing," she whispered, inching closer, until she could feel his warm breath on her mouth. She *wanted* to spill everything to him, to this man who seemed to have the kind of capabilities and self-reliance she'd only ever dreamed about. She longed to tell Sig that she didn't know how to begin taking care of herself. How the very thought of waking up alone and having to fend for herself was so intimidating it gave her chills. A man like this wouldn't be able to comprehend such debilitating dependence on money and security, though.

Would he?

"Say it," Sig said.

"Say what?"

"The thing you're not sure you want to tell me."

This moment, this night, officially felt like a dream. There was nothing but his eyes. The warmth of his presence. The quiet lull of their voices. The unique . . . knowingness between them.

"My mother sent me to music camp when I was six. On opening night, I watched a demonstration of the harp. I saw it played once. Later that night, I snuck back into the instrument room and . . . I just knew how to play. It was like a language I'd learned and forgotten, but it all came back to me." She wet her lips. "They caught me on the security camera and it was sent to my mother. And then all her friends. It was even featured on the news."

He laughed quietly. "Damn."

"Yes." The longer she hesitated to say the rest, the more her pulse pounded. "It's funny, though, when you're a prodigy in one thing, it doesn't necessarily make you good at anything else. Whether it's tennis or schoolwork or making friends or . . . just plain common sense. And I think people were disappointed by that. By me not being very . . . well rounded. You know?"

"No," he intoned, shaking his head. "I don't know. I can't imagine you disappointing anyone."

They moved closer to each other simultaneously, neither one of them seeming to be conscious of it. "I've got the harp and . . . I've gotten comfortable with that being all. I've gotten too comfortable, maybe, and that's easy to do when . . ."

"You have money."

He understood. Maybe he couldn't relate, but he wasn't judging her.

Still, the extended state of vulnerability was making her feel jumpy.

"Anyway . . ." Chloe ordered her upper lip to curl flirtatiously. "Why would I go to Boston when I'm having so much fun being driven around by a chauffeur, stealing champagne, and making trouble in Darien?"

"I don't know." Slowly, he closed that final inch, hesitated, finally brushing their lips together, turning her insides the consistency of clouds. "Maybe you could find a different kind of fun in Boston," he said, his voice noticeably deeper, his left hand lifting to cradle her cheek, his thumb pressing to her chin, as if he planned on tugging it down. While kissing her. So he could use his tongue?

Did she want that?

Yes. God, more than anything. The anticipation for him was so strong and familiar already, it felt like it had always existed.

"Can I kiss you, dream girl?"

Head. Spinning. "You haven't even called the tow truck yet."

"Fuck the tow truck."

"Yeah," she breathed.

"Excuse me," said a voice that belonged to neither of them. "Ms. Clifford?"

The golden moonbeam shower around them fizzled and vanished. Who would intrude on something that felt so momentous? Chloe's head moved like it was underwater, her fuzzy brain finally registering that the bartender was standing behind the couch, to her left. "Oh." She could still feel Sig's eyes locked on her profile. And was that the sound of his jaw popping? "Yes?"

"I couldn't help but notice you're enjoying a bottle of champagne, which is *fine*, of course. You're most welcome to do so. I just need you to sign for it."

She blinked. "You do?"

"Yes, in order to bill the appropriate parties."

"Aren't drinks part of the membership?" Chloe asked.

The man was already nodding. "Most of them are complimentary, Ms. Clifford. But this time you happened to grab a special edition Möet Impérial." He paused. "That's a two-thousand-dollar bottle of champagne."

Chloe's mouth fell open as she turned back to face Sig. "And you didn't even like it."

When Sig's eyes flooded with amusement, Chloe decided she'd kiss him really good.

Tonight.

As soon as possible.

"Your signature, Ms. Clifford," prompted the bartender.

"What happens if I don't sign it?"

"Well . . . I don't know, really. I'll probably just ask you to sign it tomorrow."

"Right. Because I'm always here. I'm never not here." She banished intrusive thoughts of endless routines. Cycles without cease. "Stalling sounds good. It'll give me time to figure something out." She chewed her lip. "My mother is not going to be happy about this," she whispered to Sig, panic beginning to trickle into her bloodstream. "Alcohol makes a woman's face look as bloated as a waterlogged corpse—she said that to me just this morning. When she's not happy with me, life becomes very difficult. Even more restrictive than it already is. And you heard him, he said '*this time*, you happened to grab a special edition,' meaning they know about all the other times I stole."

"Of course, they know. Do you think *you* go anywhere unnoticed?"

She batted her eyelashes at him. "Are you saying I'm pretty?"

"No, I'm saying you're fucking beautiful."

Her pulse scattered. "If I ran out the door right now, would you run with me?" she whispered.

"Set the pace, Chlo. I can keep up."

Big kisses were in his future. Big.

"On the count of three." She reached out and curled her fist around the neck of the champagne bottle, noticing the way Sig eyeballed his charging phone, as if judging the distance. "One, two . . . three."

They lunged in different directions—Chloe toward the glass patio door that led to the golf course, Sig for his phone and her charger, ripping it out of the wall without missing a beat. Even though Sig took a detour, he still managed to reach the door at the same time as she did, which was her first lesson about hockey players. They're fast as hell. Also, apparently, they were down to make some trouble. And that's what they did, sprinting across the golf course holding their possessions and laughing loud enough to wake the dead.

Was this a date?

Sure, she hadn't exactly been on *hundreds* of them, but this? It was making her puny, prior experience feel like child's play. Or perhaps a foreword. A note left and forgotten once the real story starts to unfold.

"Where are we running to?" he asked, keeping pace beside her. Although she had a feeling he could probably run twice as fast.

"I've never been to the Carolinas," Chloe shouted. "Let's head there."

His laugh echoed across the dark, empty golf course and she couldn't wait any longer to kiss him. Maybe because he'd not only put up with her shenanigans but seemed to be enjoying them. Maybe because he laughed at her jokes. Or maybe just because she felt unexplainably drawn to him in a way that made her chest feel odd and tight. She'd always been one to follow a whim, but this wasn't one of those times. This was a time unlike any other.

She slowed to a jog behind the clubhouse and took a long sip of champagne for courage, before turning around and finding Sig outlined by a purple sky, rugged and intense and knowing. That's what it was about him—he seemed to know this was the moment, because they both took a giant step toward each other and collided, his head dipping down, slanting and elevating her expectations to a degree that would never be met again.

Maybe not by anyone but him.

Chloe had been kissed before, mostly by guys that she'd known since elementary school and not so subtly nudged into dating later in life by her mother, because they "came from good stock." Well, apparently, they'd never come from a family of good kissers.

Sig did.

Lord God Almighty, he did.

He crushed the strands of her hair in his hands and loomed above her, which should have led to an aggressive kiss, but it didn't. It led to a slow rocking together of lips, a teasing lick of his tongue, an appreciative sound . . . and oh, she opened, she let him press his tongue inside her mouth and lick it left to right, the growling upward movement of his kiss dragging Chloe up onto her toes. And she lost it. She simply lost it. Burrowed her fingers into his thick, wild hair and moaned her enjoyment at him, arching her back—and only *then* did he get aggressive—and that consideration made her feel safe, made her feel heard and seen and appreciated.

Hot and dainty, too. Like a sexy lion tamer.

There was a good eight- or nine-inch height difference between them and yet, she could feel the tight coil inside of him, the way he tried to keep a lid on his basest impulses. To keep the pace without going too far. She could sense all of that in him and God, God, she just wanted to climb him for it. For being hungry, but respectful. Proactive, a man who takes initiative, confident enough to know she wanted to be kissed, but not overly so. Not so much that he'd press that advantage.

Sig Gauthier.

She could have gone on kissing him for days. Weeks.

But the need in both of them eventually began to spike.

They broke away to pant, drag in breath, and dive back in, hands beginning to roam. Hers got adventurous first, to be fair. She clawed at his T-shirt and scrubbed her palms down to his belt buckle, making him hiss.

"Can I touch you under your—"

"Anything. Anywhere. Any fucking thing you want."

"Thank you," she managed, sliding her palms up his bare abdomen while he licked his lips. Watched her. Flexed his stomach. Closed his eyes when she rode her hands over his pecs, letting his head drop back a little. "You're incredible."

His eyes were a little glazed when he leaned back down, settling his mouth on top of hers, breathing. Breathing. "I'm coming on too strong. I know I am. But I'm begging you to take me home and say that again while I'm fucking you, Chloe." He gripped the outside of her thigh and massaged it, before letting his hand ride up just beneath the hem of her skirt. "If you're not ready for that, we can keep this little skirt on while you ride my face. I'll be blessed either way."

Oh wow. *Oh wow.*

Newly bloomed hormones were popping up like greenery in spring.

Was he rude to say those things? Out loud?

Maybe. Maybe so. She wished he'd keep talking forever, though.

Take me home and say that again while—

"Home," she gasped, a bucket of cold water dousing her from above. "Oh my gosh, I'm supposed to be home right now. There's a dinner." She broke from his embrace, spinning in a circle. "I promised . . . I was supposed to be home in time to take a shower. Oh shit."

Chloe remained suspended in animation for a few seconds, considering the consequences of missing the important dinner during which she'd be meeting her mother's new boyfriend. If there was anything on this green earth worth courting her mother's passive aggression, it was this man, but her mother had been calling from St. Tropez for weeks raving about this new guy. It sounded serious. Chloe had promised several times that she'd not only be there, but she'd also be on her best behavior—and letting her mother down would only lead to weeks of silent treatment.

"I'm sorry, but I have to run."

She turned on the heel of her sneaker and took two jogging steps, before her feet were suddenly dangling in the air. Sig's forearm was looped around her midsection. He'd lifted her clear off the ground and she hadn't even heard him move.

"You're so *fast*, Sig Gauthier," Chloe praised, patting his forearm.

"Yeah, thanks." He hugged her back against his chest, that truly magical mouth moving against her ear. "You weren't going to leave without giving me your number, were you, Chlo?"

She thought back twenty seconds. "I guess I was."

"Nah." She could feel him digging for his phone with his free hand. "Let's hear it."

He couldn't see her smile. Maybe that's why she let it explode across her whole face.

She recited her number. He called it, his muscles relaxing slightly when the chimes went off noisily in her purse. "Go to your dinner. I've actually got something, too. But you're going to call me afterward. I need to see you again. Tonight."

Remembering the way he kissed, a shiver passed through her. "I live with my mother."

"Don't worry, I'll find us a nice place." His open mouth rode over the slope of her shoulder. "I wouldn't lay this body down in anything but the best sheets, Chlo. The only rough thing you're going to feel is me."

She bit her lip to catch a moan. "You really have a way with words."

"I don't usually use them this much. It's . . . you." He wrapped his other arm around her, hugging her from behind and she felt an unexpected prick in her throat. "It's you, okay? Don't blow me off."

"I won't," she whispered. "I couldn't."

"Good."

He nuzzled the crown of her head, hesitating briefly before loosening his arms.

Chloe blew a kiss over her shoulder and jogged for the parking lot, already counting the minutes until she saw Sig Gauthier again. There was no way this dinner was going to be a fraction as interesting as him and what he made her feel.

Oh, but she was wrong.

CHAPTER THREE

Sig pulled up to the lavish estate and raked a hand down his jaw, hoping to drag the dopey smile off his face. No chance of that, though. Hell, smiling was the last thing he'd expected to be doing before a rare meeting with his father, but here he was.

Chloe Clifford.

Son of a bitch.

Meeting the girl of his dreams wasn't on his bingo card when he woke up this morning. He didn't have some mental archetype of how his dream girl would look. How she would act. Make him feel. None of that. Up until the lobby of that country club, he'd been fine being single. Getting a little action on an as-needed basis, but never feeling pressed to commit.

But Chloe?

Yeah, he already knew he'd commit to that. Fucking *hard*. She already wanted to come to Boston, didn't she? He'd just do the long-distance thing until she decided it was right for her. And he'd *make* it right. He'd bring her down to Boston and show her everything. Every corner. She didn't think she was built to thrive there? He'd help her believe the opposite.

Sig unbuckled his seat belt, because the stiff nylon was adding pressure to a chest that already felt like a powder keg. He rubbed at the twinge at the center, but it wouldn't go away. Something happened tonight. Something important. God, he couldn't wait to see her again.

Might as well admit it, too. He couldn't wait to fuck her.

He shook his head on a pained laugh as his cock started to fill and extend, testing the denim fly of his jeans. Not a good time for a hard-on, but he'd been fighting one since she'd opened her mouth for his tongue and rubbed her belly against him. She liked making trouble outside of bed. What kind would they make inside of one? The goddamn filthy kind, if Sig had his way. He didn't know any other way to fuck and something told him she wouldn't mind being thrown into positions those country club boys could only dream about.

Get this dinner over with.

Track down the girl. No. *Lock* down the girl.

Take her back to Boston tomorrow, if she was willing. If not, he'd buy a new truck so he could make the three-hour trip as often as necessary. It wouldn't be easy during the season, but nothing worthwhile was easy, was it?

When Sig was ten, his mother couldn't afford to buy him hockey gear. With the tryout approaching in just a few weeks, he'd gotten on his bike and tracked down every secondhand, beat-up pad, helmet, and jersey in the county. He'd actually tried out for the under 11s team in mismatched skates. And when the other kids had made fun of him in front of his mortified mother, he'd informed them they were all pampered pussies who needed their parents to take them shopping. No one had bothered him after that—and Sig had kept that attitude all his life. One he'd developed for his mother's benefit, but over time, had become his method of thought. Of dealing with his lack of funds or his lowball contract.

Occasionally, he looked at one of his higher-paid opponents and thought it would be nice to make eight figures. To buy a vacation house in Hawaii. Drive a Porsche SUV. But his mind would come back with *but you don't need it.*

Parting with his faithful ride would suck, but breaking down again between Boston and Darien would suck more. Even the AAA mechanic he'd eventually called out to the country club parking lot had pondered out loud if the old bucket of bolts was worth saving. At least the guy hadn't taken long to arrive—only twenty minutes—so while he was late for dinner, he wasn't *that* late. Which was good. Because the sooner this dinner was over, the sooner he could find Chloe and finish what they'd started.

God, he was going to make her fucking scream.

Sig breathed through his nose for another minute until his erection subsided, then got out of the truck, his boots crunching in the crushed shell driveway. On his way to the twenty-foot-wide porch, adorned on both sides by sculpted bushes, Sig passed a fountain, smirking at the cherubs spitting water at one another. The woman who owned this house had probably paid tens of thousands for those weird, naked angels. Unreal.

He turned his attention to the house. How many people actually lived in this mansion perched right on the edge of the cliff, overlooking the Sound? If the answer was any less than ten, this much space was unnecessary. The entire Bearcats team—and the coaching staff—could live in this place comfortably.

Did Chloe live in a house similar to this?

Ignoring the way his neck tightened at the definite possibility, Sig rang the doorbell, took a deep breath, and braced.

With the distance in their geography, not to mention the pandemic, Sig hadn't seen Harvey in almost six years. Prior to that, when Sig turned eighteen, he'd been required to track the man down, since Sig's mother hadn't kept in contact. Over the years, the relationship between Sig and Harvey was strained. Contentious. Truthfully, he didn't know if there was any benefit to seeing Harvey. As far as Sig was concerned, the man was an unrepentant social climber who married for comfort—read:

money—and this woman had to be nothing more than his most recent target.

Still, despite all his father's faults, part of Sig couldn't seem to quit his stubborn attempts to bond with his father. Even if that connection was tenuous. Small. Harvey had been as absent as a father could be, but Sig had always dreamed of looking up into the stands and seeing a dad. It was a need he couldn't seem to shake, no matter how old he got. How successful. On the rare occasions his mother flew in from Minnesota to watch him play, her presence meant just as much. So much that he hated himself for wanting more. Especially since he never quite found any common ground with the man who'd fathered him.

Shaking off his nerves, Sig rang the bell and immediately rolled his eyes at the grand *bong* sound that nearly shook the marble foundation of the porch. Self-important much?

A woman in a uniform answered the door, smiling brightly as she gestured him inside.

"Good evening, you must be Mr. Gauthier. Please come in. Everyone is in the parlor waiting for dinner to be served."

"Great. Thanks."

He stepped into the foyer, which was more like a ballroom with its domed glass ceiling and sweeping staircase in the center of the room. Following in the maid's footsteps, he walked by a table boasting a giant vase, bursting with white flowers. Pedestals lined the room holding various sculptures, each tastefully lit from above by frosted globes. On the far end of the room, the entire wall was made of glass, the view something out of a movie. Jagged rocks forming the coastline, wind-whipped grass, the body of water beyond, gently illuminated by a lighthouse.

Inadequacy prodded at him, more insistently than he'd felt it in a while. Even if the Bearcats renewed his contract for ten times the amount of his current salary, he'd never be able to afford a house like this. This was generational wealth. Money he couldn't comprehend.

You don't need it.

There was a sound coming from somewhere in the house and it stopped Sig in his tracks. Music. Gentle music. It wasn't an overly familiar sound or instrument, but something about it made his stomach clench, though he wasn't sure the curious shift in his ribs came from enjoyment—because damn, the music was the most beautiful he'd ever heard—or something else. And he didn't have a lot of time to think about it, because before he could reach the parlor, his father and a woman in her fifties stepped out of the room to greet him.

Harvey had changed since the last time Sig saw him, a lot more silver in the temples of his jet-black hair, his gaze sharper than the lapels of his suit jacket. The blond woman he escorted fit into her surroundings in a cream-colored dress that wrapped and folded in places that made no sense to Sig, sapphires winking at him from her earlobes.

"Son," Harvey said warmly, coming forward to wrap him in an embrace.

A little embarrassed by the hope that rippled inside him, his instinctive search for that elusive bond, Sig returned the hug briefly and clapped the older man on the back. "Harvey. Good to see you. Sorry I'm late. Had some car trouble."

"Oh dear," the woman said, holding a glass tumbler with both hands. "Is everything okay now?"

"Yeah, fine. I called AAA and got the old girl up and running again. Thanks."

Based on the wrinkle of her brow, car trouble and AAA were foreign concepts to this woman.

"Well, we're all here now. Isn't that nice?" Harvey stepped back and gestured proudly. "Son, please allow me to introduce you to Sofia, the goddess of my heart."

Sig gave his father a dry look. "Very nice to meet you, Sofia."

"Likewise. I've heard such incredible things about Harvey's son, the professional hockey player. Let's get you a drink, so you can tell us *everything* there is to know." There was something familiar about Sofia's graceful mannerisms as she swept aside and gestured for Sig to precede them into the parlor, but he couldn't quite put a finger on what. Or maybe he didn't want to put the clues together yet. Ignoring the bolt tightening in his gut, he followed Sofia's wordless directive, entering another expensively decorated room, that light and sort of ethereal music growing louder. Louder. "We thought it would be nice if Chloe played for us while we waited for dinner to start."

Sig's throat burned like he'd swallowed acid, the world moving in muddled motion, as if he'd jumped out of the window and into the freezing cold Sound, his body encapsulated in pressure from all sides. His hands were notorious for being steady, but they shook now. Shook so noticeably that he shoved them into his pockets to hide them instinctively.

That was his first and most regrettable mistake.

He'd play it over and over again in the months to come.

Hiding.

He never should have hidden a damn thing.

Especially when Chloe's fingers froze on the strings of her harp and he caught the horrified shock in her gaze as she saw his reflection approach in the picture window. In that moment, he should have announced to the room that he'd met Chloe earlier that evening and there was something happening between them. Something real. But he let the seconds tick by. Tick, tick, tick, while Chloe waited for him to react. Out loud.

He couldn't find his voice, though.

Couldn't wrap his head around their bad fortune quickly enough.

Their parents were dating. His father. Her mother.

Chloe turned slowly in her stool, blinking at him. Opening her mouth, closing it.

God, she was spectacular. She'd showered, twisted her blond hair up into some kind of style at the back of her head, little pearls peeking out everywhere. She had on a short, cream-colored silk dress and no shoes. And on top of every amazing thing about her—her wit, her warmth, her beauty—she had the ability to produce that music?

Our parents are dating.

"Honey, I can't wait another second. Let's make this a celebration dinner, shall we?" Harvey crowed behind him, his father coming up beside Sig to press a crystal rocks glass halfway filled with golden liquid into his hand. Then Harvey wrapped an arm around Sofia's waist, both of them smiling from ear to ear. "Chloe. Sig. We brought you both here tonight to announce that we're getting married." He laughed tearfully while looking into Sofia's face. "By the spring, we'll be husband and wife."

Sofia raised her glass in a salute. "And you'll each gain a sibling!"

The resulting roar in Sig's head rivaled the crashing waves below.

RISING FROM HER stool in front of the harp and walking to the dining room was a challenge. Her legs weren't working like they normally did. Not at all. Why would they be? She'd just found out that her soon-to-be stepbrother and the man she'd kissed passionately on the golf course just over an hour ago were one and the same.

And oh, stranger things had happened in this corner of the world. There were only so many blue-blooded rich people in this neck of Connecticut and they all insisted on marrying each other. Rumors of kissing cousins were not totally uncommon. It's not like she and Sig had been aware of their impending connection at the time he kissed the face off her. It could be their secret, right? No one ever had to find out.

Except . . . the fact that she'd never be able to kiss him again was positively terrible. In the short time they'd spent together, Sig had made her feel more than any member of the opposite sex *ever* had. She'd been breathless about seeing him again later. Sneaking out and making love with this rough-and-ready hockey player who said things like *sit on my face.* But who also looked at her like she might be hiding angel wings beneath her clothes.

Sig sat directly across from her now with lines of strain around his mouth and eyes, his fist curled tightly around a fork. Staring at her beneath drawn brows. They needed to talk. For some reason, she had this overwhelming belief that he'd know exactly what to do. She couldn't imagine this man being uncertain of anything.

"Pancetta and pear puff, Ms. Clifford?" asked their chef, Yuri.

She leaned back to give the chef access to her place setting. "Oh yes, please! Thank you."

A smiling Yuri used a silver tong to place the puff pastry onto Chloe's plate. Pancetta and pear puffs were her favorite. With her stomach twisted in knots, she wouldn't be able to eat, but she didn't want to be rude when the chef had gone to such an effort.

Chloe realized she was staring without blinking at Sig, her lungs having ceased to operate. Commanding herself to breathe, she dragged her attention toward Harvey and Sofia who were laughing with each other at the corner of the banquet table.

It didn't escape her notice that Harvey was sitting at the head. Just like that?

The whirlpool that had become her stomach turned faster.

"Harvey, dear. We are ignoring our children," Sofia admonished with a grin, batting her fiancé on the arm. "And after we brought Sig all the way here from Boston. In a car that apparently couldn't make the journey!" She picked up her drink and swirled the ice around slowly. "One would assume a professional athlete might arrive in something a little more ostentatious, like . . . oh, I don't know. A yellow Lamborghini."

Briefly, Chloe widened her eyes at Sig in what she hoped he interpreted as an apology. She wished she could tell Sig that her mother didn't mean to be condescending or backhanded with her compliments, but Sofia's barbs were often more tailored than her couture wardrobe.

Sig replied, "My truck has been with me through a lot. Been loyal to me since I turned sixteen and I won't reward her for that by sending her to a scrapyard." Sig cleared his throat and attempted to stop looking at Chloe, but he couldn't manage it any more than she could stop staring at him. "Anyway, light blue is more my color."

Not . . . because of her eyes.

Right?

No.

He wouldn't dare. Not after finding out they were going to be related by marriage.

"If I had my pick of cars," Chloe said, "I would choose one of those big old Cadillacs that looks like a boat going down the road. Some of the seniors at the club drive them."

"Why?" Sig asked, his tone amused, but his expression . . . not. At all.

"If I got into an accident in one of those ships on wheels, I wouldn't even feel it. The other car would probably just bump right off."

Sofia laughed, long and loud. "And that, dear Chloe, is why you have a chauffeur."

Heat stained her face. Briefly, she looked at Sig to clock his reaction. No change, apart from a deep groove forming between his brows. "Do you want to learn to drive, Chloe?"

"I don't know. I haven't really thought about it. Not in a while. But . . ." She looked back over her shoulder toward the front of the house, as if she could see his truck parked in the driveway. "Yes, I think I would. Very much."

"We'll stick with having you driven by a professional," Sofia said, dismissing the idea with a flap of her hand. "Sig, how do you find Boston?"

"On a map, usually." He ignored the resulting laughter from their parents, keeping his gaze locked on Chloe. In fact, he didn't seem to care at all that his overt attention might start to become noticeable. "When did you say you're getting married? Is there already a date in mind?"

"Ah! Well." Sofia clutched her drink close to her chest and looked adoringly at Harvey. "We're angling for spring, of course."

"So, roughly . . . eight months from now," Sig supplied.

"Yes," Sofia answered. "That should give me enough time to convince my friends to return from abroad and suffer through our glitzy little affair, don't you think, Harvey?"

"You could convince the moon to become the sun, sweetheart."

Chloe shielded her face with a cupped hand, so Harvey and Sofia wouldn't see the gagging face she sent in Sig's direction. His lips twitched briefly, before he settled back into dark intensity. A contemplative expression that told Chloe he was thinking a million miles an hour.

Eight months.

That was . . . a surprisingly long time. Her mother was usually a little more impulsive, especially when it came to planning her own exchange of nuptials. She had three ex-husbands to show for it, including Chloe's father. Not to mention two broken engagements.

In fact, now that she really took the time to observe Sofia and Harvey together, she noticed a whole host of differences in her mother. Had Sofia ever looked so relaxed? Her waistline wasn't pinkie thin, as usual, and for that, she looked much healthier. Had a glow, even. Her hair was down loose. She hadn't covered her grays, and those lighter strands were weaving through the crown of blond hair that matched Chloe's.

Was Harvey good for her mother?

Was this time different?

And if so, *why* did this time have to be different?

That frustration, which was admittedly selfish, caused Chloe to shift in her seat, scooting in closer to the table. As a result, the inside of her right foot brushed the toe of Sig's boot and her stomach sucked in on reflex, a throb capturing her entire body in one big constriction. *Whommm.* Across the table, his eyelids drooped and he slowly dragged a breath in and out.

"Of course, you'll both be part of the wedding," Harvey said, oblivious to what was taking place on the other side of the table. "A big part, actually. Sig, I know we haven't exactly been close, but I was hoping you'd agree to be my best man. Asking a mere friend simply doesn't seem right when I have a son."

Sig blinked several times, turning to face his father. "You're asking *me*?"

Harvey beamed. "Yes, son." His smile dimmed slightly. "I know we haven't been on the best of terms over the years, but Sofia . . . well, she has a way of making me hope again." Growing visibly misty eyed, Sofia squeezed his arm. "What do you say, Sig? Stand by my side while I marry the woman of my dreams."

Was it Chloe's imagination or was there a touch of suspicion, skepticism, in Sig's eyes as he observed the happy couple? Did he not find their relationship authentic?

Sig seemed to realize everyone was waiting for his response. "If it works with my game schedule, I'll . . ." He massaged the back of his neck. "Yeah. I'll do my best."

"Fabulous!" Sofia cried, holding up her glass. "And, Chloe, do I even need to ask you? You'll make such a stunning maid of honor. I've already booked a girls' weekend in Paris so we can be fitted for our gowns by Margaux Tardits. As if we'd go anywhere else!"

"Great," Chloe said, feeling like she was on an out-of-control conveyor belt that continued to roll faster, faster and she couldn't reach the off switch. She was six again, being thrown onto the stage in front of a packed auditorium, no plan, just told to play. *Play!* "Paris will be a lovely escape over the winter."

"Indeed. Perhaps we can arrange a performance while we're there. I'm sure any number of venues would love to host you. Haven't you always wanted to play the Palais Garnier?"

"I . . ." Had she expressed interest in that at some point? She must have. Although sometimes it was difficult to tell where her wishes ended and her mother's began. "Yes, I suppose I would."

Her eyes drifted to Sig's across the table and whatever he saw caused a muscle to hop in his cheek. "What about Boston, Chloe? Have you ever thought of studying there?"

A hush fell over the dining room.

Sofia lowered her drink to the table. *Clink.*

It was on the tip of Chloe's tongue to say no, to please her mother and keep the dinner pleasant, but . . . something stopped her. Maybe it was Sig's foot settling itself against hers beneath the table. As if to pass on strength or encouragement. Or maybe it was the overwhelming sense of isolation she'd been feeling lately. Her loneliness didn't make any sense when she was surrounded by people at the club, instructors, tennis partners. Friends she'd known since birth who already owned their own homes in the area. Some of them were married, having babies, taking over charities from their parents. Living the life their parents had envisioned for them.

But Chloe had an unusual skill. She played the harp like she'd been born with the strings attached to her fingers. It was her most treasured escape. The elegant instrument drew her, cocooned her, nurtured her heart and soul. She loved it beyond measure.

It also meant she was stuck in this . . . in-between place.

Too promising in the music world to settle down and stop training, performing.

But too sheltered to really explore what was *possible* for her in music.

Or in life.

She'd been in this triangle existence for years, being driven between lessons, home, the club. She was at her mother's beck and call. She kept the peace, did as she was told. And lately her skin had started to feel too tight, like she couldn't move or breathe inside of it. What was the point of having this talent and not being free to achieve anything with it? Or see what she was capable of?

I'm twenty-five years old.

Oh my God, I'm twenty freaking five.

The need for change—for rebellion—had been brewing inside of Chloe for some time, but this man, this unexpected force of a man across the table, was kicking down the final blockage between Chloe and her courage. Perhaps because he was so obviously bold and confident and outspoken. Perhaps because his presence was so steady that it steadied her, too.

Their meeting wasn't an accident.

It had been for a reason.

Time sort of slowed down as that belief registered, before it sped back up in a big way.

"Yes, actually," Chloe said, keeping her gaze fixed on Sig. "I've always wanted to attend conservatory at Berklee."

Sofia's laughter wasn't as carefree as before. "There are world-class instructors in Connecticut, Chloe. Our *home* is here. We can't simply pick up and move to Boston."

"Why is it assumed that you would have to move with me?"

As soon as Chloe asked that question, she wished she hadn't, because she knew what was coming. A list of everything that made her helpless and incapable. "For one, dear, you don't know how to cook for yourself. Neither do I. That's why we have the incredible Yuri." Sofia paused to smile blithely at the chef as he circled the table. "You don't have any experience or knowledge of what it takes to live alone. The transportation system is a bear."

"It truly is," Harvey agreed. "A *bear*."

"And cities can be dangerous. If you don't need to live in one, why would you?"

"To try. To experience. To see if I'm able to do it—"

"But what if you're not?" Sofia asked, nose wrinkling with sympathy. "We have such a lovely life here in Darien. A safe, contained one. There's no reason to take risks."

"*I'm* in Boston," Sig said, his voice landing like a judge's gavel. "She'd be safe."

Silence reigned. Outside of Chloe's head and chest, anyway. Inside those two places, it sounded like the cluttered notes of an orchestra warming up.

"Son . . ." Harvey began, visibly uncomfortable by the shift in the evening's mood. "Don't get in between them."

"He's not," Chloe found herself saying. Loudly. And she found in that moment that she didn't like anyone questioning Sig. She wanted to run over to his side of the table and pat his big shoulders to make up for it. "He's not getting in between anything. I . . . want to go to Boston. I've been invited to train at Berklee and they've even offered to waive the tuition." Whatever the amount happened to be. She should probably look into that. "So . . . that's what I'm going to do. I've already decided."

She hadn't really decided. Not until the declaration had left her mouth.

But once it was out there, *oh God*, the way the pressure released from her chest like a valve had been twisted in the right direction.

"Well. What an interesting plot twist." Her mother looked at her serenely, but the snap of fire in her eyes was ominous. "If you go to Boston, Chloe, you'll do it without my money."

Just like that, her stomach filled with hot, bubbling concrete.

There it was. Money was the roadblock she couldn't go past.

Without money, she wouldn't be able to rent an apartment, wouldn't be able to simply add food to her family's tab at the country club. She'd be helpless and broke. And she had no idea how to survive like that. She didn't even know how to live alone *with* money. Not yet.

"I'll help you get started, Chloe," Sig said, drawing her attention with a meaningful look. A look that said, *Hey, don't listen to them, you got this.* "I'll find you a safe place to live and show you how to get around. How to order takeout or cook. Whatever you want." Sig looked at her mother, openly confused. "A free ride at her dream school is a huge opportunity, right?"

"Money isn't the issue," Sofia responded sweetly.

Harvey scrubbed a hand down his face. "Sig, please. You are overstepping."

"No, he isn't. He's offering support . . . and that's exactly what I need. I think maybe I've needed it for a long time. And . . . how hard can it be to make pancetta and pear puffs, right?" Chloe noticed the affront on Yuri's face and immediately backpedaled. "Very hard, obviously. I'll start with Pop-Tarts."

Yuri softened. "Pop-Tarts make a delicious pie crust in a pinch," the chef whispered, winking at her.

A gust of air blew into her chest at that subtle show of solidarity. "Thank you."

Sofia threw up her hands. "Chloe, I forbid you to go. Don't you care that I won't be able to sleep at night because I'll be worrying about you? Do you care about me at all?"

Guilt threatened to capsize Chloe, but she wouldn't let it. The decision to go somewhere on her own felt too good. Too freeing. Honestly, she was having trouble stopping herself from running straight out the door into the night.

Why was she stopping herself?

Abruptly, Chloe pushed back from the table, upsetting her silverware.

"I think I'll go pack."

Sig popped the pancetta and pear puff into his mouth, speaking while he chewed, and Chloe found that lack of manners *delightful*. "Don't forget your toothbrush."

WHAT THE FUCK are you doing?

Sig followed a buoyant Chloe to his truck with her haphazardly packed bag thrown over his shoulder, awestruck by the way she bounded around in the moonlight, smiling at him as she danced in a circle, a princess who had been freed from her ivory tower.

But he was no valiant knight, was he?

Nope.

He shouldn't have done this. Shouldn't have forced them into a situation where they would be spending an untold amount of time together. Not when they were going to be stepsiblings in eight months' time. Not when he wanted to touch her, drive himself inside of her, make her his home. He had to be out of his mind volunteering to show her the ropes in Boston. Stark raving mad.

And yet, there hadn't been a chance in fucking hell he'd have left there without her.

Simple as that.

Chloe was his responsibility now and he couldn't imagine life any other way.

What had life been *before* tonight? He could barely remember.

"Sig," Harvey called from the doorway, forcing him to stop and turn around. To wait for his father to come storming out after him. "What do you think you're doing?" Harvey asked through his teeth, a vein throbbing front and center in his forehead. It wasn't lost on Sig that Harvey was echoing his own thoughts, but probably for a far different reason. "Are you deliberately trying to ruin this for me?"

Yup.

Very different reasons.

"I'm sorry," Sig said, keeping his voice low. "I didn't mean to interrupt you in the middle of ripping off another wealthy chick."

Harvey blanched, rocking back on his heels. "Oh, right. That old chestnut." For several seconds, he remained quiet and studied Sig. "You never fail to let me know exactly what you think of me, do you?"

"I only know what you did to my mother."

"Jesus, you think you know everything." There was something curious in his tone. Like a message Sig couldn't decode. "You were a *newborn* at the time, I'll remind you."

Not for the first time, Sig wondered if he was missing an important part of the story when it came to his parents. How their relationship had ended in disaster and why. After all, Harvey had never offered his side of the story, no matter how many times Sig asked. But didn't the truth lie in the fact that his mother had ended up poor, unable to afford basic necessities for them?

"I grew up with the effects of what happened," Sig rasped, the pulse in his neck racing. "How she had to scrape by while you used her money to trap your next target."

"Look, I've made mistakes, but I'm different now. I've changed."

"And yet your taste in women has stayed exactly the same. Rich."

"Yeah? Looks like the apple doesn't fall far from the tree." Harvey split a look between Sig and Chloe where she stood waiting at the passenger side of his truck. "Listen to me, I'm marrying her mother. That's the situation." He studied his son hard. "If you have some kind of romantic interest here, you better think again. Her mother would disown her before she weathered a scandal like that. Is that what you want?"

Sig wasn't sure why he denied what happened . . . or was happening between him and Chloe. Nothing about it felt remotely wrong. But that comment about the apple not falling far from the tree had fucking stung. So had the threat of Chloe being disowned. Because of him.

"I'm only helping her out. She wants to go to Boston and I know Boston. That's all it is."

"You better hope so."

"And you better hope you're marrying Sofia for the right reasons," Sig said, taking a step into Harvey's space, rocked by protectiveness for Chloe. If Harvey swindled Sofia, he swindled Chloe, by association. "Or we're going to have a big problem."

A glint shone in his father's eyes. "Noted."

Sofia appeared in the doorway behind Harvey, fresh drink in hand.

Based on her pinched expression, she'd overheard every word of their conversation. "Harvey has told me everything about his past, just in case you think he's keeping secrets from me. He's not. We have been open books with each other." Sig highly doubted that, but God, she was speaking with so much confidence. "On the off chance there is anything to find out, my lawyers will find it as they craft the prenup. They're very protective of me."

Sig didn't doubt it.

He also didn't doubt they would find something. More than what Harvey had told Sofia.

It was only a matter of time, right?

Maybe this marriage would never take place at all.

Hope expanded his ribs for the first time in an hour.

"I'm glad you have people looking out for your best interests," Sig said, ignoring his father's snort.

"If only we could say the same for my daughter."

Sig drew back at Sofia's dry comment. "Come again?"

Her head tipped left. "Give me a little credit, Sig. I have eyes. I doubt you've volunteered to play Chloe's host in Boston purely out of the goodness of your heart." She sipped her drink extra slowly while the implication sunk in, finally bringing the glass down to her hip. "This is your last chance to leave alone, the way you arrived. Your last chance to consider how an . . . unconventional relationship might affect your career. Not to mention the life I've built for Chloe. Look around. You don't think she'll wish to return to this sooner or later?"

Sig almost caved. Because, yeah. Fuck. He'd been so bowled

over by Chloe and how she made him feel, he hadn't stopped to consider that maybe he was causing damage by taking her away, instead of helping her enrich her music career. Her life. But then he glanced back at Chloe over his shoulder and saw the determined set of her shoulders, the added confidence in her jawline. Her aura of optimism. How could keeping this person with him, near him, be bad? What was he supposed to do? Leave her there and simply hope their parents drifted apart naturally? Leave . . . *them* to chance?

Can't do it.

He'd make sure their relationship stayed aboveboard. He'd do nothing to cause her harm. Not to her life or career. Not to his, either.

He'd find the willpower to keep himself in check.

"If Chloe wants to come home, I'll drive her back here myself," Sig said gruffly, backing away. "Bye, Dad. Great seeing you, as usual." Once he reached the truck, he set Chloe's bag in the middle cab and skirted around the front bumper to open the passenger-side door for her. Once in, she tested the cracked leather seat and looked around, sniffing the air, obviously used to getting into the back of freshly scented limousines, instead of beat-up trucks with a smelly hockey bag in the back. Would she change her mind at the first sign that she was leaving this ultra-wealth behind? Because he could give her comfort, safety, and new experiences, but he couldn't give her this palace overlooking the water.

But then she beamed a smile at Sig, gave him a thumbs-up, and he told himself never to underestimate her again. As of now, she was leaving that kind of treatment in the rearview. "Let's get you to Boston, Chlo," he said a moment later when he started the truck. "Right after we stop at the club and pay off your champagne bill."

"You're going to pay it?"

"As long as they'll take a check."

"They do! Hooray!"

And he told himself to never underestimate Chloe's ability to spend money, either.

No, he'd learn *all* about that in the coming months.

"Is there a Sephora in Boston?" she breathed. "I've always wanted to go to one."

What the hell was that? He shrugged. "Probably."

It wouldn't be long until he knew more about Sephora than hockey.

More about the harp than fixing trucks.

More about Chloe than he knew about himself.

He'd love every goddamn second of it, too.

Even if he could only love her from a safe distance.

For now.

"Sig," Chloe said quietly.

His windpipe tightened because he knew what was coming. "Yeah?"

Several seconds of silence passed. "I know we only met tonight and maybe it's premature or even . . . inappropriate to ask after everything that has happened." She gripped the nylon of her seat belt with both hands. "But what does all of this mean for . . . us?"

Us.

The us that could have been.

The us they might very well never be.

What was the definition of *us* when it came to them?

As much as it burned, Sig didn't have an answer to that. He only knew he would die before jeopardizing Chloe's future when he could never, not in a million years, offer her the same level of wealth. Hell, he felt sick taking her away from it right *now*. If he didn't believe she truly wanted to experience life on her own terms, he wouldn't have driven her an inch out of the driveway. But his father and Sofia were right, she could return to Darien at any time. Probably would. Who would leave this kind of dream existence forever?

Even if she could get used to a regular life . . .

She was on course to become his stepsibling.

Having her in Boston was going to be full-time murder on his sanity.

Yet having her three hundred miles away would be worse.

For now, all he could do was wait. Hope Sofia realized she was marrying a grifter. Hope she called off the wedding . . . and freed up Sig to pursue Chloe. Romantically.

In the meantime . . . "We're going to be friends, Chlo." He forced himself to grin at her, the muscles of his cheeks barely capable of executing the feat. "Best friends."

They looked across the cab of the truck at each other with stark acknowledgment in their eyes, as if they'd both made it at the same moment, albeit very reluctantly. It couldn't be. *They* couldn't be. And then they both went back to staring out at the road, regret filling the air that separated them, Sig's heart heavier than an anvil in his chest.

CHAPTER FOUR

One week later

Sig slowed to a stop and waited in the hallway, watching Chloe disappear into the apartment, the sound of her happily chatting with the Realtor echoing down the polished stairs. Golden sconces glinted on the walls. Piano music drifted down somewhere from the top floor. A woman pushed a noticeably expensive baby carriage into the lobby below and he watched both doors lock behind the woman soundly, securely, exactly as they would behind Chloe.

They'd looked at an apartment in a different part of town prior to this and there'd only been one door separating the lobby from the street. Not to mention, the apartment was on the ground floor. He'd all but carried a protesting Chloe out of there over his shoulder.

This was more like it.

He'd sleep at night with her in this place.

And it was going to cost him a fortune. On a monthly basis. Already, the five-star hotel he'd put her in since arriving in Boston would have been enough to buy him a new truck, but he'd loved picking her up out front, watching her emerge from the glittering lobby while a man in a starched uniform held the door open for her. Giving her that experience, that security, made him feel accomplished. Made his blood pump with purpose.

Doing mental math, Sig took two steps and tested the railing with a shake, making sure it didn't wobble, then he entered the apartment behind the pair of women.

Two dead bolts on the door. Good.

Sig paused between the entrance and the living room, trying his best to see the sizable sunlit space, the high ceilings, the chef's kitchen, the view of the North End neighborhood. But all he could see were the marble columns and cherubs and sweeping staircases of her home in Darien. This apartment was only a fraction of the size in comparison—

"Sig!" Chloe cried out from one of the bedrooms. "Come look!"

He went without thinking, wanting to see what got her so excited. When he found her in the master bedroom, she was pulling open a large drawer that appeared to be hinged to the wall. "What is it?" he asked.

"It's a laundry chute," answered the Realtor. "She'll have a designated space in the basement where her clothes will compile until they're ready to be washed. It's an old-fashioned fixture, but one the residents love. It will save her from having to carry a heavy bag up and down the stairs from the basement."

Basement? "There's no washer-dryer in the apartment?"

"It's a landmark building. There are certain plumbing restrictions."

"Yeah, Chloe," Sig said, shaking his head. "I don't know . . ."

"Hellooo," Chloe called down the shoot. "Is anyone home?" With a laugh, she closed the drawer and straightened, directing her attention at the Realtor. "Who does the laundry once it's down there?"

The Realtor blinked at her. Seconds ticked by. "Uh. You do."

Chloe was incredulous, but also . . . visibly thrilled. *"Really?"*

"Y-yes."

Sig almost lost his train of thought in the face of her excitement. "I don't like the sound of her in the basement."

"I do," Chloe countered. "I've never been in one."

"I assure you, it's secure. And very elegant."

Chloe looked crestfallen. "Oh."

Sig would be confirming that before any paperwork was signed. "Let's talk, Chlo," Sig said, dipping his chin toward the hallway, indicating that Chloe should follow him. A few seconds later, they were alone in the kitchen, Chloe moving from cabinet to drawer to sink like a ricocheting beam of light. He had to hook an arm around her waist to cease her movements, drawing her to a stop in front of him. Close enough that he could look down into her face and trace the rim of black around her blue irises. But he buried the urge to trace her cheekbone with his knuckle. To lower his mouth to hers and sip at it, nuzzle it, kiss it.

He did none of that, but he'd been fighting the battle all week.

Would it ever get easier?

This week, every moment of daylight he'd been afforded between practice and games had belonged to Chloe. Going over the train route she would take to Berklee. Taking her to meet her new instructors. Eating meals together. Taking her to Sephora for the first time—a two-hour ordeal he'd pretended to hate, but handing over his credit card and purchasing a bunch of goop and sparkles had earned him a bouncing hug that he could still feel. That he *never* wanted to stop feeling.

"Do you like this place?" he asked, voice husky from strain.

"It's gorgeous," she whispered, looking around while a trench slowly formed between her brows. "What does it cost to buy an apartment like this?"

"We wouldn't be buying it," he informed her patiently. "We'd be renting it."

"Renting. Ohhh." She gave an exaggerated nod, as if she'd just been let in on a great secret. "And what does that cost?"

"You're not going to worry about that."

Her gaze zipped up to his. "Are you sure?"

"I'm going to handle it while you're training at the conservatory." He thought about the dreams she'd confided in him over French toast yesterday morning. How she thought it might be time to take baby steps out of training and become a practicing member of her chosen field of music, something her mother never seemed inclined to let her do. Pursuing a place in an orchestra, instead of playing exhibitions where she was billed as a prodigy to come observe and gawk at. "Eventually, when you're placed with an orchestra, you'll take over."

A shadow passed across her face. "You have a lot of faith in my ability to be placed with an ensemble."

"Yeah." He gave in. Brushed a hand down her hair, teasing the soft ends with his fingertips. "I do."

Her eyelids dropped to half-mast at his touch, their chests rising and falling simultaneously. "Will you teach me how to do laundry?"

"As long as the basement isn't a murder trap, yes. Let me check it out first."

She considered him. "You're going to be a little overprotective of me, aren't you?"

A little? If he signed a lease on this place, he would be installing a third dead bolt before the ink was dry. "What makes you say that?"

"Well." The Realtor appeared at the far end of the kitchen, her eagle eye zipping back and forth between Sig and Chloe. How close they were standing. Especially after they'd introduced themselves as future stepsiblings. "What do you think of the place?"

Chloe galloped toward the woman. "We'll take it!"

"I want to see the basement first," Sig growled, stomping after her.

It didn't matter that he would probably have to stretch financially to pay rent on this place, as well as his own. Not to mention, he was still making mortgage payments on the house he'd bought for his mother upon signing his current contract. But, hey. He'd sell memorabilia on eBay, if necessary. Get the guys to sign some shit and make some extra cash. Plus, he had a few high-ticket items he'd collected over the years that would be in demand at auction.

And he'd pray the Bearcats offered him a decent contract for next season.

Bottom line, Sig would do whatever it took to give Chloe this place.

His entire life, he'd told himself *you don't need it*. That he didn't require nice things.

But Chloe . . . she was the first nice thing he couldn't live without.

Two weeks later

Chloe sat on top of the washing machine with the blue bottle of detergent in her lap and tried very hard not to look smug. Sig would be arriving any moment to commence their first laundry lesson and he was going to be shocked to find she'd already bought soap. *Shocked.*

That day had been a good one already and this was going to be icing on the cake.

She'd woken up to a wine-soaked, apologetic text message from her mother, offering to send Chloe a small weekly allowance. Chloe could see the offer for what it was. A very strategic amount that would give Sofia access to her plans, her progress, but not a large enough cash flow that Chloe wouldn't miss the luxuries of home.

Chloe's first instinct had been to refuse the money, because this move to Boston was supposed to be about discovering her independence, but ultimately, she'd decided to accept the cash. She'd only been in Boston for two weeks—long enough to know everything cost money. *So much money.* And she was already relying on Sig for too much. Asking him for spending money on top of laundry lessons, Sephora spending sprees, rent money, and everything in between?

Out of the question.

Her spine straightened at the sound of bootsteps coming down the basement stairs, every cell in her body running in haphazard circles, pulse skittering. Sensitivity attacked her breasts before he even came into view, but when his big frame filled the doorway, she didn't even know which direction her heart traveled. North? South? Both? Mainly that it dislodged and floated out of position, made lighter and heavier at the sight of him in jeans, a blue puffer jacket, boots, and a Red Sox hat.

"Hey, Chlo." He crossed his arms, propped a shoulder against the doorjamb. "Whatcha got there?"

"Laundry detergent," she said primly. "No big deal."

"Wow. Did you go to the store?"

"Yes. I also bought olives and coffee."

"Breakfast of champions."

"The store two blocks from here has an olive *bar.* You get to fill your own container. I couldn't just bypass that." She wrinkled her nose. "I'm going to be eating olives for weeks."

Chuckling, he pushed off the jamb and walked in her direction. "But at least you got detergent . . ." He winced when he got closer and picked up the bottle. "Ah. Hate to break this to you, but this is fabric softener."

"*What?*"

"Still important. Just not the main event."

She looked down at the overflowing laundry basket on the concrete floor, deflated. "What am I going to use to wash my clothes? I'm on my last pair of—" She cut herself off before she could say the word *panties*, but when his gaze climbed her thighs and teased the apex of her leggings, it was obvious Sig knew what she'd been about to say.

"We can't have you going out without them, can we?" His tongue rested on his bottom lip a moment and she got the sense he was trying to control his breathing. What a coincidence—she was doing the same, because he smelled *incredible*; it was a struggle not to yank him closer by his lapels and inhale the cloves and pepper that was his signature scent. "Don't worry, I brought a couple of Tide Pods from home." He unearthed them from his jacket pocket, holding them up. "You're safe from indecency."

"Is it indecent to forgo underwear?"

"If someone *knew* you'd forgone them, yeah. It would be a little indecent." He took the fabric softener bottle away from Chloe, setting it on the neighboring machine . . . and then he framed her waist in his hands, lifting her off the machine and settling her down in front of him and tipping her chin up with a finger. "And I'd know you weren't wearing any. I might start thinking about things that I shouldn't."

Chloe swallowed. So many throbs in so many places. "Guess we better start washing."

Neither one of them moved for several seconds, then his fingertips skimmed down her throat and away, so casually, as if they hadn't left fire in their wake.

"First thing we have to do is separate lights and darks," Sig said, tone hoarse, nudging her basket with his toe. "If you put in a red shirt with a bunch of white laundry, you'll end up with a lot of pink shit. Believe me, I learned that the hard way."

"Are you a self-taught laundryman? Or did your parents teach you?"

Sig was quiet for a second. "It was just my mother and I growing up. Harvey wasn't really in the picture until I hit college—and only because I tracked him down out of curiosity. Then again, he's not really the type to pass on laundry tips, is he?"

"No," Chloe said slowly, studying him. As deeply as she felt she knew Sig after such a brief window of time, the truth was, she didn't know a lot about his past. And God, she wanted to know every detail of every single day that led up to creating this person standing in front of her. This professional athlete who carried Tide Pods in his pocket and championed her new start and installed extra locks on her door. "Your parents divorced when you were young?"

"They were never married, actually," he said, a hint of color flushing into his cheeks. He hunkered down and started dividing her laundry, prompting Chloe to kneel and follow his lead, putting whites in one pile, colors in another. "My mother grew up with money, a big family, but her parents didn't approve of Harvey. And I guess they were right, since he ended up leaving shortly after I was born. I'm not sure if my mother resented her family for never accepting Harvey or if him leaving just scored her pride and she couldn't face them, but . . . we moved away from them after Harvey bailed. My mom wanted to make her own way, without their help. But she never liked talking about the circumstances." His brows drew together. "I've got a lot more questions than answers when it comes to how I grew up."

"I'm sorry, Sig."

"It's okay. If I'd grown up all posh like you, I wouldn't be able to teach you how to do laundry now. See?" He winked at her. "Everything happens for a reason. My mom was too busy working two jobs to teach me how to wash clothes, so I did what any hockey player would do. I asked my coach. His wife came over and showed me the basics."

"How old were you during all of this?"

He squinted an eye. "Seven, maybe?"

"Wow," she whispered, only vaguely aware that they'd gravitated together over the course of Sig's story and now their foreheads were almost touching. "Did she teach you anything else?"

Sig nodded. "How to make chicken and dumplings."

"I don't know what that is, but it sounds really good."

"I'll make it for you one day."

"No." She shook her head. "You're doing enough for me."

"I'll never . . . do enough for you, Chloe." He turned his face away on a dry chuckle, as if he couldn't believe he'd made that statement out loud. "What about your father? What's his story?"

Chloe hummed in her throat, trying not to be obvious about memorizing the shape of Sig's hard upper lip. "There was a very messy divorce with my mother when I was a toddler. She got custody—and the house. He remarried and had two more children. They live on Long Island, and I've never met a single one of them. But I speak to my father a couple times a year." She bit the inside of her cheek. "Every once in a while, an article is published about him in one finance journal or another. He mentions me every time. That his oldest child is a harp prodigy."

Sig studied her closely. "You don't like that."

She shrugged a shoulder. "He's never even come to a performance. It doesn't seem right that he should get some kind of credit for it, you know?"

"Yeah. Absolutely fuck that." He nudged her forehead with his own. "You going to let me come to one?"

Her heart crammed its way into her throat. "Will you?"

"Damn right I will."

She was suddenly smiling so wide, it hurt. "Okay."

"As long as you come to a hockey game."

"Damn right I will."

Now he was smiling, too. How did she get here? Doing laundry in a basement in Boston with this beautiful man? Two weeks ago, she couldn't have imagined it. Now, she couldn't imagine being anywhere else.

"What about your mother?" Sig asked quietly, his hand lifting to brush back her hair, but dropping before he could complete the action. "It's hard to get a read there. She obviously cares so much about you . . ."

"But the vibes are giving Disney villain? Yeah." She searched through her mom-related discomfort for the right words. "It's complicated with Sofia. She wants what is best for me. She was simply brought up in a world where inconveniences don't exist. If you want a situation to look a certain way, you just pay to have it tailored to your taste. When she can't have what she wants, she leans on cash harder and harder to maneuver people. Including me. She's my mother, though, and I love her even though she is far from perfect. And kind of scary." They both laughed softly. "It's like, I know if I needed her, she would be there. I also know she'll find a way to maneuver me into a place that makes her comfortable again." Chloe looked up into Sig's eyes, wanting to absorb the understanding she already knew she'd find there, finding the distance between their heads had dwindled. "She can't help it."

Chloe could see the moment he realized how close their mouths were, the intimacy of the setting. No matter what they did, they seemed to end up here. On the verge of making a wrong move. One they wouldn't be able to take back.

Slowly, they pulled back from each other and finished sorting the laundry. He walked her through how to add soap to the machine, which buttons to press, then eventually how to work the dryer. While they talked about everything from favorite breakfast foods to hockey injuries, Chloe hopped back onto the machine and waited for her first wash to finish. Sig was directly in front of her with his hands propped on the corners of the machine, his thumbs inches away from the outsides of her thighs. A little close, maybe, but . . .

Had they tacitly agreed not to fight the need to be near each other?

Or was that her imagination?

Chloe was halfway through a question about Sig's college days when the spin cycle started. And it started with a vengeance. The violent shaking began so suddenly, a laugh flew from her mouth and continued . . .

Until she saw the stark hunger transform Sig's face. His attention had locked in on her breasts. Namely, the way they were being jostled with every sharp movement of the machine, her cleavage jiggling in the neckline of her T-shirt.

"I should get down," she said, breathless.

"Yeah. You should." The resonant whir of the washing machine nearly drowned out his words, but somehow, they were still loud in her ears. Like she alone had the ability to hear him under any circumstances. "God, I wish we'd never gone to that dinner, Chlo." His palms hovered a centimeter above her thighs, before he rested them there, skimming them upward toward her hips. "I've never wished for ignorance, but I wish we didn't know what we know. I wish I'd just taken you and ran."

"Me too," she whispered, reaching up and threading her fingers through his hair, making him bury his face in the crook of her neck with a groan. His hip blades were pressed to the insides of her knees now, her center aching for pressure, friction, even though she knew it wasn't allowed. None of this was. Still . . . "If we'd run away, where would we have gone?"

"Sweden."

Am I floating? "Sweden?"

"You could play in the royal philharmonic orchestra there." He rubbed his lips up and down against the side of her neck. "I could play hockey."

Her head fell back, neck unhinging. "You've thought about this?"

"Thought. Obsessed. Whatever you want to call it." Sig rolled their foreheads together, looking down. Watching her breasts shake with increasingly labored breath. "You grew up pampered, but that's not how I would have treated you in bed. I'd have fucked you like the world was ending." He dropped his mouth to her breasts and licked each slope, before slowly dragging his tongue up the side of her neck and laving a circle beneath her ear. "It would have been ending, because another one would have been beginning. Ours." He cursed beneath his breath. "I'm sorry."

"You can't be sorry," she managed, her eyes still crossed from that lick. From his words. That night had been as meaningful to him as it was to her. The start of something undefinable. "You didn't do anything wrong."

"Maybe not." He dragged her an inch closer to the edge of the washer, but stopped, his jaw giving a tight pop. "But Christ, I better go before I do."

Before she managed to focus, Sig had left the laundry room, his boots pounding up the stairs toward the building exit, leaving Chloe boneless and heartsick on the shaking washer.

CHAPTER FIVE

Two months later

Sig sat in the front row of the concert hall, thanking God it was dark.

Because he was pretty sure his jaw was in the vicinity of his knees.

Tonight was Chloe's first student showcase with Berklee. It wasn't the first time Sig had put on a tuxedo, but the only other times he'd worn a penguin suit, he'd been at the ESPY Awards, surrounded by other athletes roughly his size. Not tonight. He was by far and away the biggest motherfucker in attendance—and sitting in the first row with a bouquet of roses crushed in his lap, he was probably blocking everyone's view of Chloe playing the harp onstage. There was no greater crime, because she was . . .

Eyes closed, she tilted her face and her cheek caught the light, her fingers moving fluidly over the strings, lips moving with the notes, verbalizing sound in a way no one else could interpret, playing what had to be the entrance music to heaven. This wasn't normal. She was better than everyone else, right? Didn't the audience realize that?

Oh *Jesus.*

His heart was going to rip a hole in his chest.

How had he managed to stop himself from touching her since that day in the laundry room? It was a daily struggle, due to the sheer amount of time they spent together, but Harvey's voice always echoed back to him before his hunger could take over. *Her mother would disown her before she weathered a scandal like that. Is that what you want?*

No. God, no. Because Sig couldn't match the life Sofia could provide for Chloe.

Not yet. Maybe not ever. With the contract deadline approaching in the next few months and rumblings of a change in ownership going around the locker room, he had no idea what the future held for his career.

No player ever really had a guarantee of a holy grail contract, right? He was no different.

None of this stopped him from falling for her. Deeper and deeper. Did it?

Every day—every *single* day—he swore he'd reached the pinnacle of his feelings for this woman and then he was proven wrong. Even last week when she had her period and answered the door sobbing in sweatpants and cradling a mug of soup, he'd been fucking mesmerized.

"Do you know that when birds fly into closed windows, they're usually attacking their own reflection? It's all just a big mistake and sometimes they die for it."

He cataloged the situation the way he registered the positions of each defender on his way down the ice. "Did a bird fly into your window?"

"Yes."

"Do you want me to go check if it's okay?"

"Yes. I'm scared to do it myself." She sighed down at her soup, *stirred it, and seemed frustrated by the fact that it was soup in the first place. "I have my period."*

"Oh. Maybe you should go lie down."

"I tried that," she groaned, head falling back on her shoulders. "Still cursed."

Sig was not adequately trained for this. He was a fixer. Hockey was nothing but a series of problems that needed to be solved—fast—but he couldn't just get rid of this problem or fight his way out of it. That sucked. "I'm going to go downstairs and make sure the bird flew off, happy and alive, and then I'll be back with a solution."

"That's what you think."

"Go try lying down again."

"Okay."

She cried her way to the couch, set down the soup, and fell face forward onto the cushions. Sig felt helpless on his way back down the stairs and out of the building, where he stopped short, raking a hand through his hair.

Bad news: the fucking bird was dead.

"Jesus Christ." He paced a little, ignoring the passersby that snapped pictures of him with their phones. As soon as the coast was clear, he hunkered down and used a tree branch to dig a bird grave, lowering tweetie into it with a few muttered words of remembrance. Swiping dirt off the knees of his jeans, he made his way back up to the apartment, letting himself in. "Good news, I didn't see the bird anywhere. It must have flown off."

Chloe sat up, looking hopeful. "Really? Because you were gone a long time."

"Yeah, well. I was doing a really thorough search."

"Oh." She pressed a hand to her chest, tension ebbing. "Thank goodness."

"Yup."

"Do you want to watch a movie with me?" She picked up the remote. "I was thinking of putting on A Star Is Born."

A tearjerker. In her state? Terrible plan. "How about a comedy?"

Her eyes turned glassy. "Maybe that's a better idea."

Sig went over and sat beside Chloe on the couch, smiling when she situated the blanket so he could have half. For the first forty-odd minutes of the movie, he bit the inside of his cheek while she struggled to find a comfortable position. And then he threw out every last ounce of his common sense and dragged her sideways into his lap, tucking her head beneath his chin and slowly, hesitantly, rubbing her belly with his knuckles.

She sighed happily and didn't move for the next hour, except to laugh.

And it was the happiest and most capable he'd ever felt . . . ever.

Now, as she played the last note of her song, concluding the concert, he stood up and almost decimated the bouquet of roses, trying to clap while they were still in his hands. When Chloe appeared to be searching for someone in the crowd, he almost shouted, *Who are you looking for?* That way, he could track that person down and take them to her.

Turned out, it was him, though.

Him.

As soon as she spotted Sig, she sucked in a breath and waved, before finally exiting the stage, leaving him standing there with a knot in his throat, as the applause died down. His row had almost cleared completely by the time he remembered Chloe had gotten him permission to go backstage after the show—and he went there now, wanting to see her, of course, but also wanting to get the fucking roses out of his hands before they were as lifeless as tweetie.

Sig made his way to the stage door and gave his name to a security guard, waded through a sea of well-heeled people accustomed to classical music and Thursday night concertos—and he finally caught sight of Chloe.

Surrounded by dudes.

Musicians.

Vaguely, he recognized a lot of them from the show. Violinists, pianists, and whatnot.

One sweep of their rapturous expressions told Sig all he needed to know. They were down bad. Every one of them. She dazzled them effortlessly with her constant motion and animated hand gestures and those gorgeous, expressive eyes. And they were all sorely out of luck. Because no one got close to Chloe. No one but him.

A gut instinct as destructive as it sounded.

Sig cleared his throat as he got closer to Chloe and her group of admirers. He watched her stop midsentence, turn and launch straight into him, wrapping both her arms around his neck, the front of her body molding to his muscle. Making eye contact with every single member of her fan club, he lifted her off the ground and kissed her temple.

"Hey, dream girl." He squeezed her closer. "You were incredible."

Don't even think about it, he mouthed at the quartet of guys. *I'm as mean as I look.*

They paled, before all moving in opposite directions at once.

Chloe didn't notice because her arms were still slung snugly around his neck, the side of her cheek pressed to his shoulder. "Did you bring me flowers?"

Sig hummed. "There should be at least one or two left intact."

"Big hockey hands. Fragile flowers," she murmured, smiling. "Not a match."

He tightened his hold that final degree, making her gasp in his ear—and he went too far. One of many times he would go too far with Chloe. God help them both. "These hands can handle fragile things just fine when necessary, Chlo."

Over the top of her head, Sig could see people were beginning to take note of their too-long embrace and he reluctantly set her down. She stared at him for several seconds, probably replaying his comment and wondering if he'd meant it like it sounded. Eventually, however, she visibly shook herself and looked around. "Oh." She reared back. "Where did everyone go?"

"I don't know." Sig shrugged. "Weird."

Four Months Later

Chloe sat in the stands of Boston Garden listening to the sounds of the Bearcats wrapping up practice. She'd become a regular at games, but not so much training. Today was a special occasion because Sig was going to give her a driving lesson afterward. She wasn't the only person spectating practice—several reporters were there, as well as a group of people taking a tour of the arena. Dozens of team administrators and coaches stood in groups on the outskirts of the ice, gesturing to the players, conferring.

She'd brought a book to read, but it sat in her lap unopened, her hands cemented around the spine, squeezing. Her heart knocked in her rib cage. Sig was so incredible out there, she couldn't seem to tear her eyes off him long enough to find her page. His behavior during practice differed from games. For instance, he was smiling a lot more today. *Talking shit*, as he called it, to his teammates. And yet he still stopped on a dime, spraying ice in a chilly plume. Still moved like a magician. Just switching back and forth from amused and jocular to devilishly fast and capable within seconds.

Flashbacks from the last four months came to her in snippets. Sig sitting in the front row of her performance holding roses. Sig passed out on her coach, exhausted after a game, covered by a fleece Barbie blanket. Sig showing up at a nightclub and dragging her out onto the sidewalk, claiming he wanted to see her home safely, when they both knew he didn't want her talking to other men. And so it went, this man being a massive fixture in her life.

Daily joy and daily . . . discomfort.

Like right now, she was so slick between her thighs, her vagina could pass for a miniature waterslide. There'd been a near incident yesterday when she'd overslept and woken up to Sig standing above her bed, looking worried, holding paper cups of coffee.

Assuming she'd been dreaming—because, honestly, she couldn't remember a night where Sig *didn't* star in her dreams, anymore—she'd arched her back and purred for him to get into bed and wake her up properly.

He'd almost complied.

Almost.

His muscles had stiffened, his pupils expanding, and he'd set her coffee down. She'd watched him thicken in the front of his jeans and reached for the growing ridge, but he'd strode out of the room before her fingertips could make contact. The slam of the front door alerted her to the fact that she was, indeed, very much awake. Not dreaming.

She already knew they were going to pretend it never happened.

And she hated that.

They talked about everything, but they avoided the topic of their attraction to each other like the plague.

A loud slam shot Chloe's heart up into her mouth.

Sig was vying for the puck with one of his teammates—Corrigan, she saw.

A whistle blew somewhere, ending the play, and both men looked up at Chloe. Corrigan grinned around his mouthpiece, using the end of his stick to salute Chloe, while Sig glared at him from two feet away. She saluted back, regardless.

Then Corrigan rapped his glove against the glass. "Let me get your number, though."

Sig took out his legs with a hard sweep of his stick, leaving Corrigan flat on his back. She couldn't make out the words her future stepbrother said while bending forward over his prone teammate, but a lot of them seemed to begin with "F." None of this surprised her, and it probably should.

No, it *definitely* should.

The coach brought the Bearcats together at the bench for some feedback from several members of the staff, after which they exited the ice through the tunnel.

"Ms. Clifford, you can follow me," said a security guard in a blue windbreaker to her left, smiling at her from the concrete steps. "You can wait for Mr. Gauthier by the team exit."

"Okay, thanks."

Ten minutes later, Chloe stood at the end of a long, brightly lit tunnel by a set of double doors, not far from the locker room. She could hear metal doors slamming, yelling, laughter, running showers—and just as she finally opened her book to read a few pages, Sig emerged from the chaos, hair wet, still in the process of pulling on his T-shirt. As in, no shirt yet.

Nothing to cover his smooth slabs of muscle. Or the tattoos she'd never seen.

Or that black trail of hair under his navel.

One of the shirtsleeves got caught and he cursed, twisting the fabric to correct the angle, and everything flexed at once, including his eight-pack . . . and she dropped her book. Probably went through puberty a second time, too. Adult puberty. Oh no. No. This accidental flashing was taking place way too soon following the wake-me-up-properly incident. Her hormones were multiplying like rabbits. How was she supposed to learn how to operate a motor vehicle in this state? How was she supposed to *breathe*?

Finally, he got his shirt down and continued his long-legged stride in her direction. "Hey, Chlo." He hesitated in front of her, but after a brief check of the empty hallway, ultimately leaned down to kiss her cheek. Once. Twice. "Sorry, I tried not to keep you waiting too long."

"It's fine," she said in a rush, goose bumps shivering down her back. "I'm reading."

He looked down at her dropped book and raised an eyebrow.

"I got to a scary part," she explained. "A jump scare. It flew right out of my hands."

"I see." He swiped a hand through his wet hair. "You ready for your driving lesson? We're going to use the underground parking garage."

"The one beneath the arena?"

"Yeah. It's empty." He ran a knuckle down her cheek. "No one for you to crash into."

"Oh, really?" she deadpanned. "What about the walls?"

"They can rebuild those."

Chloe broke into a laugh.

Sig's gaze traveled from her mouth to her eyes. Back down. "Listen, about yesterday—"

"There she is," said a voice behind Sig—one that caused him to roll his eyes. Corrigan.

And a second voice. "Stop trying to sneak her out of here before I get a chance to say hello." Mailer.

Collectively known as the Rookies. Or the ORGASM DONORS, according to the matching sweatshirts they often wore.

"Hey, Chloe," Mailer said, drawing even with her and Sig, shoulder to shoulder with Corrigan. Both of them were . . . hot, frankly. Tall and stacked. Corrigan with his wild reddish-brown hair and beard, Mailer with his ice-blue eyes and shaved head. To put it simply, however, they paled in comparison to Sig. From her point of view, anyway. Someone else might disagree.

That someone would be wrong, but they were entitled to their opinion.

Chloe smiled. "Hey, guys."

"Don't encourage them," Sig muttered.

"We don't need encouragement," Corrigan said, trying to slide in between her and Sig and getting an elbow to the chest for his effort. "Ow."

"What brings you to practice, Chloe?" Mailer asked, watching Sig's elbow out of the corner of his eyes, poised to block it. "Stop hiding your true feelings. You can tell them you came to watch me."

"Actually, Sig is going to teach me how to drive."

Corrigan did a double take. "You don't know how to *drive*?"

"Do you like your nose where it is?" Sig snapped. "Because I'd be happy to relocate it for you." He gave Chloe a reassuring look. "Plenty of people in Boston never learn how to drive. That's what the trains and buses are for."

"You're not going to teach her in that old truck, though, right?" Corrigan asked, obviously placing very little value on his life.

That moment marked one of the two times she'd seen Sig look less than 100 percent confident and in charge of his surroundings. The other time had been at the country club. When they'd walked into the lounge together to charge his phone and he'd seen the luxury she took for granted.

"I love his truck," Chloe blurted. "I never would have met Sig if it wasn't for that truck."

The Rookies exchanged a confused glance.

"But . . . really? I thought your parents were getting married. Isn't that how you met?"

"Yes," Sig said, emphatically. "It is."

Mailer looked like he was doing math. "So . . ."

"I'm confused," Corrigan added.

"Confused is your default," Sig shot back, steering Chloe out of the tunnel and into the parking lot. "Let's go."

"I love your truck," she whispered up at his set chin.

"Nah, they are right about this one thing. It's time for a new one."

"No." She dug in her heels, literally, but he merely picked her up and kept walking. "If you try and get rid of that truck, I'm going to handcuff myself to the wheel."

Humor was slowly drifting back into his expression. "I'd get a much higher price if you were included in the deal, dream girl. In the billions, at least . . ." He looked over his shoulder, presumably to make sure they weren't being followed. Then he hefted Chloe up so the fronts of their bodies were pressed together, her toes dangling in the vicinity of his shins. "Never mind, you're priceless," he grumbled, rubbing their noses together. "A high enough number doesn't exist."

Then he set her down, grabbed her hand, and kept walking.

Chloe floated on a breeze behind him, her body twisting in the air like a windsock.

"Don't get rid of the truck, Sig." She tugged on his hand, giving him her most pleading look when he turned around. "You love it. You told me it made you feel free. When your mom was working late and your house felt quiet, you'd go drive around and listen to sports radio in your truck and feel less lonely. Remember? It's part of you. It's . . . freedom, you know? For you *and* me. Please don't listen to those guys."

"I want to give you nicer things, Chloe. What you're used to."

Neither one of them addressed the fact that giving her nice things wasn't the traditional role of a stepsibling. Or that it was something a spouse might say. The irony went unnoticed. Or ignored, rather. "Out of everything I've ever had, you are the nicest." She let those words fly right out of her, unchecked. "And the truck is part of you. Keep it."

They were standing at the passenger-side door of said truck now, toe-to-toe.

There was something about the way Sig looked at her that said he was replaying her statement in his head on repeat. Good. Good, she was desperate and sexually frustrated today—maybe that made her too honest. And maybe it rubbed off on Sig.

Briefly, he looked back over his shoulder at the arena, turning back to face her with a locked jaw, leaning down to speak against her temple. "I'll keep the truck as long as you never give another man your phone number. How does that sound?"

Heat slithered up her thighs. "Sig . . ."

"Just make the promise. Don't think about why you shouldn't."

"I promise."

His mouth dipped to her neck, exhaling against her rioting pulse. "That's a good girl."

Her sex flexed so dramatically; she choked on a moan.

Seconds ticked by while she reeled, and Sig visibly struggled to get himself under control.

Finally, he opened the passenger door and boosted her inside, giving her a long, starved look while he engaged her belt buckle. "Maybe we should put off the driving lesson for another day."

Chloe closed her eyes and nodded. "Good idea."

Sig accepted a slap on the back from Burgess while sitting in the last row of lockers. He was taking his time getting dressed after practice, because he had an uncomfortable phone call to make and he didn't want to put it off any longer. And call him crazy, but there was something about the stench of freshly used hockey equipment that he found comforting.

When Sig heard the final locker slam, he rooted through his duffel bag and took out his phone, smacking it against his palm a couple of times, before hitting the third speed dial on his list, just below Chloe and Burgess.

Rosie. His mother.

It rang three times before she answered. "Hi, Sig."

"Rosie. Hi."

Sig couldn't remember the last time he'd called his mother by anything besides her first name. That formality had a lot to do with the way he'd been raised. Act like an adult. Tough it out. Suck it up. That had been the rhetoric at home and on the ice. At home, those lessons had been out of necessity. Mom wasn't home to make school lunch or drive him to practice, so he'd figured it out himself. Sig didn't hold a single ounce of resentment over being treated like an adult so young. Nah, he was stronger and more capable, thanks to that. Upon reaching college, he'd excelled while everyone else learned to take care of themselves for the first time. He had Rosie to thank for that, along with working herself to the bone to pay for hockey, food, shelter.

Unfortunately, the formal relationship with his mother also meant they didn't have a lot of heart-to-hearts, back then *or* now. He had more meaningful conversations with Chloe in the first week of their acquaintance than he'd ever had with Rosie. Hell, anyone.

That's what was going to make fishing for information about his father so difficult. But he'd been waiting for months to get a call from Sofia or Harvey saying they'd called off the wedding. That Sofia's high-priced lawyers had turned up something questionable from Harvey's past and advised her against the marriage. That they'd decided to be friends, instead. He'd *lived* for that phone call, so certain that it would arrive.

But it hadn't.

And Sig couldn't continue to leave his future with Chloe in someone else's hands.

If he'd given her that driving lesson last night, she'd have ended up on the rear gate of his truck with her legs spread. Every time he left her for the night, it got a little harder, verging on impossible. They gravitated toward each other like magnets. He missed her voice when he wasn't hearing it. She made every single day better just by being alive. Being his best friend, as well as his . . .

Fuck. There had to be a solution here.

"How is the weather in Boston?" Rosie asked.

Sig shook his head to clear it of visions of his hands tugging Chloe's panties down to her ankles, her knees opening to let him see it all. "Right now, it's raining," he said thickly, clearing his throat hard. "But it's not too cold for January."

"Ah. Good. I'll have to get out east soon for my annual trip to watch you play."

"Just let me know the game you want to see and I'll handle the rest," he said, automatically, knowing she'd probably wait until closer to the end of the season, as usual. She'd once explained she wasn't one for crowds or public events and needed time to psych herself up for the spectacle. "Is everything good with the house?"

"Better than good. Great. You know how much I appreciate what you've done for me, Sig. I don't say it nearly often enough."

He was already shaking his head, wishing he hadn't asked about the house. It almost sounded like he'd called for a pat on the back. "It's no problem. But listen, I called for another reason." He rubbed the back of his neck hard. "There's something I was hoping to ask you about."

The slightest hesitation ensued. "Oh?"

She already knew. He'd asked so many times before and been stonewalled.

"Yeah." He took a centering breath, stood, and slowly walked a path in front of the bench. "I know you don't like to talk much about Harvey. Or that whole mess back in the day. But, uh . . . I'm still curious about what went down. I always will be, you know? I can't help it, and now . . ."

Rosie's sigh emerged a little shaky. "Sig, I would really like to leave the past in the past."

"I realize that. I do. Could you just answer a few questions?"

"I'll try."

Sig glanced at the ceiling in relief, quickly decided which questions to prioritize. Maybe it was best if he started easy. "How long were you and Harvey in a relationship before you got pregnant with me?"

"Oh . . . about a year, I would say. Off and on. It was rocky at the best of times. But so was every other relationship among my friends." She laughed lightly, as if reminiscing, but her humor faded quickly. "Back when I still lived with my parents and life was simple—but only as long as I dated the men they approved of."

"And they didn't approve of Harvey."

"No. They'd already picked someone else out for me. Bobby Prince. And I tried to make that work, but Harvey always wormed his way back in. That's his way. He's a love bomber. You're so dazzled by his attention, you don't realize he's only seeing dollar signs."

"That's what I wanted to ask you about." He paused, trying to organize his thoughts. "At that point, your money was coming from your parents. How did he get access to it?"

"Sig, I would really like to move on from this for good, you know?"

Why was this always the point where she balked? The details of how Harvey allegedly took Rosie's money and hightailed it, leaving her alone and pregnant, seemed destined to remain muddy and indecipherable.

It was on the tip of Sig's tongue to explain to Rosie why he needed this information so badly. To tell her about Chloe for the first time ever. But he didn't. He wanted to know they could be permanent first. Talking about his girl out loud to his mother? He needed more freedom to do that. He needed forever to be in the bag, otherwise sharing her felt premature. Or like he was jinxing his chances of making them work.

Sig cleared his throat. "Did your parents offer to support you— us—after Harvey left?"

"With strings attached. There were always strings." She made an impatient sound. "We did all right on our own, didn't we, Sig? It wasn't so bad."

"No." He sighed. "No, Rosie. It wasn't bad at all. I wouldn't change anything."

Frustration was biting into his ribs. He'd reached another dead end. That much was obvious. He could push, but he was always hesitant to upset his mother. She was the only family he had and he wanted to remain on good terms. Still, he didn't want to end this phone call with nothing. He just needed a crumb. *Something* he could use to look into Harvey's background himself. Not only to prevent him from rendering Sofia, and thus, Chloe, penniless . . . but because if he didn't do everything in his power to stop the wedding, he'd regret it his whole life. "Do you happen to know any of the women Harvey dated after he left Minnetonka?"

This wasn't a question he'd asked before and it seemed to momentarily throw off his mother. When she recovered, her tone was almost bashful. "Well, I'll admit to doing some light internet stalking in a moment of weakness. Harvey and I retained one mutual friend—for a while, anyway. I've lost touch now. But they did delight in telling me he'd moved on to some beautiful heiress down in South Carolina, just months after he took off."

Had Harvey conned this heiress, too? "Do you remember her name?"

"I'm embarrassed to say that I do. But . . . well, he made an impression, I guess. The jealousy must have burned her name into my brain. It's Ulla Franklin."

Now it was burned into Sig's memory, too. "Thanks, Rosie. I'll let you go now."

"All right. Thanks for calling."

"Don't forget to give me a date to visit."

"I will, Sig. Bye now."

"Bye."

After hanging up, he remained eerily still for a moment, asking himself if he was really prepared to take the next step. One he'd been on the verge of pursuing for a while. It seemed extreme. No, it was. But he'd go to every extreme possible for Chloe. She was worth every effort available to him.

Sig scrolled to an email he'd received from his agent, David, a week prior. A response to a message Sig had sent the man asking if he could recommend a private investigator. Now, he clicked the phone number, which was highlighted in blue, and put the phone to his ear.

"Hello?" asked a voice on the other end.

"Hi. Is this Niko?"

"Who's calling, please?"

"My name is Sig Gauthier. You were recommended by my agent, David Malone."

"Right." Fingers tapped on a keyboard in the background. "What kind of investigation are you calling about?"

Five months later

Sig let himself into Chloe's apartment, freezing in place when he saw her standing less than five feet away . . . holding a cake. Covered with lit candles.

Behind her in the kitchen lay a mess of epic proportions. Pans and batter and filthy utensils on every surface. Hell, Chloe herself looked like she'd been doused in flour.

This couldn't be what he thought it was.

The very possibility weighed him down with so many emotions, he almost turned and walked out of the apartment. Her smile kept him there.

"What is this?"

"It's your birthday!"

Suspicion confirmed. She'd made him a birthday cake.

Oh fuck.

He'd been stung by a swarm of wasps in the dead center of his chest. He had tremendous balance, but just then, it was deserting him, so he tried to make it look casual when he closed the door and leaned back against it, using it to stay upright.

"You made that yourself, Chlo?"

Dumb question. He'd seen the kitchen. But words were failing him.

"Yes." She presented the cake higher, proud, but also worried. He could see that. She was worried he wouldn't like it? "No one ever talks about how hard it is to crack an egg. And then getting the broken piece out of the bowl? It's like . . . ugh. It just doesn't want to be caught, you know? Just when you think you've trapped that sucker, boom, it's gone."

Growing up, his mother had done everything she could to make the day special with limited resources and Sig treasured the memories of those slices of Entenmann's and cups of grape soda.

And his mother had called this morning. But it had been . . . damn. Almost a decade since the last time he'd celebrated his birthday with someone else.

To have it be Chloe?

To have her go to this much trouble?

And yet, he should have expected it from her. Because as much as he tried to do things for Chloe, she supported him, tended to him, in the ways she knew how. Never failing to be at his home games. Sending him audio of her playing the harp after a loss on the road. No words, just song. Just the presence of her—exactly what he needed.

Defending his truck.

Making him ice packs and propping his foot up on her little pillows. Sometimes he didn't even need ice, he just rubbed a part of his body and winced, hoping she'd fuss over him. He'd never had anyone fuss over him. Chloe did.

I love you. I love you so much. To my dying day.

"It's the most incredible cake I've ever seen in my life, Chloe," he said, finally finding his voice. "I can't believe you did this for me."

"You should." She flicked a look at the cake. "Do you really think it's incredible?"

"Yes."

She squinted a blue eye. "I definitely didn't get out all the eggshells."

"They'll add texture."

She laughed, pleasure bringing color to her cheeks. "Blow out the candles. Make a wish."

Sig leaned down, looking her in the eye while he made the wish. A wish he couldn't guarantee would ever happen. A wish that seemed to get further out of his reach the more time passed.

I wish for this same exact birthday next year, except you'll be wearing a wedding ring.

Mine.

Chloe turned on a heel and headed for the kitchen, presumably to cut the cake. "Don't tell me what it is, or it won't come true," she sang over her shoulder.

That's what I'm afraid of.

CHAPTER SIX

Now

"An actual zebra with a whistle would be better at your job, ref!" Chloe shouted at the top of her lungs, her sentiments echoed by the seventeen thousand Boston Bearcats fans in the arena behind her. "How do you *sleep* at night?"

"If he's smart? With one eye open," Tallulah drawled beside her in the front row. "You are easily the most terrifying fan to ever wear a pink, bedazzled, personalized jersey."

"Thank you," Chloe whispered, her voice catching a little when Sig used the sleeve of his uniform to wipe away the blood coming from his nose, as casually as one scratched an itch. She slapped the glass partition to get the ref's attention. "Last time I checked, slashing was a penalty! Did the visitors pay you in cash or Venmo?"

"At least Sig got to punch the other guy in the face," Tallulah pointed out, even as her gaze remained glued to her fiancé, Burgess Abraham, who defended the crease with his signature scowl.

"Not hard enough," Chloe muttered, realizing she was nervously worrying the hem of her pink Gauthier jersey and tried to stop, but in the dozen or so Bearcats games she'd attended since moving to Boston, she'd never actually seen blood oozing from Sig's face. Shouldn't he be taken out of the game? Or at the very least be examined by the trainer?

As if sensing her spiking nerves, Sig looked over at her and winked.

I'm fine, he mouthed.

Chloe melted back into her seat with a relieved exhale. Of course Sig was fine. It was just a little blood and her . . . confidant/guardian/future stepbrother/etc. could handle anything—and she meant *anything*. Low water pressure in her shower? Sig fixed it. She didn't know which combination of trains and buses to take to the conservatory? Sig arrived with coffees and showed her the perfect route. Her landlord banged on her door, demanding she pay the rent and she'd already spent half of it on cream blushes? Sig knew exactly what to do.

He was so wonderful, sometimes she cried about it in the shower.

The only thing Sig *couldn't* do was kiss her.

Chloe was trying to smile through the pressure in her breast when a man knelt in front of her, smiling in an apologetic way. "Sorry, I just don't want to block the game," he said, gesturing at the furious matchup taking place over his shoulder. "I'm Irving Randell from the *Boston Globe*. I don't officially report on the Bearcats yet, but I'm hoping to one day. Right now, I'm kind of a grunt. However, I *do* moderate the message boards." He dipped his chin at Chloe. "Have to say, you've been a real topic of conversation lately, Miss . . ."

Chloe started to answer, but stopped when Tallulah leaned over with a wary expression. "A topic of conversation how, exactly?"

"Usually, the hockey message boards are trade speculations or fans complaining about calls from the night before—"

"As they should," Chloe said earnestly.

"Yes. But a thread popped up recently titled 'Pink Jersey' and the response was . . ."—he made an explosive sound—". . . wild.

It's the longest message board thread to date. As in, *ever*. In the history of the *Globe* website." He squinted at Chloe. "You're at every single home game and your presence has even been noted by fans watching from home. Mainly, because of your . . . enthusiasm in the stands. People want to know who you are."

Chloe was distracted by the violent scuffle taking place over the man's shoulder. Thankfully, Sig wasn't involved in this one. "Oh, I'm—"

"Wait a sec, Chloe," Tallulah interrupted, squeezing her arm. "Maybe you should talk to Sig before you answer any questions."

Irving raised a dark eyebrow. "So you *do* know Sig Gauthier? Personally?"

The fascination in the man's tone finally captured Chloe's attention. Had he actually said there was a thread on the *Boston Globe* website concerning her pink jersey? "If people want to know where I had my jersey made, I'll share the Etsy shop!" She brushed at the sleeves. "As far as I'm concerned, everyone here should be wearing a Gauthier jersey—he's the best player on the team." Wincing, she reached for her friend's knee. "No offense, Tallulah."

"None taken," her friend responded with a dry smile.

"You're the au pair turned girlfriend of Burgess Abraham," Irving said, tossing a brief glance at Tallulah. "Right? And you're sitting with Pink Jersey. Which is why a lot of people have speculated, considering Abraham and Gauthier are such good friends off the ice, that maybe Pink Jersey is . . ."

"From Glinda's Glitz Haus," Chloe replied, back to being transfixed by the game. Didn't this man realize they were tied with five minutes to go in the third period? Crunch time had arrived, bitches. "Yes. It is," she murmured, distractedly. "Fast shipping. Excellent packaging, too. Are you going to plug her on the website?"

Irving opened his mouth and closed it again. "I mean . . . sure.

Sure. But I think what people are really wondering is whether or not you're Gauthier's girlfriend."

"Oh! *What?*" Chloe's heart sprouted legs and started running circles around her chest. *Gauthier's girlfriend.* Those two words side by side reminded Chloe of the cold plunge back at the country club. How it felt to submerge herself in that shockingly cold water, before running with her teeth chattering to the hot tub and warming back up again. Freezing followed by hot. That's what the phrase "Gauthier's girlfriend" did to her system. Flash froze it. Baked it.

Someday, a girl would call herself by that title.

But it wouldn't be her.

Who would she become to Sig when he eventually found someone he liked enough to date? Their relationship would have to change drastically, wouldn't it? No more falling asleep together on her couch in front of the television. No more extralong hugs that led to even longer looks, the occasional nuzzle or stroke of her hair. No more calling him just to hear his voice. That wasn't stepsister behavior. Two more months and they would officially have to stop toeing the danger line that was etched into the ground between them.

Living the life of a couple, knowing full well that could never be their reality.

Chloe forced humor onto her face, even though her windpipe had sealed itself shut. "No, I'm not his girlfriend. Of course not. My mother is marrying his father. Soon, too!" *Smile. Bigger. That's not big enough. Keep going.* "In two months, actually. I just got back from a wedding dress fitting with my mother in Paris. Wedding preparations are well underway. It's going to be the social event of the season, although people in Connecticut say that about every event, right down to the Botox parties. It really has lost all meaning."

Irving stared back at her. "You're Gauthier's . . . stepsister."

"*Future.* We're not related by marriage yet."

"So for now, you're . . ."

Friends. Best friends.

Right.

"I think you've gotten enough for tonight," Tallulah slid in, looking distinctly worried. "If you don't mind, we'd love to watch the rest of the game."

Irving shook himself. "Of course." As soon as the reporter stood up, someone screamed *puck in play.* "Uh . . ." He awkwardly hunkered halfway down, producing a white laminated rectangle from his pocket and handing it over to Chloe. "Here is my business card if you want to say anything else."

Chloe looked at the card. "Oh. It really does say 'glorified grunt.'"

The man flashed a distracted grin. "Told you so."

She shook her head. "Why would people be interested in my relationship with Sig?"

"What can I say? Boston loves a rumor. They also love black-and-white facts." His gaze ticked down to her jersey and back up. "When you can find a way to give them both, they eat it up, spoon and all."

"That doesn't sound awesome," Chloe said slowly.

"Timing-wise, it is. There is a list being published this week naming Boston's most eligible bachelors and Gauthier is right on top."

Flames erupted in Chloe's throat. The man who rubbed her back until she fell asleep some nights, the man who was slowly teaching her how to drive, the man who'd taken her to her first food truck festival and coached her through the process of frying an egg . . . was being announced as single and ready to mingle. "You're kidding. That's amazing." Irving was regarding her closely, so she forced herself to laugh, wincing inwardly when it fell flatter than a pancake. "I'm so thrilled for him."

Irving hummed. "Well. It has been nice meeting you both. Remember, if you want to expand on anything you've told me, my line is always open."

"Great," Chloe said, tucking the card into her clutch bag. "Thank you."

"No, thank *you*."

Chloe watched the reporter walk away with an increasing sense of queasiness. "This isn't going to be good, is it?"

"Probably not," Tallulah said without missing a beat.

The dread in her belly thickened. "Sig will know what to do. He always does."

Tallulah was quiet as the game clock ran out and the players cleared the ice, preparing for extra time. But the third time the Zamboni passed, she broke her silence. "Chloe, we've cried into mugs of hot chocolate together. I crashed in your guest room when me and Burgess were going through our own drama. We've witnessed each other in various states of angst and thus, I consider us close friends . . ."

"We are. You're my closest friend, besides—"

"Sig. I know."

Chloe's face warmed. Friends didn't stare into each other's eyes like it was their final moments on earth, the way she did with her future stepbrother, but what else could she call him? "I sense a 'but' coming."

"You sense correctly." After a brief glance over her shoulder, Tallulah leaned in. "Look, I've told myself this is none of my business over and over again. Maybe part of me was even afraid to ask. But the more time you and I spend together, the more I notice your relationship with Sig is very . . . unusual. And I hope you don't mind me saying that this upcoming wedding seems to be stressing you out. Which is normal! Your parent is getting married. But I guess what I'm trying to say is . . . are you stressed for a different reason?" The volume of her voice fell another degree. "Bluntly put, is there something romantic between you and Sig?"

"No!" Chloe said on a burst of air, out of pure reflex, because while she lived for what felt like stolen moments with Sig, she couldn't help but be ashamed of them, too.

Ashamed of herself.

Her mother was so in love. So gloriously happy. Sure, Chloe and Sofia's relationship had a whopping share of tension, her mother demanding details about Chloe's life in Boston before she'd deposit money into Chloe's bank account. Their Paris trip had been ruthlessly overscheduled with fittings, personal shopping excursions, and meetings with "friends" Sofia had collected on vacations over the years, but during their one-on-one moments, her mother had managed to land numerous subtle digs about Chloe's lack of survival skills, hinting that it was only a matter of time before Chloe returned to Darien. Coaxing her to come home.

Frankly, Chloe was a little nervous that Sofia hadn't done something more drastic to manipulate Chloe into moving back to Darien. She'd expected fireworks by now.

Or a bomb.

Maybe love had softened Sofia? Was that too much to hope for? Chloe had never, ever seen her mother this close to content. She'd called Chloe that very afternoon on cloud nine, thanks to Harvey signing them up for surprise salsa dancing lessons.

Yet here was Chloe, down in Boston, fantasizing about Harvey's son. Nightly.

Sometimes hourly.

Wishing and praying and obsessing over the possibility that Sig would give in one of these nights and kiss her again, like he had that night on the golf course. Just maul her to death. Honestly, she would leave the earth willingly at this point, if she could just feel his tongue in her mouth again, his grip in her hair. To have him unrestrained around her.

Sig was so controlled.

A good thing. A *necessary* thing.

On top of their parents being in love and getting married, Chloe was killing it at the conservatory. Opportunities were already beginning to open up for her, but those doors would slam closed if word got around that she was in a foggy, undefined relationship with someone related to her by marriage. Sig's profession put him in the spotlight as well, as evidenced by a reporter approaching her from the *Globe*. What if she hurt his standing with the team?

Obviously, what happened the night they met couldn't happen again. They were best friends. Some might say they were *way* too friendly. They probably needed to back off a little. And they would!

Eventually.

Chloe had kept her feelings to herself somewhat out of shame, somewhat from denial that they were doing anything wrong. Everyone had a different definition of wrong. Right? At the moment, however, with possessiveness gluing her to the plastic seat, the words "Boston's Most Eligible Bachelor" ringing in her ears, she couldn't keep the truth inside. Not entirely.

"Okay, here's the truth." She picked at an invisible string on her leggings. "We, um. We met two hours before we found out we were going to be stepsiblings. Let's say it was a very interesting meeting. One that is really hard to forget." Her throat squeezed at the memory of them running across the golf course, laughing, as if the world was wide open to them. As if they could go anywhere together without consequence. "Impossible, actually."

"You . . . kissed him."

"No. We kissed each other."

"Okay," Tallulah drew out, staring at her levelly. "Is that where the intimacy ended? Like, has anything happened since then?"

Chloe blinked. "Of course not. We'll be related by marriage in two months."

"I know." Her friend sobered even further. "I mean, technically, you wouldn't be breaking the law. You met as adults, you're not blood related. If Sig wasn't a professional athlete with a lot of eyes on him—"

"And an indignity like this wouldn't ruin my mother's social position and hinder my own prospects—"

"Exactly." Tallulah gave her a sympathetic wince. "It's . . . delicate. In so many ways. You did the right thing by stopping as soon as you found out your parents were tying the knot."

Well. That wasn't entirely true was it? Chloe and Sig might not have slept together, but sometimes she felt as though their relationship was *more* intimate than sex.

"Do you ever just wonder if maybe . . ." Tallulah started.

"What?"

Her friend seemed unsure about whether or not to continue. "The connection between you two is . . . blatant, for lack of a better term. It's palpable, like, at all times. And I guess I'm wondering if you two could get it out of your systems now. Before it is *technically* wrong to sleep together. You know, just to avoid a lifetime of wondering." She covered her face with both hands. "Am I a terrible person for saying any of this?"

"No." Chloe stared blindly at the ice. "Oh God, maybe you're right."

"No, I'm not. Don't listen to me. I am *not* right." Tallulah's expression turned even more serious. "And I'm sorry, Chloe. Your feelings for him must be really complicated. Everything *about* this is complicated."

Chloe nodded and nodded . . . and nodded some more, as if a spring in her neck was broken. "I don't think any amount of time could get this out of our systems," she whispered. "That's why we agreed to be friends only."

"Then you made the best decision," Tallulah said quietly.

"It doesn't feel like it." She attempted a smile, but it dropped like it weighed as much as an elephant. "Do you think I can bribe the *Globe* into canceling Boston's Most Eligible Bachelor list? And do you think they would accept unopened lipsticks as a bribe?"

Tallulah's throat shifted with a swallow. "Oh, honey."

Two bodies slammed into the glass. When Chloe saw that one of them was Sig and he was the victim of an obvious cross-check and the whistle didn't blow, she surged to her feet and slapped a frustrated hand on the glass. "Are you serious, ref?" The arena went nuts with boos and catcalls. "Your mom called. Even she thinks you're a hack!"

CHAPTER SEVEN

Walking into the friends and family waiting area after a game was always a mindfuck.

Burgess stopped talking to Sig midsentence and beelined for Tallulah and Lissa, drawing them both into a hug. Some of the younger players broke off, heading for a group of their friends. Or their parents. But mostly, his teammates reunited with their wives. Babies or toddlers in miniature jerseys. Everyone separating into family units, murmuring to one another and making plans. Saying things like, *I can't wait to get into my pajamas.*

Sig had Chloe.

She was always waiting for him after home games, standing off to the side in her pink jersey, purse tucked beneath her arm like a proper society girl, watching his teammates reunite with their loved ones. Struggling to smile, the same way he did. Because their relationship wasn't an easy one to define. Nothing about it was easy.

Was she a friend? Yes.

Was she *only* a friend. Nope.

Was she family? Sort of. Not yet, but . . . verging.

Sig stood in silence at the set of doors leading from the tunnel to the waiting area, composing himself. It was always necessary for him to do this. To take a moment and remember why he couldn't simply walk up to Chloe and kiss the face off her, the way a lot of his teammates were doing with their wives. In a parallel universe, where their parents weren't engaged, he was carrying Chloe out to his truck right now, cursing the fifteen-minute ride to their house, because he couldn't wait to be inside of her. His girl. His everything.

They weren't in a parallel universe, however. This was real life—and there was only one of those. And so, Sig climbed the same mental mountain he climbed after every game. He scaled the sides of it until he reached the plateau, also known as his personal purgatory. The place where he couldn't have Chloe, but he couldn't for the life of him stay away from her, either. Not for a single day.

Which had made the last four days miserable while she'd been in Paris with her mother. The very sight of her right now was like walking again after ninety-six hours of being paralyzed.

What was the correct way to greet a woman you loved with every fiber of your fucking soul, but couldn't have?

It was getting harder and harder to figure that out.

Chloe was beginning to look uncomfortable by herself in the coupled-up family area, which propelled Sig into motion. He hefted his gear bag more securely onto his shoulder and wove through a few groups to reach Chloe, who softened at the sight of him. Just kind of exhaled with her entire body, wringing her hands briefly before giving him a quick hug. Way too quick.

They didn't hug like that when they were alone.

People were watching, though. Wondering about their dynamic. Why Chloe came to every game like a devoted girlfriend, when in fact, she was his future stepsister. Yeah, they wondered about his relationship with Chloe for a damn good reason.

He wondered about it, too. Day and night.

Mainly about how much longer he could embody this obsession with Chloe without having a nervous breakdown. Niko, the private investigator, was still in the process of verifying the preliminary facts and the case, not to mention sifting through Harvey's plethora of past relationships, which was taking time. A lot more time than Sig and Chloe had.

"Hey," he said, letting her go from their brief embrace. Feeling eyes on his back. "Thanks for coming."

She gave him a prim look. "I don't think the refs were very glad to see me."

He chuckled, remembering her indignant pout on the other side of the glass.

Indignant and beautiful. God, so fucking beautiful.

"Nope," Sig responded. "Pretty sure every ref in the league has your face pinned to a dartboard in their kitchen."

Humor was slowly beginning to replace the tension that was always between them at first. The moments that held the empty space where a kiss would be, if they were free to express themselves honestly. "With their poor eyesight? I'm not worried about them hitting a bull's-eye." She scrutinized the lower half of his face, her gaze snagging on the bandaged cut on his nose. "Is it bad?"

"Nah. I've cut myself worse shaving."

With her attention fastened on his jaw, she hummed quietly.

Sig moved a little closer. As much as he dared in this setting. "What?"

"Nothing," Chloe murmured. "I've just never seen you shave before."

He swore his heart was beating in his stomach. Every time. She did this to him within seconds *every time*. "Would you want to watch me shave, Chlo?" he asked, after a brief check over his shoulder. To make sure no one was within earshot.

Slowly, her eyes climbed up to meet his. "Yes."

It took an effort to keep his breathing even. Was this a crazy conversation to be having in the friends and family area after a game? Absolutely, yes. Was it odd for him and *this* woman? No. Not at all. There was nothing typical about her. Or them. There might be dozens of people scattered throughout the room, but when they were standing this close and no one else could hear them, anything went with Chloe. And he lived and breathed to find out what she would say and do next.

"If you shave for me," she said for his ears alone, her tone playful now, "I'll let you help me decide what I should wear for the first day of my new mentorship tomorrow."

He dismantled that statement piece by piece, examining every part of it.

"Hold up. You're starting a new mentorship tomorrow?"

She nodded, a smile blooming across her mouth. "My instructors told me they were trying to land me a mentorship with the first chair harpist at BSO." Boston Symphony Orchestra. "I got the email while I was in Paris. They are going to take me on."

Sig tried not to stare at those lips. Failed. "When were you going to tell me this was in the works?"

"You're busy with the season."

He scoffed. "On day five of Hell Week, you texted me that you wanted French toast, so I brought you out for French toast, in between practices. In a sweaty T-shirt and shorts." He tamped down on the urge to lean down and kiss her forehead. "You know damn well I'm never too busy for you, Chloe. Why *really* didn't you tell me?"

Her smile dipped. "Because I'm nervous and I was thinking of backing out."

Again, he struggled not to reach for her. "Okay. We'll talk it out."

"All right, Bearcats fam," called the arena's maintenance guy, Augie. "We're turning the lights off and going home, if you don't mind making your way to the parking lot."

"Night, Augie," Burgess boomed to Sig's right, throwing the man a salute. "Thanks."

Everyone followed the captain's lead, shouting their thanks at the maintenance man, while filing out into the team parking lot. Once they reached Sig's truck, Chloe exchanged a hug with Tallulah and Lissa. Sig fist-bumped Burgess. And then Sig was boosting Chloe into the passenger seat of his truck, wincing as he always did when the damaged leather touched her thighs. "Don't even start grumbling about a new truck. Not again," she said, preemptively, checking her appearance in the rearview, her pinkie dragging a U-shape beneath one of her eyes. "This one is perfect."

It physically burned to drive her around in this beat-up old thing. She used to have a designated town car and a *chauffeur*, for fuck's sake. "It's time for a new one."

She clicked her seat belt into place. "Only if you want to find me handcuffed to the steering wheel."

Sig glanced over his shoulder at the parking lot to judge how alone they were. Whether or not anyone was watching. When he found them to be out of everyone's view, he ducked into the truck, bringing his forehead an inch from Chloe's and listening to her quick intake of breath. Memorizing the way she closed her eyes, her lashes making spiky patterns on her cheeks. "Are you implying you own a pair of handcuffs, Chloe?"

"Maybe," she said on an exhale—and he wished he could feel that breath on his entire body. Against his chest, below his waist. *Everywhere.*

Sig nudged her forehead with his own. "I'm not in the mood to play games after four days without seeing your beautiful face. Give me a better answer."

He could see his words absorbing into her skin. Could *sense* the intake. "Are you implying I might have cuffs for recreational purposes?"

"Do you?"

"When would I manage to use handcuffs with a man?" She wet her lips, nearly grazing his mouth with her tongue. So close but so far. "I can't go home with anyone when you always show up at the bar to take me home yourself."

"I promised to look out for you."

"You might have taken that responsibility a little too far, don't you think?"

Sig's heart paused midbeat. "Do you want me to stop?"

She shook her head rapidly. "No."

His heart kicked back into gear. God, he wanted to ruin that pink lip gloss. Kiss her until it was smeared all over his mouth, chin, and tongue. "Okay then."

"Okay then," she breathed unevenly. "Just so we're clear."

Break. Now. Time for a break.

Jaw clenched tight enough to snap, Sig removed himself from Chloe's space and ducked back out of the truck. He put his hands on his hips and paced in a slow circle, attempting to bring his pulse back to a normal rate. He'd only managed it slightly by the time he got into the driver's side and fired up the engine.

Being this close with Chloe on a near constant basis was torture at its most pure and he would volunteer for it until the day he died.

No one was going to have the honor of being Chloe's companion but him.

But how long could they go on like this without giving in?

Sig didn't have an answer to that. But he knew one thing very well.

He had to figure out a way for them to be together.

There simply wasn't another option. Chloe ending up with someone else?

Not a fucking chance.

Sig glanced over to double-check that Chloe had put on her seat belt, even though he'd witnessed her engage the buckle, before pulling out onto the road. Traveling in the direction of her apartment.

Finally, he'd composed himself enough to speak. "Back to this mentorship. When did you decide to do it?"

"Well." She sat up a little taller on the seat. "I'm going to continue at the conservatory, as planned, but my instructors . . . they say there is nothing else they can teach me."

Pride rocked into his chest. Not only had she left her life of luxury behind and moved to an entirely new city, but she'd adapted quickly to living alone, commuting, making friends, like Tallulah. Proven herself and thrived at Berklee, exactly as he'd known she would. "Damn, Chlo."

"Yes. But that implies there is something this mentor *can* teach me. Right?"

"Uh-huh. That tracks." He glanced over to find her looking deep in thought. "You don't want to find out if there is something you don't already know?"

"I guess I do," she hedged. "But it's been a long time since anyone pushed me, Sig. I've always just naturally been a badass on the harp."

He chuckled. "The baddest."

"What if it's like that movie *Whiplash*? Where the instructor tortures me psychologically so he can break me down and rebuild me in his image?"

"Easy. I will fucking kill him."

"Ooh. Promise?"

Heat swamped the back of his neck at the thought of her being bullied. "*Yes.*"

He sensed, rather than saw, her smirk. "Her name is Grace

Shen and by all accounts, she's a consummate professional. You can stop committing mental murder now."

At the news that Chloe's mentor was a woman, his blood ceased to boil, but the possessiveness remained at a simmer. It always did. Ready to rollick at a moment's notice. For instance, what if Grace had an assistant who didn't find it unprofessional to ask Chloe on a date? There were too many variables . . . and as long as they were just friends, Sig had a blade hanging above his neck at all times.

"Are you really going to shave for me?" Chloe asked, distracting him.

Speaking of blades near his neck. "Have I ever said no to anything you wanted?"

"No," she said, not hesitating.

"You said if I shaved for you, you would let me help you decide what to wear to your first mentorship meeting."

"I did say that." He was certain that he caught her shivering in his peripheral vision, her voice significantly softer when she added, "I could do a quick fashion show for you when we get home . . ."

Sig couldn't respond. He was too busy trying to keep his dick locked in neutral. As always. It was a losing battle and he knew, as always, he'd be leaving her apartment hard as nails tonight, just like he did every other time. But there was a pretense to uphold. They were best friends who would eventually be related, but weren't quite related yet, having an innocent fashion show at eleven o'clock at night in her bedroom.

Totally normal.

Nothing to see here.

CHAPTER EIGHT

Whenever Sig graced her apartment with his presence, Chloe had to refrain from doing an embarrassing little dance. Sometimes she gave into the urge and let her excitement at being around him show. Oher times, like tonight, when they'd already pushed their limits a little too far, she held back out of necessity.

Still . . . having Sig over was the best. THE BEST.

He sauntered around like a cranky tiger, straightening picture frames and folding up throw blankets. Frowning at all the crumpled-up Sephora bags in the trash can. Grumbling. Checking her cabinets to make sure she had enough food.

Chloe really did her best not to stare as he completed these rituals, but not staring at Sig Gauthier was like going to the beach and ignoring a brilliant pink-and-orange sunset.

In his sweatpants, Bearcats hoodie, and wet, freshly showered hair, he was the sun itself, as far as Chloe was concerned. The meaning of the name Sig meant "a victory that brings peace and protection" and that definition couldn't be more accurate. He was thoughtful and encouraging and, oh yeah, superprotective. Most important, however, Sig believed in her. In a way she'd never experienced from someone she loved.

Sure, she knew her mother believed in her musical abilities, but Sofia never took an active interest beyond bragging about them or scheduling her an audience where Sofia could bask in the accolades afterward. Similar to Chloe's estranged father, Sofia used these performances as a social tool. A magic trick to pull out of the bag at parties or a way to meet interesting people abroad. Since coming to Boston Chloe had started to ponder the possibility that her mother had never pushed her to take bigger chances with her music because she wanted to keep Chloe at home, under her thumb. Meanwhile, Sig asked Chloe what she wanted. She never had to worry about an ulterior motive with him. With Sig, there was nothing but safety.

Emotionally, at least.

She was eons away from being satisfied physically. Sig had lit a fuse six months ago in Connecticut and she was getting dangerously close to the end of it.

Trying to ignore the way her pulse thumped, Chloe leaned a hip against her kitchen table, watching him do his rounds a few yards away in the kitchen. "I don't think I even congratulated you on winning tonight."

"That's okay. I know you're pumped when we win." He took an empty Pop-Tarts box out of the cabinet, showing her the lack of contents with a frown, before tossing it onto the counter. Instead of continuing his search as usual, he braced his hands on the counter, staying silent for a few beats, before looking over at Chloe again. "Burgess is officially retiring after this season. He told me tonight before the game."

Goose bumps raced down Chloe's arms.

Burgess "Sir Savage" Abraham was an institution. A Bearcats legend and one of the most beloved figures in Boston. Sig's idol turned close friend. Tallulah's future husband. Hearing that he would no longer be part of the team Chloe had grown to love with her whole heart over the last six months was . . . expected, yes, since he'd recently faced a back injury and he was approaching his late thirties. But the news was still like a blast from two shocker paddles.

"Oh my gosh." She pushed off the table and entered the kitchen, approaching Sig slowly. "How do you feel about that?"

"I don't know." A muscle hopped in his jaw. "Mostly sad, I guess."

"Of course."

"I'm nervous about the changes that'll need to be made."

"Like . . . you taking over as captain?"

Sig grunted. Hesitated before nodding.

As much as she hated how unsettled Sig was clearly feeling, she couldn't help but soak in the fact that he was confiding in her. No one had ever chosen her to be the keeper of their worries and concerns and fears. It was just another reason she treasured this person above all others. How could she not? He'd worked his way up to the highest level of his profession. He wasn't just born with a heap of talent, like her. No, he'd honed it with his blood, sweat, and tears, day after day. And while she crowed to anyone who would listen that Sig was the best player on the ice, he never said it himself. He just . . . showed it. Showed up.

Sig Gauthier *always* showed up.

Chloe thought carefully before speaking. Thought about what he'd said to her in the car. Wanted to say the exact best thing, like *he* always did. "Burgess is ready. And you're ready. You're each ready for different things and you're both well prepared for them."

He cut her a sideways look. Swallowed. "They're not going to love me the way they love him."

I'll love you enough for this whole city.

She firmed her chin. "Oh yes, they will. They love players who sacrifice everything for the W, so they'll love you most of all." Throat aching, she inched closer, close enough that she could lift onto her tiptoes and press her lips against his shoulder through the padding of his sweatshirt. "Give them a chance. More importantly, give yourself a chance."

His throat worked for several seconds, before he rasped a chuckle. "When did you start saying shit like, 'sacrifice everything for the W'?" Amusement lightened his eyes. "Didn't I find you at a freaking country club?"

A genuine smile exploded across her face. "I've evolved!"

He straightened from his lean against the counter and faced Chloe, taking her by the wrists and walking her backward through the kitchen, then into the dining area, his heat already making contact with her skin, straight through their clothes. "Next you're going to be spouting off my stats for the season and quoting Gretzky."

"You miss 100 percent of the shots you don't take."

"Oh my God." Sig threw his head back and laughed. "*I* didn't even know he was the one who coined that phrase. How did *you* know?"

"It's common knowledge!" They were in the hallway now. The one that led to her bedroom and Chloe's heart rate was bouncing like a rubber ball in her veins. "Also, it's written on the beer koozie of the man who sits behind me at the games." She gave a solemn nod. "He has season tickets, so I see that beer koozie *a lot.*"

Sig slowed them to a stop, right on the threshold of her bedroom, searching her face with an expression she couldn't name. Somehow like . . . bewilderment? "What the hell am I going to do about you being so cute? Huh?"

Words spoken earlier that night came back to her in a wave.

The connection between you two is . . . blatant, for lack of a better term. It's palpable, like, at all times. And I guess I'm wondering if you two could get it out of your systems now. Before it is technically wrong to sleep together.

You know, just to avoid a lifetime of wondering.

A lifetime? Of never knowing what if felt like to be consumed by this man?

Was she delusional to ever have thought such a thing was possible?

"Maybe you should listen to Gretzky . . ." With her conversation with Tallulah ringing in her ears, Chloe went up on her toes and whispered against Sig's chin, "And take a shot."

Strained surprise rippled at the corners of his mouth, his thumbs digging into the pulses of her inner wrists. "*Chloe.*"

She gave him several beats to accept the invitation, but his restraint only seemed to intensify. Hiding her disappointment with a blithe smile, Chloe extricated her wrists from his hands, though it took him a few seconds to release her—and even then, she could feel him struggling not to snatch them back. That struggle allowed her to hope.

Hope for what, though?

What are you doing?

Unclear. She only knew the phrase *get it out of your systems* had continued to circle her thoughts until it unleashed a sort of . . . permission. A dangerous sort of bravery.

"So, I'm a little bummed . . ." Chloe said, turning and opening the door of her walk-in closet.

Seconds ticked by. "Why?"

"Because I have a specific top I like to wear for good luck, but I forgot to pack it last time I was in Connecticut," she said, entering the space. Hesitating. Taking a deep breath. Then stripping off her pink Gauthier jersey, slowly, so slowly, savoring the fact that Sig was watching her disrobe from the entrance of the closet, probably shocked, but unable to look away. Heard his hands smack and brace on the sides of the frame. The creak of wood as the pink material dropped to the floor. His hitched groan. "It's a black-and-white pattern, has long sleeves and this high, ruffled neck. Silk." She looked back at him over her shoulder, her knees turning to jelly at his expression—the embodiment of pure hunger. Yearning. The same kind she felt, without cease. "I've always played the harp best when I'm naked. And that blouse makes me feel like I'm wearing nothing at all."

His chest rose and plummeted, his words tangling up in one another. "When and . . . where did you play the harp naked?"

"All the time." Hanging on to her courage, she removed a forest-green button-down from her rack of clothes, examined it, and hung it back up. "When I used to have one in my bedroom."

"The harp is in the parlor at your other house," he grated.

"We have three harps."

He scrutinized her, jaw grinding, very visibly trying to keep his thoughts on track. "Do you miss having access to one at all times, the way you did when you lived with Sofia?"

Chloe had just taken a pair of cigarette pants off their hanger with the use of unsteady fingers, but she paused to breathe in and out, consider the question. "Yes, I miss having a harp with me at all times. But I like my freedom in Boston more."

The trench between his brows remained. "Glad to hear it."

Sometimes she could tell that Sig was recording and cataloging things inside of his head, but she never knew when, where, or how he would unearth them for future use. For instance, a month ago she'd tripped on an uneven floorboard in the hallway outside of her apartment. Sig had wordlessly caught her by the back of her sweater before she could fall down, setting her back upright and going about his business carrying groceries inside. But a couple of days later, she'd left for barre class and found him on his hands and knees fixing the floorboard, while the shame-faced super stood nearby.

She breathed her way through the seemingly endless round of warm shivers, the delight of having his eyes on her nearly bare back. "What do you think I should wear, since I don't have my lucky blouse?"

"You look amazing in everything, Chloe."

"You don't have to sound so irritated about it."

He made a sharp sound. "Irritated doesn't begin to cover it."

"Explain what you mean."

"The fact that other men get to see you look so beautiful . . ."

She tried to hold her breath, but couldn't. "Keep going."

His explanation came out in a gruff rush. "I don't think it would piss me off half as much if I was the one who knew what you looked like without clothes on."

Chloe closed her eyes and let the rush of exhilaration travel from the crown of her head, down to her curled toes. She wasn't supposed to enjoy Sig's jealousy, right? How many articles and cautionary Reddit tales had she consumed about male behaviors that constituted red flags?

So many.

When she stopped to think about how involved Sig was in every aspect of her life, she knew the boundaries were blurred enough to be nonexistent. Yet she *loved* him crossing those lines. His possessiveness turned her on. In fact, she *craved* those too-brief glimpses of it, because she could never feel caged or crowded by Sig. Not the man who'd shown her how to spread her wings. How to navigate the city, buy food for herself, make online payments (when she remembered).

As much as he guarded her like the crown jewels, he supported her independence.

It was only occasionally she wanted to be pinned down and told she belonged to him.

Okay, fine. She wanted that constantly.

Obviously he wanted that, too, so why couldn't they give in? Just once.

"Should I keep stripping so you can find out?"

His breath rasped in and out. "Yes. God help me."

Chloe held up the garment in question, even though her arm was shaking. "I'll probably wear these with a simple white button-down. Since I'm going for professional."

Sig nodded. She turned briefly to watch a line snap in his cheek. "Try it all on."

The small muscles of Chloe's sex drew in tight on themselves. "Okay," she murmured, undoing the front snap of her black bra. Exposing her breasts to the cool air of her closet, watching excitement turn her nipples to hard pearls as she drew the straps down her arms. Off.

She didn't turn around. She was too afraid his intensity would cause her to combust.

Already she was on the verge, just having his gaze lick her back like a flame.

And when she reached for the closest white button-down shirt hanging on the rack, she knew Sig caught the full profile of her left breast. Knew it for sure by the low sound of hunger he emitted, the splintering sound the wood doorframe made in his grip.

"You'll wear a bra with that tomorrow, right?" Sig asked, noticeably struggling to keep his voice even. Stopping to breathe in and out between the fifth and sixth word.

"Yes," she answered, pulling the shirt on over hypersensitive skin, fastening the buttons with shaking fingers. "I just don't feel like hunting up my nude one right now."

"Good."

The silence between them stretched, but it was far from quiet inside their bodies. Minds. Chloe knew on instinct she wasn't alone in that. Her heart was loud, knocking into her ribs, and intuition told her Sig was in the same state. They were a messy pair. *Everything* about what they were doing was messy but stopping seemed impossible.

Chloe bit down on her bottom lip until she felt pain, needing to distract from the hunger yawning in her belly. How it reared its head when she bent forward slowly, pushing her leggings down to her knees. Then, lower, to her ankles. She needed him to look at her mostly bare backside, the way he was doing now. She needed him to see the minuscule black thong she'd worn after touching herself to fantasies about him that morning, the tight fit against her sex making her think of him inappropriately all day.

Every time she sat down or stood up.

Sig was openly panting behind her. Not hiding his lust. Not for the moment.

That's why she couldn't turn around. If she saw it and couldn't slake it, she'd die.

"Christ, you are so goddamn gorgeous." She heard him swallow a jagged groan. "I want to wrestle you down and fuck you so bad, I'm shaking. Are you happy?"

Sound rushed in her ears.

It might have been her, though. Gasping for air. She couldn't be sure. "No. Yes."

"Give me the next best thing. Pick up that jersey and drag it up between your beautiful legs."

Chloe's knees dipped, the erotic command sending every ounce of blood in her body rushing south. Had she initiated this? Yes. But the need tightening its grip around her was more intense than she could have imagined. Would it kill her to only experience this once and then stop? Possibly. Maybe she'd been shortsighted to even try. "Sig . . ."

"Tell me you don't want more of this, too."

"I do. I do so bad." She started to tremble, her nipples so tight they felt like they were being pinched in between two powerful fingers. Lust took the driver's seat, then, propelled there by the raw desperation in his tone. Closing her eyes, she bent forward another inch and picked up the jersey, pressing the cool mesh to her inner ankle and slowly, slowly trailing it up the curve of her calves, the insides of her knee, whimpering when she reached the sensitive inner portion of her thighs.

"Good girl. If I can't be between your thighs, let me enjoy having my name there." After a moment of heaving breathing, his voice dropped another octave. "Press it where we both wish I could put my cock, Chloe."

A sob wrenched from her throat and she was forced to stabilize herself by slapping the flat of her left hand onto the wall while her right one pulled the jersey upward another two inches and pressed. Hard to her core. Hard enough to make her breath escape in a shudder.

"Goddamn," he rasped. "Does it feel good?"

Chloe could barely see the closet wall in front of her. Everything in her world was a blur of shapes and colors, the waves of need growing larger, more powerful. "Not as good as you would feel."

"*Fuck.*"

She dropped the jersey out of necessity, bracing both hands on the closet wall now, using all her strength to squeeze her thighs together, even if that only made the ache intensify.

"Sig, I can't have you anymore, without *having* you. I can't do it anymore."

A few seconds passed in silence. "I'd rather torture myself with you than be with anyone else." He cursed under his breath and she sensed, rather than saw him take a step in her direction, his fingertips just barely grazing her spine. "Come here."

She turned and barreled straight into his chest, knowing he wouldn't budge an inch, sighing with equal parts frustration and relief as he wrapped her in his arms, holding her like letting go was an unthinkable concept, his hands stroking her hair, up and down her spine.

"We'll stop," he said against her temple, before rubbing his cheek on the spot. Hauling her closer, higher until her toes were barely brushing the ground. "I let it go too far and now I'm hurting you. We'll stop."

"It's still going to hurt tomorrow."

And the day after and the day after that.

"Don't say that, Chloe. I'd rather die than hurt you."

His words did nothing to diminish the hopeless feeling inside of her. For the last six months, she'd had this secret belief that Sig would find a way for them to be together. That everything in her life would work itself out, like it always had. However, along with her new and expanding awareness that life outside of Darien wasn't designed for her enjoyment came the realization that . . . life *didn't* always work itself out.

She was in love with Sig.

And they might not end up together.

That was reality.

Every day, she fell deeper, too. Maybe . . . maybe she needed to find a way to put the brakes on before she went careening over the side of a cliff.

Maybe it was time to start thinking about dating?

Why did the very idea make her stomach shrink to the size of a pea?

Holding on to the last thread of her courage, Chloe pressed her tongue to his neck and licked up that thick cord of muscle that caused her so many sleepless nights. "We could give in just once," she whispered. "No one would know."

Sig pulled back just enough to meet her eyes, letting her see the agony, the regret, the lust. All of it. "Feel me, dream girl." He jerked her right leg up around his hips and tilted his lower body, grinding upward and lifting her higher, to the very tip of her big toe, until her vision went totally black. "You think I could stop at *once*? I'd *never* be able to stop. I'd be hiking up your skirt at their wedding reception. I'm already an addict and I've never even gotten a hit."

"Taste me." Liquid heat pooled between her thighs. Preparing. Every underused muscle below her belly button cinched up and twisted. "Everyone already suspects us."

"Yeah, but *I* know I'm doing right by you, Chloe." He dropped his mouth over hers, his frustrated breath heating her lips. "I'm not giving in unless it's right. Unless I know that I'm not dragging you into something wrong. Something that could hurt you. Your future."

"Drag me. *Please.*"

He interlocked their lips and moaned.

Chloe's heart went wild. She held her breath. This was it. This was it. Damn the consequences. They would burn alive now and figure out a plan tomorrow. Sig would know what to do. He'd know how to turn what they were into something socially acceptable, so it wouldn't bring shame to her family name or hurt any possible advances in their careers. So they wouldn't have to be judged by everyone in their lives and everyone they ever met in the future. How could something that inspired this much love inside of her be so bad?

"Sig, please. Just take me to bed."

"Jesus Christ. Don't you think I want to? Feels like I've spent my whole life wanting to get inside you. I fucking *belong* there." Avoiding her eyes, he set her down and backed off, raking five unsteady fingers through his hair. Pacing out of the closet and into her bedroom. Stopping. "I have to go before I let us do something we can't take back, Chloe."

With that, he took one final agonized look at her, his gaze blazing a path down to her naked thighs, before he turned on a booted heel and strode for the door.

Still stunned, she stared at the space he'd occupied, the sound of the front door opening finally forcing her into motion. Leaving? He was just going to *leave* after she'd made herself completely vulnerable? "When I said I can't do this anymore, I meant it," she called, speed walking after him. *Stop talking. You're keyed up. You're going to say something you'll regret.* But the voice of reason was a lot quieter than her sexual frustration at that very moment. "Having you and not having you at the same time . . . I can't live like this anymore. It's torture."

Just outside the apartment door now, he spun around, regarding her with guarded shock. Dawning panic. "*Chloe*—"

"I think we should both start dating other people," she blurted, watching his left eyebrow hoist very slowly, and very dramatically. "Not that *we* were ever dating, but you know what I mean. Maybe it'll be easier to be best friends if we have separate, healthy romantic lives, you know?" A scalding hot iron branded the insides of her throat. "There won't be so much . . . of an expectation for us to be everything to each other when we simply *can't* be everything to each other. We can't keep pretending the way we are is normal."

He stared back at her like he couldn't comprehend anything coming out of her mouth.

"You know, you made the list of Boston's Most Eligible Bachelors." The words scraped the walls of her throat like hot sandpaper. "It's perfect timing."

More confusion lit his eyes. "I . . . what? How do you know that?"

"It doesn't matter."

"What a coincidence. Neither does some ridiculous list." He tunneled frustrated fingers through his hair. "I'm coming back in so we can straighten this out."

He started forward, but she shook her head adamantly. "There is nothing to discuss and . . . listen, I just want to be alone. Good night, Sig."

Closing the door on his stricken expression was one of the hardest things she'd ever done in her life. But despite the tears burning in her eyes and the hormonal wreckage that was her overwrought body, Chloe couldn't help but feel proud of herself. At least she'd tried. At least she'd been brave in calling out the problem by name, in detail, even if the effort didn't pay off.

It was comforting to know she'd gotten stronger.

If only she could stop being weak for a man who obviously wasn't meant for her.

CHAPTER NINE

Sig was really taking a huge chance driving his junker from Boston to Darien—and the ancient engine was making its grievances known. But Chloe wanted her good luck blouse for tomorrow, so she was going to get the goddamn blouse. As long as Sig had a single breath in his lungs, if she wanted something, he'd go get it for her.

No questions or debates.

Not even if she'd spit roasted his fucking heart tonight and left it out to bleed.

He needed to speak to his father. Immediately. There were only two months remaining until the wedding . . . and now he'd lost Chloe. Lost her in a capacity he'd never really had her, but reason didn't make the gaping wound in his chest any smaller or less excruciating.

Sig blindly took the exit to Darien, his tires squealing as he took the left onto the service road that would take him toward the Sound—and the Clifford residence.

The worst part about tonight was he'd hurt Chloe.

Had she been the one to strip nearly naked and beg to be taken to bed? Yeah—and he'd be replaying every second of that adult game of peekaboo until he was old and gray. But the fact that Chloe started it didn't matter. Sig was the one with the inside information. He was the one keeping his father's past to himself, hoping it would derail the wedding. Even if that happened, Sig would still be so fucking worried about being able to provide for Chloe that he wouldn't give himself the privilege of sleeping with her until he had a secure contract with the Bearcats. Money and security to offer her.

Chloe knew none of that.

She only knew she'd been denied.

That truth sat in his stomach like a dozen bricks. He could barely remember the three-hour drive, because he continued to replay not only what happened earlier, but over the course of the last six months since Chloe moved to Boston. God knew their relationship had never been easy. How could it be? There was enough sexual tension between them to fill every hockey arena in North America. But in the beginning, when he'd rented her the apartment and showed her around Boston, he'd kept his filthy hands to himself. Mostly. He'd left her place without watching her strip, at the very least.

He didn't speak to her like he spoke to her tonight.

Press it where we both wish I could put my cock, Chloe.

Sig squealed to a stop at a red light and rolled down the window, letting cold air into the truck so he wouldn't arrive sweating. Maybe he shouldn't have made this impulsive trip to visit Harvey. Hell, he hadn't even called first. But he kept hearing Chloe say *I can't do this anymore.* Kept hearing her suggestion they date other people. So, no, he couldn't put this visit off. He was running out of time.

There was one disaster he could avert right this moment, however.

With the light still red, Sig picked up his phone and quickly pulled up the necessary contact, tapping dial. His agent, David, answered on the fourth ring, his voice groggy and disoriented from sleep. "No, Sig. I haven't heard from the Bearcats about an offer yet."

Sig ignored the grind in his stomach. "That's not why I'm calling. I need you to do something for me and it's urgent."

"At one thirty in the morning? You don't say." A long-suffering sigh. "What is it?"

"I need you to get me off Boston's Most Eligible Bachelor list. Like yesterday."

"Why? That kind of thing only serves to raise your stock."

"First of all, you obviously haven't spent much time in a locker room with athletes. That kind of thing gets you absolutely crucified. But second . . ." Sig trailed off, knowing he couldn't give David the real reason. "Look, you'll have to take my word for it. I need to *not* be on that list."

Chloe would hate it, no matter what she said to the contrary. In fact, Sig had a hunch that this stupid list was the real reason tonight had ended like it had. A dinner bell being rung over his head would make her jealous. It would drive her crazy. And he didn't do that kind of shit to her. End of story. As far as Sig was concerned, there was nothing eligible about him.

He'd been locked down tighter than Fort Knox for six months.

"Do you have a girlfriend or something? What reason am I giving them?"

"I don't know." The light finally turned green and Sig hit the gas, sailing through the intersection. "Tell them I'm morally opposed to being objectified."

David groaned. "What a waste of good looks."

Sig rolled his eyes. "Just shut it down, will you?"

"I'll do what I can."

Minutes later, Sig pulled up to the mansion on the Sound and killed the engine, the bricks in his stomach growing heavier as he looked up at the reminder of what Chloe had given up by moving to Boston. By dropping everything and coming with him at a moment's notice. Trusting him wholeheartedly.

He'd vowed to himself that he wouldn't let her be sorry.

Tonight was the first time he'd felt on the verge of failing her.

They were in love, he and Chloe. Deep, twisted, enduring love. They hadn't said the words out loud, but their actions spoke for themselves. She showed up to every game, she lit up whenever he walked into the room, when she had a bad day, she called him. Cried into his neck. Called him with good news, too. Celebrated by popping champagne into the phone and begging him to come over and dance with her. She was everything joyful and sacred in his life.

And he wanted to marry her more than he wanted to live.

Sig took his phone out of the cupholder and texted his father. *I'm outside. Need to talk.*

A light came on in the upstairs window a few seconds later, followed by Harvey's silhouette peering down at the circular driveway.

Impatience gnawed at Sig's gut.

Dammit, he'd been so confident that this relationship between Harvey and Sofia would fizzle out before a wedding could even take place. They were still together, though. Happy, too, according to Chloe. Had Sofia's lawyers simply not done a thorough job of investigating Harvey's past? If he had, wouldn't Harvey be out on his ear by now?

If Sofia's lawyers had come up empty, would Niko have no luck, too?

Sig didn't know, but there was one avenue he'd yet to take—and it was a long shot. Nonetheless, he was taking that shot tonight.

His future with Chloe was at stake and he was getting desperate.

As soon as Sig saw Harvey emerge from the house in a robe, rubbing his hands together against the cold, Sig climbed out of the truck and walked in the direction of his father. They met at the side of the fountain, Harvey eyeballing him like he'd lost his mind. Maybe he had.

"It's the middle of the night. Is something wrong? Is Chloe okay?"

Jesus, the mere suggestion that something could be wrong with Chloe made Sig's stomach pitch sideways, upsetting the bricks he'd been carrying around all night. "She's fine. I'm sure she's sleeping in the glow of the Home Shopping Network right now."

Harvey ceased blowing warm air into his hands. "How do you know how she sleeps?"

"I know because she told me," Sig responded in a hard tone. "Don't make implications about my relationship with her. You don't know the first thing about it."

"I know you're too close to the woman who will one day be your stepsister." Harvey paused, his expression wary. Scrutinizing. "She calls to speak with her mother and you're all she talks about."

Sig tried to keep his features neutral, but he could barely swallow after hearing that.

Why was he hedging the truth, though? Hadn't he come here tonight to plead for his life? It burned to beg this man for anything. He'd do whatever it took to stop this wedding, though. Not only so he could be with Chloe, but so this man couldn't potentially deplete another woman's finances under the guise of being a loving husband.

"Fine." Sig shifted right to left, crossing his arms tight to his chest. As if to mitigate the physical cost of saying the next part out loud. "There is something between me and Chloe. I won't pretend that isn't true."

Harvey slowly closed his eyes. "Jesus Christ."

"We met at the country club when my truck broke down that night. A lot happened before we . . . knew. I was shocked to see her playing the harp when I showed up. She didn't expect me to be your son, either. It's a fucked-up situation, but . . ." He had to stop so he could struggle through the detonations going off in his chest. They were being set off by talking about his feelings for Chloe openly. Out loud. God, it felt great. Scary, though, considering it might not make a difference to the man standing in front of him. "But there's *nothing* fucked-up or wrong about me and Chloe, okay?"

"Isn't there?" Harvey snapped.

"No." Sig shook his head. "It's the purest thing I've ever felt in my life. It's like I've loved her since I took my first breath."

"Love," Harvey said flatly. "You *love* her?"

"I *exist* for her." Sig's lungs shrunk to the size of straws, air scarcely passing through them in a rattle. "I've never asked you for anything in my life . . . Father. I'll never ask you for anything again. Except for right now. I'm asking you not to marry Sofia. I know you won't admit out loud that she's nothing more than a mark to you, but if that's the case, I'm asking you to please move on. Please. Pick someone else."

When Sig had admitted to existing for Chloe, he could have sworn his father's eyes had softened. They were hard now, however. Glittering with irritation in the moonlight. "You still really believe I'm just here to con Sofia out of her money." Harvey took a stiff step in his son's direction. "If the heinous shit you believe about me were true, don't you think Sofia's high-powered estate lawyer would have found it? Nothing about my past set off alarm bells. The report came back squeaky-clean. Sorry to disappoint you."

There was Sig's confirmation. Sofia's lawyers *had* concluded their investigation.

Squeaky-clean. Was this man's depravity all in Sig's head? No. No, he'd lived through the poverty this man had inflicted on his mother. Experienced it himself.

"Sig, I'm in love with Sofia as much as you're apparently in love with Chloe."

Impossible. He couldn't feel a fraction of this. He wouldn't even be standing.

Sig didn't say that out loud. Couldn't. Hope was slipping through his fingers.

"I'm asking you for the last time," Sig rasped. "Please."

"Please call off the wedding to the woman I love?" Harvey scoffed. "No. You can't ask me to do that. And Chloe's relationship with Sofia is decent right now, despite what you've already done to ruin it, whisking her off to Boston with no warning." He dropped his voice even lower. "Now, I'm proud of what you've done in the hockey world, but you're a free agent come the end of the season, son. That doesn't sound like a lot of security. Not like Sofia and this world can offer her. Sofia loves her daughter. But I'll remind you what kind of shitstorm would erupt if something like this went public. You need to consider how your actions now are going to affect Chloe's future. Or her relationship with her mother and Darien, in general."

"Not a minute goes by that I'm not thinking of how *everything under the sun* affects her," Sig said through his teeth.

Harvey appeared to be taken aback by his vehemence. "I'm marrying Sofia, Sig. What can you possibly do once that happens? Marry your *stepsister*? Jesus, Sig. Pull your head out of your as—"

"Watch yourself," Sig cut in quietly, causing the man to snap his mouth shut. "You might have the upper hand tonight, but you haven't earned the right to speak to me like that."

After a tense moment of eye contact, Harvey broke first, sighing. "I don't want this to come between us. I don't want it to come between Chloe and her mother, either."

Sig studied Harvey hard and asked himself the same question he always did. Was this man genuine or was he all an act? A game player? It irked him that he couldn't get a read, when he was usually adept at making judgments of someone's character. Was his head too clouded by the past to see Harvey clearly? Was there an ulterior motive in play here or was it all in Sig's head? If only his mother didn't shut down every time Sig tried to speak to her about the past, all the circumstances surrounding her relationship with Harvey, maybe he'd have answers.

"Fair warning, I've hired my own investigator. If you have any skeletons in the closet, I'm going to rattle them." He walked backward toward his truck, maintaining eye contact with Harvey the whole way. "You won't hear the word 'please' from my mouth ever again."

His father flinched, ever so slightly, but Sig caught it. "You won't find . . . anything you can use."

"We'll see." Sig started to climb back into the driver's side of the truck, but he paused with a growled curse, remembering the other reason he'd driven three hours. "Listen. I need you to get me a blouse out of Chloe's closet. Black-and-white silk. High, ruffled neck."

"*What?*" Harvey exclaimed.

"Just do it."

Ten minutes later, the truck engine blasted to life and Sig got back on the highway to Boston, blouse draped over the passenger seat, the words "you won't find anything you can use" echoing loudly in his ears.

He refused to believe that was true.

Because if it was, where did that leave him?

Without her. That's where.

A place he couldn't fathom being.

CHAPTER TEN

Chloe peeked her head into the building to make sure the coast was clear, before sneaking into the vestibule and soundlessly opening her mailbox. A stack of envelopes and a Free People catalog dropped into her hand and she quickly stuffed the mail into her purse, making a mental note to show them to Sig later. Just to make sure there wasn't anything important, like a bill. He was always complaining about bills being paid late, but nothing ever really happened when they were late, as far as she could tell.

Except for the rent.

Now when *that* was late, her landlord let her know all about it. In fact, that was the *only* time she ever saw Angry Raymond. On the seventh or eighth of the month when the rent check hadn't been dropped off yet, he seemed to sense when she entered the building and he would spring forth from his apartment like a haunted jack-in-the-box, shouting words like "late fees" and "grace period."

Holding her breath, Chloe climbed the first few steps, wincing when the step let out a tiny whine—and like clockwork, Raymond shot out of his doorway like a demented whack-a-mole character in socks and sandals.

"Ms. Clifford—"

"I know. I know. I'll drop it off tomorrow!"

"It was due last week."

Chloe gasped. "It was?"

His withering sigh was mightier than the North Wind. "Why don't you give me Mr. Sig's number. I'll sort it out with him."

She was already shaking her head. "No, we cannot tell Mr. Sig. Mr. Sig does *not* need to know."

Chloe knew the exact look Sig would give her if he found out the rent was overdue. She'd seen it before. Three times to be precise, which didn't seem like a lot until you considered she'd only lived in Boston for six months. He'd tilt his head to the right and narrow his left eye. "What am I going to do with you, Chlo?" he'd ask, fondly exasperated.

A heavy weight settled on her chest. She hadn't heard from him since yesterday, when she'd half kicked him out of her apartment, which was *highly* unusual. He usually sent her a good morning text, a filthy meme, or simply showed up with breakfast. *Something.* Yes, she was standing firm on what she'd said. The romantic nonromance that complicated their relationship was becoming too painful to bear. But that truth didn't stop her from missing him in epic fashion, as she did now. Worrying she'd acted too impulsively and hurt their bond.

Please don't let me have done that.

"I think Mr. Sig *does* need to know," said her landlord. "He is the responsible one."

"You wouldn't really squeal on me, would you, Raymond?" Chloe didn't even have to force a hitch into her voice. "I just used a teeny tiny bit of my rent money to buy eye creams—"

He threw up his hands. "*Eye creams?* More than one?"

"Yes! You must test them out to know which one is right for you! But wait until you hear how I'm going to solve this." She came down a step and attempted to engage her landlord with a conspiratorial smile, thanking God when he blushed at least a little. "I'm giving online harp lessons. I gave one just this morning, actually."

Not that she'd run it past the university.

Had Chloe committed a crime by setting up her laptop in the practice room before anyone had arrived and gave a quick little one-hour lesson to Brandy in Duluth? No.

Although . . . probably.

"I'm giving another one tomorrow and then I'll have enough in my account to cover the rent." She wiggled her calloused fingers at him. "I'm working on it—I promise."

Raymond hedged. And he harrumphed.

Almost there. I'm going to buy myself one more day.

The last thing she wanted was to bother Sig about her late rent. After all, he was already depositing enough money into her account every month to cover the payment. Expecting him to shell out even more cash wouldn't be cute.

"You have until tomorrow. Then I'm calling Mr. Sig."

"It won't come to that, I promise! Have I ever broken a promise?"

"When you sign a lease, you promise to pay the rent *on time,* so technically—"

"Oh, Raymond!" Laughing, she reached down from her perch on the stairs to tickle his chin, watching a red flush spread up to the bald patch on the crown of his head. "You're such a stickler for the rules. I love that about you."

"You do?"

"Yes." She pressed both hands to her heart. "We need more people like you in this world. There would be less chaos."

"Meanwhile," he mumbled, still blushing, "the chaos is coming from people like you."

Considering his tone had lost a considerable amount of its bite, Chloe chose to laugh at that. "Well, somebody has to do it, right?"

A grudging smile from the landlord. "I guess so, Ms. Chloe."

Crisis averted. "I have to run now, Raymond," she called down to the landlord while jogging up the stairs. "I have an appointment with my new mentor in half an hour and I'm going to be late."

"I'm sure you'll manage to talk your way out of it!" he shouted up at her.

Chloe unlocked the door to her apartment and hip bumped it open, throwing her purse onto the kitchen table and running for the bedroom. She probably could have just remained downtown and killed time between conservatory and the first meeting with her mentor, but she wanted to come home, freshen up, and change, so she could put her best foot forward. Unfortunately, she was about as good with time management as she was with money management. In other words: stone-cold rotten.

"You can still make it on time. Just change and go," she murmured to herself, already undressing on her way into the bedroom. Her line of sight was compromised by the shirt she pulled off over her head, but as soon as she lowered it, her footsteps came to an abrupt halt.

Laying on the bed was a blouse.

Not just any blouse, though. Her lucky blouse.

Slowly, her hands raised to cover her mouth, the air in the room turning heavy, the pulse in her temples beating faster. Louder. The muscles of her throat drew in on themselves and she couldn't manage a swallow. There was only one explanation for the blouse being here, in her bedroom in Boston, but she took a giant sniff of the air to compound her theory, letting Sig's pepper-and-clove scent coast down the walls of her lungs, electricity spreading to her fingertips.

Blindfold her and set her loose in a room with ten thousand people and she would find him every single time. Those were the signature aromas he'd left to signal he'd been there.

Sig had gone to Darien last night to retrieve her lucky blouse.

Six, maybe seven hours of driving. More if there was traffic. And all that after she'd told him they should start dating other people. Not to mention, he'd only finished competing in a little something called a professional hockey game.

Chloe's heart pumped so fast, so furiously, she worried the tempo might be dangerous.

Why did he continue to give her reasons to be in love with him when it hurt so badly?

A lucky blouse was such a silly, superstitious thing, but he'd recognized it was important to *her*. Sig took her seriously. He listened to her. He delivered. Every single time. A rock-solid presence in her life that never failed her. Ever. Meanwhile, she continuously asked for advice, groceries, and extra rent money.

Chloe crept forward toward the blouse and picked it up, finding the front pocket slightly raised. She tucked her fingers inside of the silk and removed a folded note.

> *I'm sorry, dream girl.*
> *Go knock them dead.*

A wounded sound left her, accompanied by a whoosh of breath and she simply spun into motion, unbuttoning the black-and-white blouse, putting it on, and refastening the buttons at top speed. It was either move as fast as possible or stand stationary for the rest of her life, bleeding internally over what he'd done. The gesture, the note, his scent, the fact that he'd been in her bedroom while she wasn't home. The fact that he'd called her dream girl, a nickname he'd started calling her the night they met.

If she didn't move, move, move and get out of her apartment, she'd lie down and die, because love was meant to be a glorious thing, but sometimes she wondered if loving someone and not being able to acknowledge and act on it could suffocate her to death.

A few minutes later, Chloe was dressed. She tossed the mail out of her purse onto the table, shouldered her purse, and tapped down the stairs in a low pair of heels, all while calling an Uber. Any other afternoon, she would take public transportation, but she was already going to be late at this point and any delays would cause her to miss the meeting entirely.

Thankfully, she'd managed to beat the brutality of Boston's rush hour and within ten minutes, she pulled up in front of a corner residential building in Beacon Hill. The awning read *The Tudor.* Um, what? Was she in the right place? She'd expected a music school or a Berklee-owned rehearsal space, but that's not what this was.

Chloe triple-checked the address listed in the email from her conservatory instructor and climbed out of the Uber with a murmured thank you to the driver. A doorman asked for her name, verified she was on the visitor list, guided her to the elevator, and hit the button for the penthouse—and okay, even having only a fleeting concept of money, Chloe knew the top floor in this building had to be wildly expensive. Apart from being the first chair harpist with the Boston Symphony Orchestra, who *was* this mentor?

The elevator doors opened to reveal a pretty Chinese woman who appeared to be in her early forties kneeling in front of a grand piano. She was willowy and elegant—and she was slamming a high heel against the gleaming hardwood floor with enough force to summon a demon from the pits of hell.

"You're late, Chloe Clifford." She pointed the heel at Chloe. "You better hope you have the talent to make up for it."

Chloe almost swallowed her chin. "I guess you'll have to be the judge of that."

"Oh, I will." The woman stood up and, walking toward Chloe with an extended arm, realized she was still holding the high heel—a Louboutin, by the way—and dropped it so she could shake Chloe's hand. "As of now, I'm your judge, jury, and executioner."

"Oh dear."

"'Oh dear' is right. I'm Grace Shen, and you're mine now." She ended the incredibly firm handshake, turned on a heel, and stalked past the grand piano. "The harp is this way."

Chloe hustled after her. "What is your grievance with the Louboutin?"

"It belonged to my girlfriend. She sent me a WhatsApp message from Berlin just before you arrived. She decided to take a position with the Philharmonic." Grace shot her a too-sweet smile over her shoulder. "And one beneath a cellist, as well. A *cellist*," she repeated with a groan. "Four strings? Not exactly brain surgery, is it?"

"Well . . ."

"Now, forty-seven strings and seven pedals?" Grace stopped on a dime, turned, and gestured to one of the most beautiful harps Chloe had ever seen in her life, made even more majestic due to its position in front of a panoramic view of Boston. "That's a little more like it, right?"

"Yes," Chloe breathed, dropping her purse, her fingers already beginning to tingle. "Holy Connecticut, this is an antique. You *play* this?"

"That is its purpose. To be played."

"But—"

"Look at your fingers. They're shaking with anticipation. If this were sitting in the Smithsonian, you still wouldn't be able to walk past this instrument without playing it."

"Yes, but I would fully expect to serve jail time." Chloe ran the tip of her index finger down the gilded column of the world's most beautiful harp, marveling over the leafy motif that appeared to be hand-painted. "It would be worth it."

"Funny. Have you been to jail?"

"Not yet."

A laugh shot out of Grace, followed by a long pause wherein, without even turning around, Chloe could feel her new mentor considering her closely. "I'd like to hear Handel. Passacaglia, please."

There was only one other thing in this world that could make her heart speed at a relatively similar tempo to Sig—and it was the instrument sitting in front of her. The baroque piece rolled out in Chloe's mind like a red carpet being kicked long, unfurling with a smooth whip, and her fingers lifted on their own, elbows pointing outward and firming. Confidence straightened her spine. This was her world.

Unlike her relationship with Sig, she knew how to navigate these strings, as if she'd been born nestled inside of them. When she'd been lonely as a child or an adult, isolated by the prodigy label, this is where she'd escaped. Into the notes. They were always there for Chloe and they were there for her now, her mental gymnastics stilling while her fingers gently plucked the opening notes, wind filling the sails inside her chest, the full, timeless sound of the antique wrapping her in melancholy and elation, all at once.

She lost time, vanishing into the romantic piece as she tried to communicate her love to the harp, to show it her appreciation for being so beautiful. For letting her play its strings.

When she finished, it took her several moments to open her eyes, her spine slowly losing some of its stiffness, her fingertips still buzzing from the experience.

"Fine, you're worth my time, Clifford. But if you're ever late again, I will beat you with my ex-girlfriend's shoe."

"Fair enough."

Grace sighed.

A ribbon of smoke sailed over Chloe's shoulder and she turned around to find her new mentor hitting a vape. "Save your judgment."

"You won't get any judgment from me. I spent seven hundred dollars on eye cream instead of paying my rent this month."

Grace looked horrified. "You *rent*?"

"Well." Chloe turned partially on the stool. "I live there. Sig rents it for me."

"What is a Sig?"

Chloe released a gusty sigh. "The most perfect human on earth."

"Right." Another hit of the vape. Before Grace could say anything else, a dog started barking somewhere in the back of the cavernous penthouse. "Goddamn it."

"You have a dog," Chloe breathed, rising to her feet. "What kind?"

"It's *also* my ex-girlfriend's. And do I look like a breeder? I have no clue what kind it is. It's got fur and I have to take it for walks. Like, *consistently*." Grace pushed Chloe back down onto the stool. "You can pet the damn thing in a second, but I'm going to read you the riot act first. I don't know if you noticed, but I'm not really the inspirational guru type. I'm doing a favor for a friend by giving you some guidance. *They* think you're worth the effort. With your talent and Connecticut blue blooded-ness, they think you're BSO material. But if I'm going to put *my* time into you, Clifford, I need to know that you want to be the best. Because I won't accept any less than that."

No one had ever spoken to her like this. Her first instinct was to apologize to Grace for wasting her time and ask politely to please, please pet the dog, but something stopped her. Maybe it was the need to play the golden instrument from heaven again. Or maybe . . . maybe it was months of watching Sig play hockey.

Watching him sweat and bleed and sacrifice his body for a little black puck. For his teammates. For Boston.

What would it be like to apply herself with that degree of tenacity and succeed?

She'd sort of coasted on her God-given talent her whole life, but she could see, could feel that this dynamic woman would be the one to push her to the next level. If Chloe wanted it. If she worked hard enough.

"What does the best mean? What does it look like?"

"First chair, bitch. Principal harp. What else?"

"*You're* first chair for the Boston Symphony Orchestra."

"Yeah, but I'm restless. I'm a nomad. I won't be here forever. For instance, Berlin is calling my name pretty loud right now. I don't lose easy, especially to a cellist." Her smirk faded, leaving a serious expression behind. "If you want a shot at the spot, Clifford, you need to be above reproach. I can't stress that enough. You show up on time, work your ass off. Do not shit where you eat. Do not give the powers that be a reason to doubt your character. Swift said it best, keep your side of the street clean. And when the situation calls for it, you schmooze with donors. The BSO prides themselves on a virtuous image. Is that you?"

"I don't know about *virtuous*. I mean, I like to go out . . ."

"Of course. We all do. You just have to be quiet about it."

This sounded quite arduous. She could keep things status quo, couldn't she? Finish conservatory, find a nice position with the orchestra that wasn't so front and center. No pressure, no one's reputation riding on her back, continuing to coast on the prodigy status. When she'd decided to come to Boston, first chair hadn't been her goal, anyway. It was too lofty. Too grueling for someone who could have an easy life, regardless of her job. Or was that her mother speaking?

Was this her sign to find out what she was really capable of?

"Can I have a day to think about it?"

"Actually, I'd *rather* you took a day." Grace stowed her vape. "It proves you're not going to take what I said lightly. We'd be working *hard*."

Pressure built in Chloe's chest, but she smiled through it. "How was the piece?"

"Decent. But you could be a bit more technical. I'm all for your weird, loopy dream state, but you dropped three notes. That won't fly when you have an orchestra behind you. We're going to need a higher level of concentration."

Wow. Three notes?

Breathe. Breathe.

She didn't have to do this. Her instructors at Berklee rarely pointed out errors.

"You don't like hearing you made mistakes."

"I'm just not used to it."

"Can you *get* used to it?"

"If I can't, what does that say about me?" Grace shrugged at her, paced to the window, and stared out at Boston, arms crossed.

"Have you seen *Whiplash*?" Chloe asked.

Grace cast her an exasperated, sideways look. "You don't think I'm as scary as Terence Fletcher, do you? I'm not." She fluttered her eyelashes. "Or am I?"

Chloe gulped. "I—"

The dog barked—and kept right on barking. "You wouldn't happen to want a side gig as a dog sitter, would you?" Grace asked. "I can pay you in eye cream or cash, your choice."

Dog sitter. *Her?*

In her mind's eye, she could see Sig shaking his head. *No way, Chlo. Absolutely not.*

Was she responsible enough to care for an animal?

God no.

But maybe caring for a living, breathing creature would be a crash course on learning how to be a responsible adult. Maybe if she could keep a dog happy, walked, and fed, she'd feel more capable of being a mentee of this dynamic, motivated woman. Maybe she'd be able to envision herself as first chair for one of the country's most illustrious orchestras.

Because right now, she couldn't.

"Sure. I'll take the pup." Chloe forced a smile. "How hard can dog parenting be?"

Famous last words.

CHAPTER ELEVEN

Sig used his teeth to rip a piece of tape, smoothing the clear adhesive over the opening of a cardboard box containing a signed game jersey. His dining room table was covered in autographed pucks, Bearcats pennants, and one broken stick, made famous by Sir Savage snapping it in half over his leg after a loss to the Rangers. When sold, that stick would catch a decent price. So decent, Sig might have to encourage the captain to break a few more before he officially retired.

Thank God he had this shit to keep him busy, because he hadn't spoken to Chloe all day and he had a constant sense of something being undone. Like he'd woken up late and missed practice, only worse. Much worse. Did she . . . *like* the space he was trying to give her?

Disturbed by the possibility, Sig snatched up his phone and called the private investigator for a second time. On his first attempt, he'd left a voicemail, but hours had passed, and he was eager for an update. Way too eager to wait hours for a call back.

Luckily, the guy answered on the second ring. "Mr. Gauthier."

"Like I said, Sig is fine."

"That's right. Sig." Fingers tapped a keyboard in the background. "I was just getting ready to call you. We might not have the kind of progress you wanted, but we have some answers. Give me a moment to put my notes together."

Sig tried to swallow the sudden dryness. "Sure."

He blew out a silent breath at the ceiling. Not for the first time, he experienced a wave of guilt over siccing an investigator on his own father. And by association, his mother, because Niko's research could inevitably turn up information about her, too. Reminding himself that Harvey had been absent the first eighteen years of his life and that his mother was withholding important details about his past didn't do much to assuage the unwanted discomfort.

Just because Sofia was a controlling mother and Harvey was a status chaser didn't make them bad people, did it? If Sig uncovered the means to stop this wedding, would he be able to pull the trigger so easily? Harvey and Sofia seemed genuinely happy with each other. Chloe remarked on it constantly. "My mom is on cloud nine." If he found something that proved his suspicions that Harvey was a serial swindler, however, he'd be honor bound to bring it to Sofia. Not only to protect Sofia—and Chloe—from financial harm . . . but to stop this marriage from happening.

Sig's goal from the outset had been to put the brakes on the relationship that was keeping him from Chloe. Was that selfish?

Not if he truly believed his father posed a threat—and he did. Didn't he?

Sig could still see his mother hobbling through the front door after working the night shift at a gas station. She'd cursed the name *Harvey* on a daily basis. Blamed him for leaving them penniless and struggling. Sig wasn't imagining those darker days. He'd lived them.

"All right. Here we go." Sig braced while Niko took a centering breath, his chair creaking in the background. "I was able to locate Ulla Franklin, your father's second wife. Took some time to convince her daughter that I'm not the boogeyman, but she finally put Ulla on the horn. Fortunately or unfortunately, depending on your viewpoint, she only had nice things to say about your father, Harvey. Oh, she said he's an unrepentant flirt with a taste for the finer things, but . . . she said he didn't mind signing a prenup. He brought his own money into the marriage and he left with it."

"He brought my *mother's* money into the marriage," Sig corrected.

"I hear you. Anyhow, according to Ulla, he never made a play for hers. They parted on decent terms, though they lost contact years ago."

Sig was caught between shock and disappointment. And maybe something else. Just the tiniest hint of relief. Relief at the potential proof that his parent wasn't a bad guy after all. Relief he didn't necessarily want to feel. "Is there a way to speak with my mother's family—"

"Only if you want to go through six lawyers. My initial introduction email was greeted with a threat of a lawsuit. They want nothing to do with an investigation into your father."

"Does that seem a little extreme to you?"

"More than a little," Niko said, tapping on his keyboard again. "Look, I'm going to follow your father's trail to the next woman, but my initial steps in that direction don't seem promising. There doesn't appear to be any major financial gains since his split from your mother. He parties with guys who own yachts, but he never owns the yacht, make sense?"

"Yeah." Sig massaged his eye sockets. "Keep looking, please."

"On it."

An hour later, a distracted Sig had gone back to packing sold memorabilia, weighing each package, and hitting print on shipping labels. Slapping them on. Busywork that was becoming less and less effective in stopping him from dwelling on the fruitless call from Niko . . . and preventing him from texting Chloe. Or better yet, driving to her apartment. Evening had fallen, meaning she would be home. Probably heating up soup on the stove. Smashing up Saltine crackers to sprinkle over the top. The Home Shopping Network would be on in the living room. She'd paint her toenails later and talk to the hosts, as if they could hear her.

Goddamn, she was so cute.

Sig realized he was staring into space and dropped the tape, raking a hand down his face. He paced away from the table, his attention drawn to the keys to his truck where they hung by the front door, directly above his gear bag. Maybe he'd just drive over there and drop off some strawberry Pop-Tarts. She was fresh out—he knew that.

He also knew she wouldn't be able to find them anywhere in her neighborhood.

Technically, he had no choice but to turn up at her front door. Otherwise, what the hell was she going to eat for breakfast tomorrow? Was he going to let the girl starve?

Decision made, Sig marched into his kitchen and opened the cabinet holding a multitude of Pop-Tarts boxes. At least a hundred of them, maybe more. Strawberry only. They'd all been purchased in the North End at every deli and grocery store in a ten-block radius of Chloe's apartment. She could never find them herself. The stores were always cleaned out. All because sometimes Sig needed an actual reason to show up at her place that wasn't *I needed to see you so I could breathe*—and the Tarts were his ticket.

He'd only closed a hand around one of the boxes when the door buzzed.

Sig turned from the cabinet with a confused look, arm dropping. Who the hell was that?

Maybe it was Mailer dropping off some autographed shirts—

he'd forgotten to bring them to practice that afternoon and swore he'd get them to Sig as soon as possible.

Even though the rookie showing up at his place was odd, Sig buzzed the guy in and unchained the door to his apartment, leaving it slightly ajar. Then he went back to the kitchen and uncapped two beers, getting ready to offer one to Mailer as a thank you—

But Chloe walked into the apartment, instead.

Chloe.

In his fucking apartment.

With a bulldog on a leash, but that was somehow the *least* pressing issue.

The cold bottle of Sam Adams paused halfway to Sig's mouth, his blood pounding loudly and suddenly in his temples, the walls of his apartment beating like the ventricles of a heart. And speaking of hearts, his dropped like a boulder into his stomach. *Thunk.*

She'd never been there before. For a lot of reasons. So many reasons.

"Chlo." Sig fumbled the beers onto the counter, reached up, and slammed the cabinet containing the Pop-Tarts shut. Thankfully, due to the angle of where she stood just inside the entryway, she couldn't see the contents. Christ, how would he even begin to explain that? *I'm so lost for you. I'm so pathetically lost.* "What are you doing here?"

She stared at him for several seconds, before transferring the dog leash to the opposite hand in order to close the apartment door. "I was sitting on my couch and I just kept waiting for you to walk in. When I realized you weren't going to come, I guess . . ." Trailing off, she wet her lips. Glanced around, taking in the small living room, the old furniture, though he couldn't gauge her reaction. Could she hide her shock so easily? "I started wondering why it's a given that you'll always come to me. I can get here just as easily, you know?"

Sig didn't respond. Couldn't. He was too busy wanting to cover her eyes so she couldn't see anything else. The wires hanging down from his flat screen. The old rug under his coffee table. The dining room table full of memorabilia. *God*, especially that.

He was so busy cataloging everything in his apartment he didn't want Chloe to see that he didn't catch her staring at the two bottles of beer. Not until she said, very quietly, "Are you expecting someone?" Some of the color left her face. "Should I go?"

Holy shit.

Did she think he had a woman coming over?

"That's fine, though." She nervously flipped her hair back over her shoulder and it finally dawned on him that she was wearing her lucky blouse. The one he'd driven to Darien and collected. "I mean, we talked about this last night. You're free to date—"

"No, *we* didn't talk about it. You talked—and I agreed to nothing."

"I think your agreement was implied."

"The fuck it was, Chloe." Frustrated, he snatched up his beer and drained half of it, before firmly setting it back down. Taking a breath. "When you buzzed, I thought you were Mailer dropping something off. That's why I opened a second beer. Keep talking about dating other people and I'm going to need both of them, plus an additional five."

"You *are* getting ready to be named one of Boston's most eligible bachelors." Her smile was the fakest one she'd ever given him. "Your social calendar is going to be full very soon."

"Social calendar? There's the country club girl I know and love." He made note of the high color in her cheeks, the rapid way she was blinking. "Tell the truth. This whole eligible bachelor list is the reason you gave me that separate romantic lives speech last night, isn't it?" Slowly, Sig exited the kitchen, sauntering in Chloe's direction, studying her guarded expression extra closely for confirmation of his growing theory. "You heard I was going to be on some ridiculous list and freaked out?"

Chloe let out a high-pitched laugh, pressed a dainty hand to her cheek. "What are you carrying on about? I'm *thrilled* you've made that idiotic list."

"Are you lying, though?"

"Am I—" She rolled her beautiful eyes. "Of course, I'm not lying."

"You sure about that?" He stopped in front of her, making note of the pulse racing at the base of her neck. "Because if you were going to be put on an eligible bachelorette list, Chloe Clifford, I would tear the fucking city down."

Her eyes closed, as if those words were washing over her face like warm water. Not kissing her in that moment was painful. Even more painful than usual and that was saying *a lot*. "Sig, you're going to be my stepbrother," she whispered.

A notch formed in his throat, his hand moving on its own to tuck some strands of loose hair behind her ear, his fingertips tracing the perfect curve of her jaw. "I haven't been a bachelor since I heard your voice for the first time. I was yours before I even turned around and you know it."

"You can't keep saying—"

"Chloe."

"Yes?"

He'd pushed far enough. Time to distract her before she made another attempt to create distance between them. "Don't you think it's time we talked about the dog?"

It took her several seconds to get on the same page, because she was staring at his mouth. "Oh. Um . . . I'm surprised you made it this long without asking about my pup. It's almost like you've gotten used to my mischief." Eventually, Chloe tore her attention off his mouth and looked down at the canine. "His name is Pierre. A very chic and Parisian name for an English bulldog with breath that could kill a horse." She crouched down to scratch the bulldog's chin, a smile spreading from cheek to cheek. "Pierre slobbered all over my favorite pants. Which was fine. I can live with slobber. But then I took him for a walk and he was just digging, digging anywhere he could get his little sausage paws. Then he jumped on me. Thank goodness he didn't soil the blouse. Oh! The blouse!" She shot back to her feet, dropped the leash, and wrapped both arms around his neck. Squeezing, while he died and went to heaven. "Sig, did you really drive all the way to Darien for a *shirt*?"

Chloe's calming balm spread all over his frayed nerves. "You wanted it, so you got it."

She hummed into his neck, the vibration drawing his attention to her body, curved so perfectly against him. Tits, belly, thighs. *Fuck.* If only they didn't have the doom of their eventual relationship hanging over their heads, he'd slide his hands into the back of her panties and take a tight grip of those ass cheeks. Toss her a foot off the ground so she could hook her pretty thighs around his hips. Push down the waistband of his sweatpants and fuck her with those little ankle boots still on. He'd slide her up and down on his cock, make her play with her clit until she went limp with satisfaction. Then he'd look right into her eyes, get balls deep, and come, as far inside of her as possible, sending the message that had been etched into his bones since the night they met.

You are mine.

Chloe shifted against him, started to pull away . . . but hesitated while chewing her lip and Christ, she went back in for another too long, too intimate hug, as if she couldn't help touching him. And that proof that her addiction mirrored his caused him to slip. Again. Even after the last twenty-four hours of panic that he'd pushed too much and lost her, the words tumbled out of him, because he was a total and complete mess for this person.

"You could wrap your legs around me for a little while, if you want," he whispered against her temple, his palm roaming down her spine and pressing her into him, letting her feel what she was doing to his cock. "I'll just hold you like that. It won't go any further."

Her open mouth found the underside of his chin, letting out a stuttered exhale. "That's what I'm afraid of."

Lust and frustration warred in his gut. "Chloe—"

The dog barked.

He'd forgotten about the dog.

A whole lot of nail clicking and sniffing ensued and the next thing Sig knew, there was a bulldog headbutting him in the shin. He looked down to find two big brown eyes staring up at him. The entire row of his bottom teeth was on display, two incisors sticking up higher than the others—and he headbutted Sig again.

"Oh. Sig." Chloe's arms dropped from around his neck. "I think he's trying to defend my honor." She dropped into a kneel, taking the sides of the bulldog's face in her hands. "Aren't you, baby? Aren't you, little man? Yes! Yes, you are!"

Pierre blinked up at Sig. Once, twice. As if to say, *Your time is up, chump.*

There's a new guy in town.

"Okay, let's back up."

Sig raked a hand through his hair. Was he jealous of a dog? Yes. Yes, he was.

"Where the hell did you get Pierre, Chlo?"

"He belongs to my mentor's ex-girlfriend. She moved to Berlin to play with the Philharmonic. And a cello player."

"Why do *you* have him now?"

"Grace—that's my mentor, who I love. Oh, Sig, she's a force. Truly one of a kind. And she has an eighteenth-century harp crafted in France that feels like I'm playing silk. But she doesn't want a dog. I think it's painful because she misses her ex, you know? Even if she would never admit it. Anyway, I offered to take Pierre for a while."

There was a lot to unpack here.

There always was when Chloe gave an explanation on anything.

He loved that about her. How she meandered on her way to the point, dropping him little hints about her day, how she felt about things, leaping between points and forgetting where she'd started. Loved her curveballs—such as showing up with a random bulldog. Classic Chloe Curveball. She loved to throw them.

Sometimes she missed her train stop and got lost in Boston—no joke, one time she'd called him from Logan Airport with no idea how she'd arrived there. Or she went dancing on a Saturday night and lost track of time, forgetting to text him her location and sending him into the early stages of a stroke. There was also the one time her smoke detector battery had died, resulting in a high-pitched beep that led her to think the building was on fire. That panicked phone call had almost turned his hair white and resulted in him putting the landlord's number on speed dial.

Who knew what she'd throw at him next time? Sig didn't know. He only knew he'd catch her curveballs as often as she wanted to throw them.

"First of all, great. I'm glad you like your mentor. Second . . . is this harp something you want?" He was already doing mental math. How much could it possibly cost? "Do you want the harp, Chloe?"

She gasped. "It's not for sale, Sig."

They'd see about that as soon as he was offered a new contract. The offer would be coming. It *would*. Although the locker
room had been buzzing this morning with the continued rumors of a management change. Shit felt so up in the air, so
uncertain, and he didn't like it one bit. He wanted stability. A
plan. "If you say so."

"I do."

"Uh-huh."

"Sig . . ." She seemed to be chewing something over. "Do you
think I'm responsible enough to care for this dog?"

"It's a little late to be questioning this now, isn't it?" Sig joked,
chucking her under the chin. When he saw she was seriously
worried, however, he matched her solemn expression. "Do you
want me to take the dog?"

"What? No! I'm keeping the dog. I figure . . . if I can prove
to myself I'm a capable dog owner, maybe I can take on more
responsibility elsewhere. You know?"

Something important and complicated was taking place in her
head, but Sig knew from experience that she'd need to explain in
her own time. He couldn't rush her.

"Let's start small. Has Pierre eaten?"

"Yes. He had a tofu teriyaki bowl from down the street. Gob-
bled it right up."

"Okay, that's fine for tonight," he said, hiding his smile. "But
tomorrow, you should probably pick him up some kibble."

"Kibble." She nodded vigorously. "I'll need to write that
down."

"You know how to search locations on your phone." He
brushed his palm down the back of her head, rubbed a circle
onto her back. "Find the closest pet store. When you get there,
tell one of the employees what kind of dog he is, and they'll
recommend a brand."

The wheels were turning. "I'm going to get him a bed, too. The biggest, most obnoxious one they have. Pink and purple. Princess in script across the back."

"Look at you. You're a natural born pet owner."

"Maybe. Yeah." Her confidence grew. "He seems to like me."

Sig scoffed. "Of course he does."

Chloe looked at his collarbone for several long, indecisive seconds, before sighing and resting her cheek there, the fingertips of her right hand brushing up, down, up, down against his triceps. His balls got heavier with every stroke, but the way she was so naturally drawn to touch him, the presence of that was worth the pain.

"Tell me about your mentor," he said, gruffly. "Grace, right?"

"Yes. Grace." She was silent a moment, as if she was recalling the events of the day. "She's very strict, very blunt, but . . . I have a feeling she wouldn't agree to see me again if she didn't think I have potential for something bigger. In fact, I *know* she wouldn't."

Her tone was almost a dreamlike murmur. The sound of her voice comforted and aroused Sig so much that he was only vaguely worried now that she'd look around at his place, his stuff, and register he didn't have enough money to support her, make her happy. Not indefinitely. Not without a new contract.

"I've been coasting on the talent I was born with. She's not going to let me do that anymore. She wants to push me and, yeah, that's scary. No one has ever really pushed me, only complimented me. Marveling over the prodigy. But as soon as I met her today, I could feel I was in the presence of someone . . . greater. I just don't know if I'm resilient enough to be challenged. Really challenged. *Whiplash* challenged, minus the abuse."

"Thank you for adding that last part."

"You're welcome." He heard her swallow. "She thinks I can

go . . . far, Sig. If I can handle the work. If I don't buckle under her instruction. Playing the harp without simply being told I'm wonderful at it all the time."

Sig tipped her chin up so he could look down into her face. "How far does she think you can go, Chlo?"

"First chair," she said quietly. "Principal harp for BSO. If I can learn enough. If I work hard. Really, really hard."

Pride rushed in from all sides. "Holy shit."

"I don't think I can do it," she whispered, studying him for a reaction.

He saw the spark of hope in her eyes, the reluctant excitement. So he didn't hesitate when he said, "Yes, you can."

Chloe looked down, then to the side. "I'm just not sure . . ." She trailed off with a frown. "What is all that stuff?" Her spine straightened a little more. "Are those signed jerseys?"

The temperature of Sig's blood started to drop as she zipped her attention back to him.

"Where are you sending them?"

CHAPTER TWELVE

Chloe felt an ominous gurgle in her stomach.

Something had simply been . . . *off* since she walked into Sig's apartment. For one, it was nothing like she'd expected. Much smaller than the luxury condo she'd pictured him returning to every night. Just like his truck, the furniture appeared to be well loved, but verging on ancient. Touches of him were everywhere, from a stack of professional athlete autobiographies to the hand-held vacuum charging on the counter.

For all his flash and speed on the ice, Sig had an old soul. He liked knowing facts, craved tidiness. Even his hockey sticks were leaned against the wall at perfect ninety-degree angles.

On the television? The Home Shopping Network.

And she wanted to ask him about that. Why he would be watching Laurie Woodruff peddle Victorian-style watches when he usually chuckled and rolled his eyes at Chloe's constant viewing of the twenty-four-hour shopping network. But then she saw the pile of merchandise sitting in neat piles on his kitchen table and the sight stole all her focus. An invisible finger of dread traced down the nape of her neck as she cataloged everything she was seeing.

An open laptop with a spreadsheet on the screen.

Boxes, tape, scissors. A weighing scale.

At least eight packed boxes, ready to ship in the corner.

Signed pucks, jerseys, rolled-up posters, helmets. A broken stick.

"Where are you sending all these memorabilia?" she prompted again, looking at him, her nerves tingling when she couldn't get a read. "It looks like you're selling it."

Sig's face was carved in stone. "It does look like that, doesn't it?"

Several beats passed. "Are you?"

Slowly, he drained the rest of his beer. "I can feel myself wanting to lie to you, Chloe—and I don't do that. So I'm just going to ask you to drop it."

"The only reason people sell things is to make money. But you . . ." She studied him closely. The line ready to snap in his cheek. The sudden lack of color in his face. "You have money, right? You're paying my rent, you bring me groceries." Her stomach was beginning to feel hollow. "You complain about my Sephora habit, but you totally enable me, too, sending me links to sales. I mean, you . . . you're a professional hockey player. I don't understand."

His jaw flexed. "You're not going to drop this, are you?"

"No."

It almost scared her how *winded* he looked. "Come here." He took her by the wrist, guiding her into the living room where he sat her down on the couch, her numb legs giving out beneath her just in time for her butt to hit the cushions. Sig took a spot directly in front of her on the edge of his coffee table, hands clasped between his knees. Head bowed. "Chloe, this is hard for me."

That woke her up. Sure, sometimes Sig suffered professional ups and downs, the occasional crisis of confidence that came from being an athlete, but he wasn't a person who hesitated. He was decisive. Always knew the answer. Right now, he lacked his usual strength and that meant he needed her. It would be a cold day in hell before she let him down after everything he'd done on her behalf. "Do you need help burying a body, because we can probably borrow a shovel from my landlord. He has some snitch tendencies, but we'll find a way to keep him quiet. Bottom line, I'm with you, okay? Whatever it is, I'm with you."

He huffed a disbelieving sound, but the affection in his eyes made it temporarily impossible to breathe. "Congratulations, Chlo. You're officially a Bostonian."

Her lips stretched into a smile. "Tell me anything right now and watch me stick."

"Yeah, I'm getting there." He raked the smirk off his face with a heavy hand. Paused. "I was a third-round draft pick. I'd injured my knee midway through last AHL season and . . . suddenly nothing I'd done before that mattered, you know? Championship titles, awards, out the window. I was just a liability. At the time, I was lucky to be fucking drafted at all, and while my contract was modest . . ." He wouldn't look at her. "It was more money than I'd ever had in my life. Enough to buy my mother a house—and she deserved it after what she sacrificed for me. I bought this place, too, and I've been comfortable. With the end of my contract coming up—"

"You've been comfortable . . . until me," Chloe said, a jolt racing down to her toes. "*I'm* the reason you're selling memorabilia."

All her life, she'd been kept inside of a bubble. That had never been more obvious than it was in this moment. This was also the moment it burst.

"I'm not hurting for money, Chloe, I just . . ." His throat worked. "The past has taught me to save for a rainy day. The Bearcats haven't offered me a new contract yet and I can't stand the fucking thought of you wanting for anything. I can't *stand* it. I told you I would support you and that's what I'm going to do."

She was shaking her head vigorously. "No. My apartment is nicer than yours."

"I don't need nice. I need *you* to have nice."

"Sig." Her temples were pounding. "Oh my God. You . . . no. You don't have time for a side hustle. You've been running this whole operation? Selling signed pucks to support *three people* while I was blowing my rent money on eye cream?" She pressed both hands to her stomach. "I'm going to be sick."

Sig's chest was beginning to heave up and down. "It's a privilege to do this for you, Chloe. Don't take it away from me."

"But I'm not really independent at all, am I? I was blind to believe I was. This . . ." She swept a hand toward the kitchen table. "This is what it really takes to earn what you're giving me and I had no part in it."

Chloe stood up on jelly legs.

Sig quickly followed suit, taking her by the elbows.

"You'll contribute eventually. Right now, you're focused on training. That was the deal. And don't minimize all the ways you've learned to be on your own. Don't do that."

Chloe acknowledged that statement with a dull nod, but she wasn't able to accept the affirmation. Not now when her reality was altering itself. Not when she was seeing every moment of the last months through a new lens. "And then I have the nerve to tell Grace I'll *think* about her mentoring me, potentially taking on first chair. That would pay . . . a lot, probably. Enough that I'd be able to support myself and take pressure off you. And I said I would think about it. Oh my God, I am so *oblivious*."

"Stop being hard on yourself. You've never had to think about money."

"Well, I'm thinking about it now. I'm not letting you do this anymore."

"Let me?" Roughly, he hauled her body up against his, his lips close enough to hers that she could taste the beer on his breath. "Chloe, I would sell my fucking soul for you and smile while I signed on the dotted line."

"But you don't have to," she whispered, sliding her fingers into his hair, nails dragging along his scalp. "You can keep your soul and have me, too." Determination spread inside of Chloe, warming her blood, firming her bones. She'd never had this much purpose in her entire life—and wow, it felt good. *Really* good. Necessary. "I'm going to work my butt off and I'm going to earn first chair. I'm going to really earn it. I'm going to do it."

Unmistakable pride moved in his expression. "You can do anything. Especially this." He traced her cheekbone with an arc of his thumb. "But you do it for you. Not me. Not because I had to sell some shit to keep us healthy until my next contract. Do it because *you* want it."

Knowing he was right, that landing a spot with BSO had to be for herself and no one else, Chloe took a moment to think, to explore her intentions and found that, yes, becoming a better harpist would satisfy her long-held worry that she'd coasted by on natural talent. Or worse, that she'd wasted a gift that gave her so much joy. Time to be sure. Time to find out what she was truly capable of.

"I'll do it for me," she said, looking him in the eye.

"Good."

"And you'll get a contract renewal for yourself. A big one—or else the Bearcats front office don't know how lucky they are. *Third round?*" Anger speared upward from her stomach into her throat, so fiercely she had to grab him by the collar of his T-shirt. "How dare they take this long to make up for that oversight? I'd like to kick down the GM's door and shove my foot up his ass. Three times. Once for each round they ignored your talent. You're only the best player *in the league*. Tell me one other player who—"

"You really meant it, didn't you?" His expression was an odd mixture of humility and adoration. "You're with me. No exceptions."

Chloe frowned at him. "I told you. I'll get the shovel."

He stared down at her. "Whatever you think I've done for you by bringing you to Boston, I want you to know you've done the same for me. I've never been the best, I've always been the assist guy. I have the speed to create openings in the defense. But I believe I'm the best when you say it. I believe that when I look at you."

"Good." She threw her arms around his neck, letting out a watery laugh into his shoulder. "It's true."

He lifted Chloe onto her toes and crushed her close. "I thought you finding this out would change everything."

"No."

"So all that bullshit about seeing other people . . ."

She pulled away wiping her eyes, mustering a sweet as honey smile. "No, that still stands. I meant that."

His eyeballs came close to popping out of his head. "*What?*"

If anything, she was now more determined than ever to have clear boundaries in her life. Look what had been going on behind the scenes without her knowledge! Going forward, she was going to have her eyes wide open. Goals would be reached, professionally and personally—and as much as it hurt, she couldn't continue to wallow in a romantic gray area with Sig. It only caused hurt and confusion . . . and in two months, it would lead to full heartbreak. Today was the day to make big moves. Big, necessary moves.

Even if she really wanted to be kissed and stroked and told more wonderful things by this man she loved more than breathing. More than the harp and every color in the rainbow.

"I really need to go, Sig," she forced herself to say. "I need to buy kibble for Pierre before the deli closes." Many things were occurring to her at once. "And I can't wait to call Grace and let her know I'm ready to lock in. You know, it's crazy! Now that I've made the decision to reach for the top, I'm excited. Not nearly as nervous as I thought I would be."

"Great. But Chloe. You're *not* dating. Period."

"You're right, I probably won't have a lot of time, now that I'll be practicing so hard. But you never know, Sig. You never know."

He boomed a humorless laugh. "You really want some poor chump to die, don't you?"

She admonished him with a frown. "Don't be violent in front of Pierre."

It was obvious from his double take that he'd forgotten about the dog who was currently napping in front of the door. "While we're on the subject, what time are you planning to walk Pierre in the morning? Not before sunrise. Right, Chloe?"

"Grace said he'll need to be walked at five thirty a.m."

"Oh, okay." He pinched the bridge of his nose. "Sure."

She mimicked his flippant body language. "What does that mean?"

"It means I'll see you at five thirty a.m.," he growled. "Did you think I was going to let you walk around in the dark alone?"

"Sig?"

"Yes."

"You seem irritated."

He visibly gathered himself. "I'm not irritated with you. I'm irritated with every man in Boston for existing."

She tried to appear nonchalant while something sharp was pulverizing her chest. "Well. *If* we hadn't agreed to date other people—"

"Nah, we didn't agree to that."

"—If we hadn't made that mature and necessary decision, I probably wouldn't feel wonderful about every straight woman in

Boston flipping open their newspaper and finding you under the word 'eligible.'"

"They're not going to see me on any list. I already squashed it."

She mashed her lips together to keep from smiling. "Really?"

"Yup."

Relief spread over the wound and she gave him her most grateful smile. "Thank you."

His sigh was long and reluctantly tender. "You realize you make no sense, dream girl."

She picked up Pierre's leash and backed toward the door. "I'll try harder."

"Don't you dare change a thing about yourself."

They smiled at each other across the apartment for long moments that made her heart feel heavy and light and burdensome and lucky all at once. Sagging with love and turmoil. Maybe her heart had more than four chambers because how else could everything fit?

"Good night, Sig," she murmured, grasping the doorknob to prevent herself from running to him. Leaping without looking. Begging again for him to relent.

To give her at least one night.

"Good night, Chloe," he said, reaching up and snagging his hair in a fist at the crown of his head, obviously gripping tight to keep from lunging for her, too. Giving in. Giving them what they both needed so badly it burned. "See you in the morning."

When Chloe left that night, she was resolved to try and move on.

Sig still had other ideas.

CHAPTER THIRTEEN

Sig sat down across from Burgess in the smoothie shop.

"You summoned me?"

Observing Sig, Burgess grunted. Leaned back and tossed a crumpled napkin onto the table. "Why do you look like warmed-over shit?"

"Had an early morning," Sig said without blinking.

"For what reason?"

"Dude named Pierre."

"Really." The Bearcats captain scrubbed at his bearded chin. "When are you going to introduce him to the team?"

"When they start allowing dogs at the games, I guess."

"Ohh, I see. Pierre is a dog. Are you enjoying yourself?"

"I'm in a brightly lit smoothie shop full of joggers, I haven't slept yet, and they don't serve coffee," Sig deadpanned. "What do you think?"

Burgess didn't bother answering that. "Does the dog have something to do with Chloe?"

"Of course, it does." An image of Chloe smiling beneath the streetlights and nuzzling her face into his shoulder made him shift in his chair, attempting to balance the heavy weight in his chest. He'd been waiting outside her building that morning at five a.m., just in case she threw him another wild card and decided to venture out early. But no, she'd emerged on time, yawning and wrapped in a blanket, smiling sleepily when she saw him. They'd walked in silence, side by side, laughing quietly at Pierre's repertoire of unique sounds, neither one of them bringing up the roller-coaster conversation from the night before.

Maybe she was still digesting everything, like Sig.

His secret had been laid on the table and instead of getting mad, she'd encouraged him.

Stuck by him.

Just not enough to refrain from dating other men.

Sig ground his molars until pain shot upward behind his eye. "I didn't want her walking the dog alone before sunrise. Could mean early mornings for a while. Not sure if she's just dog sitting or keeping him permanently, but I try not to ask for too many specifics with Chlo." He couldn't quite catch his affectionate smile before it formed. "She errs on the side of impulsive."

Burgess hummed, studied him beneath drawn brows. "That's sort of why I brought you here, man. Specifics are about to become really important, really fast. There's a team meeting tonight and everyone is going to be there. Top to bottom. The GM, coaching staff. The owner."

Sig stopped in the act of rubbing at his gritty eyes. "I wasn't notified about a team meeting."

"You will be. I got the heads-up first, because the topic of discussion will be my retirement and how the team will be reorganizing. I have the option of forgoing the meeting."

"Are you going to skip it?"

"Fuck no. I'm insulted they even suggested it." Burgess took an outraged pull of his smoothie, which was green and probably contained so many supplements that it no longer tasted like anything resembling food. "My point is that specifics are going to be important because you're going to be named captain."

Sig's back teeth glued themselves together, a combination of anticipation and nerves stiffening his joints. "They haven't even reupped my contract and they're naming me captain?"

"Maybe they want to gauge your dedication first. Talk vision." Sig nodded firmly. "If that's the case, you've got nothing to worry about. You're dedicated. Resourceful. A born leader. If I could pick my own team and had everyone in the league to choose from, I'd still pick you to replace me as captain."

"Jesus, you could have warned me this was going to be emotional," Sig said, crossing both arms over a chest that was feeling far too vulnerable this morning. "I would have brought a box of Kleenex."

"Shut it." Burgess sniffed, shifted in his seat. "I don't want to ask you about this, but I've ignored it for a long time. Now I need to know if it's going to become an issue. I've been in the league for fourteen years and things have changed. There is interest in our personal lives that didn't exist before. Or at least the public didn't have so much access to it. Now they do. Are you following me?" Burgess picked up his smoothie cup and set it back down. "What's the story with you and Chloe? Just get it out in the open so we can figure out how to keep it from biting you in the ass."

Sig hated the shame that enflamed his skin.

Shame had no place around him and Chloe, but *especially* her.

What they had felt like a miracle to him. No one else would see it like that, though. Maybe not even Burgess—and despite the fact that his captain already suspected that Sig's relationship with Chloe was romantic, he had a hard time relaying the details. Burgess never made a goddamn move out of step. He was noble to a fault. Meanwhile, here was Sig, the potential new captain of the Bearcats, torturing himself with constant visits to his future stepsister. Touching, feeling, holding her any way he could.

"The story between me and Chloe?" Sig cleared his throat, only fleetingly looking Burgess in the eye. "Our parents are getting married in two months. There can't really be a story, can there?"

"Sig. I have eyes. So does everyone else. There is something there."

"We don't . . ." Sig let out a quick exhale. "There's nothing sexual going on. We just like to be . . . *around* each other. A lot. Christ, I can't believe we're having this conversation."

"Having the hard conversation now could save you having it with someone else in the future."

Sig stabbed the table with his index finger. "The only thing that's going to save me is our parents calling off the fucking wedding, all right?"

Burgess didn't flinch. "And if they don't?"

"I don't know," Sig enunciated.

Before the team captain could respond, a bell tinkled over the door—and in walked Corrigan and Mailer.

"Jesus, not the Rookies," Burgess muttered.

Sig clocked their arrival with a relieved smirk. Corrigan and Mailer were his teammates, so he loved them in the way one is forced to love their weird cousins, but they were still considered pesky rookies. At this present moment, however, Sig welcomed their timely arrival with open arms. Burgess wouldn't pry into Sig's personal life in front of them, which marked an end to the interrogation for which he had no answers. Hallelujah.

"Well, if it isn't the Orgasm Donors," Sig greeted them, smirking.

"Well, if it isn't our father and stepfather having some quality time together," Mailer said, grabbing a chair from a nearby table, flipping it around and straddling it. "I guess our evite went to spam."

Corrigan grabbed a chair, too. "Or they got our email addresses wrong. He's FartDeathstar1 for future reference. I'm Pucksandpussy000."

"I assume the zeroes are there because you're getting none of either," Sig drawled.

"Wrong. It's because I don't leave any for anyone else."

The Orgasm Donors high-fived across the table.

Burgess looked like he was chewing metal bolts. "How did you know we were here?"

"Bearcats Reddit. Everyone knows you come here at the same time every morning, soon as your kid leaves for school." Corrigan laid a hand on Burgess's arm. "Sorry, let me slow down. Reddit is a website. Are you familiar with websites?"

"Are you familiar with broken cartilage?"

The Donor laughed, but removed his hand as fast as possible. "So, besties, what are we talking about?"

"Nothing." This from Burgess.

Yeah, no way Sig wasn't going to use Corrigan and Mailer's interruption to his advantage. "Apparently, there is going to be a team meeting tonight. Big one."

Their excitement was palpable.

As was Burgess's irritation. "Are you happy?"

In response, Sig grabbed Burgess's smoothie and took a long sip. Grimaced over the taste of grass and set it back down.

Corrigan propped his elbows on the table, leaned in to study Burgess's and Sig's faces in turn. "What is the meeting about?"

Sig didn't miss a beat. "Do you want to tell them or should I, Sir Savage?"

Not a single blink from Burgess. "You break it to them."

"Fine. I'll be the bearer of bad news." Sig let out a slow breath. "The brass has spoken. You're the new team mascots. The giant, fuzzy costumes are being sized as we speak."

"One of you was going to be the head, one of you was going to be the tail . . ."

"But you're both asses, so the new mascot has two tails. No head, whatsoever. First of its kind."

"Fitting, right? Since there isn't a brain between you."

Burgess and Sig gave each other a very mature fist bump.

Mailer and Corrigan were looking at each other. "I can't figure out how they do this," Mailer marveled. "They don't even need time to come up with ways to trash us."

"It's so natural," Corrigan agreed, shaking his head. "I guess it's just the kind of wisdom that comes from being ancient."

Sig drilled the Donor with a look. "I'm twenty-nine, motherfucker."

Mailer scooted his backward chair closer to the table. "What is the meeting really about?" He opened his mouth and closed it, as if he wasn't sure he should share something. "Speaking of Reddit, I probably went a little too deep on a thread last night, but, uh, . . . there was something about the GM. A member of his family taking over day-to-day operations? Have you guys heard anything about that?"

Sig shot the captain a look to determine if he knew anything, but he looked just as baffled as Sig probably did. "Has anyone met his kids?"

A chorus of nos.

Burgess shrugged. "Probably just a rumor."

Mailer slapped a hand onto Burgess's shoulder. "The captain has spoken. It's hearsay, I daresay."

"We can only pray," Corrigan tacked on.

"Oh shit. That was seamless." They slapped approximately ninety high fives over the table while Burgess and Sig stared at each other, mentally exhausted. "We're turning into you two right before your very eyes. How does it feel?"

"Demoralizing." Burgess sighed.

"Guys—" Sig cut himself off when his phone started to vibrate in his pocket. There was only one person who called him, instead of texting, and it was Chloe. Sure enough, her name was scrolling by on the screen, the green circle at the bottom indicating it was a FaceTime call.

Corrigan leaned over. "Who is that?"

"Is it Chloe?" Mailer demanded to know. "Answer and put in a good word for me, man."

"Sure, I'll get right on that. Never."

No way he was having a conversation with Chloe in front of this trio. But the decision was taken out of his hands when Corrigan's fingers shot out fast and unexpectedly, hitting the button to answer the call. "Chloe!" he shouted in the general direction of the device. "Let's run away together to Madagascar."

Mailer wouldn't be left out. "All three of us. Think of the possibilities."

Watching Sig's face, Burgess whistled low under his breath.

Probably because there was a vein the size of a vacuum hose beating in the dead center of his forehead. "Sorry about that, Chlo," Sig managed through a dry throat, finally looking down into the smiling face of his soon-to-be stepsister. "I'm at a breakfast meeting. Is everything okay?"

"Better than okay. My morning class got canceled because my instructor is sick, so I took Pierre to a dog park. Look!" She flipped the camera around and all he saw was a young man's smiling face. "Oops, that's Elton."

That single sip of smoothie was gurgling in his stomach. "Who the hell is Elton?"

"He's at the dog park with his bichon frise." Elton's chin was no longer in the shot and Chloe was walking around showing Sig the doggie obstacle course, but mentally? Sig was still seeing El-ton. "It's right down the street from my building. Pierre loves it."

As far as Sig could tell, Pierre was lying still as a statue by the water fountain, no intention of moving ever again as long as he lived.

"Sig," Chloe started, "how quickly can someone develop sep-aration anxiety?"

"Corrigan gets separation anxiety from Burgess," Mailer said.

"Shut the fuck up," Corrigan fired back. "You're the one who has his rookie card framed on your nightstand."

"It's a collector's item, bitch."

Elton was back in the shot now, mooning at Chloe. "I don't like that guy," Sig said, without thinking. "Is he bothering you?"

"Who?"

"*Elton*, Chloe."

"Oh! No, he's not bothering me. He asked for my number, but . . ." She dropped her voice to a whisper. "He's not really my type, so I told him I'm not interested in a date. But he said that was fine. That our dogs could still hang out!"

A stiletto-wearing demon was using Sig's brain as a trampo-line. "Oh, he just took your number for a *dog* playdate. That's what he told you, huh?"

"Yes! I should have gotten a dog before. It's a great way to make friends."

Burgess leaned in. "Mute yourself for a sec."

Sig complied. "What?"

"A bichon frise is a girl's dog," Burgess said, tapping his temple with his index finger. "Elton has definitely got a girlfriend or a wife."

"Genius." Corrigan wipes an imaginary tear. "Freaking genius."

Sig's Adam's apple was trying to twist its way out of his throat and he'd already started to dig for his keys in his pocket. "You want some company, Chlo?"

"No, I'm fine. I didn't mean to interrupt your meeting." She crouched down beside Pierre, scrunching up his face with her left hand and pointing the camera at them both. "Pierre says hello to everyone. He can't wait to meet the team. Look at the excitement!"

The dog blinked.

Chloe's laughter rang out.

The Orgasm Donors smiled, obviously, because the sound was perfect and infectious.

"I think I'll head over there," Sig said to Chloe while forcing a casual smile. "Practice isn't until later this afternoon and I want to see the dog park for myself. Looks incredible."

"It is. It's right next to a baseball field." She got distracted by the scenery, the camera filming her throat and a couple strands of blowing blond hair. "I think Elton just finished a rec league game or something . . ."

"Oh hell no. A *baseball* player?" spat Corrigan.

Mailer stood up. "Fuck that. We ride. No one's sister is dating a baseball player."

Sig jabbed the air with his finger. "For the last time, stop calling her my sister."

"Whatever she is, she's keeping it hockey." Corrigan and Mailer were already walking toward the exit of the smoothie shop. "Let's fucking go."

Annoyed or not by their presumed intervention, Sig was already following them. "I can handle this myself," he growled, once they were out on the sidewalk.

"We're a team." Mailer cracked his knuckles. "No one handles anything by themselves."

"I'm too old for this shit," Burgess declared, emerging from the shop. "But I'm not missing it, either. Let's go scare the pants off a goddamn baseball player."

Mailer frowned. "Isn't the point to keep his pants *on*?"

"You know what I mean." Burgess sighed, flipping his keys over in his hand. "I'll drive."

CHAPTER FOURTEEN

Fact: Chloe had the cutest dog in the whole park. Not up for debate.

Sure, he'd been sitting in the same spot for the last thirty minutes, but he was just preparing to make his move! That spoke volumes about his personality. Check out the scene, decide which dogs were best to avoid, and then slide into the group fashionably late. The cool new guy. Yes, Chloe could see exactly what he was doing.

"G'boy, Pierre," she called, making a kissing sound at the bulldog.

Pierre sort of melted sideways into the grass, yawning the whole way down.

"He had a big breakfast," she explained to the group of pet owners, which consisted of Omar, a senior citizen who had marched his pug into the park ten minutes ago and immediately hidden behind the sports section of the newspaper. And Elton, a cute baseball player with an impeccably groomed bichon frise.

Maybe giving Elton her phone number might have been a little premature, but it was nice to make friends based on something other than her last name. Growing up in Connecticut, her last name was always the first thing someone asked of her. *Chloe . . . ?* They would trail off leaving her name dangling in the air like a fishhook. Wait for her to complete the moniker that would determine her relevance. As soon as she said *Clifford*, the tension in their face fled.

Ah, it's fine, she's one of us.

Chloe was a little embarrassed to admit she'd taken comfort in that at one time.

Acceptance based on wealth she'd done nothing to earn or deserve.

She'd had a lot of friends in Connecticut, but never anyone she would tell her deep, dark secrets to. They were friends who got together at parties or at the club and gossiped about one another. Dropped risqué details about their sex lives for clout. Complained about wanting to get out of Darien, but not *really* wanting to leave, just to go on their next vacation.

Chloe had fit in as best she could, mainly to please her mother. However, she'd learned early that giving in to her mischievous impulses earned her points with the group. That was who she'd become. Chloe, the thief. Chloe, the charming con, able to talk her way out of trouble while everyone giggled nearby. Once, her friends had driven onto the golf course and parked in a circle facing one another with their headlights on, music blasting, a flash mob dance party, of sorts.

When the police arrived, they'd shoved Chloe in their direction as their spokesperson, and she'd tearfully explained to them they'd all gotten lost. And thank goodness the cops were there to lead them back to the road. It had worked. But it hadn't *really* worked, had it? The truth was, she'd never *actually* been in danger of getting into trouble. Her little bubble wasn't designed for anything but a scot-free existence.

Not anymore, though. Not after last night.

Her blinders had well and truly been ripped off.

"How long have you been in Boston?" asked Elton, distracting her.

"Six months," Chloe responded, pinkie waving at Pierre. Was he asleep or dead? "I'm from Connecticut, but I gratefully consider this home now."

Elton looked around, squinting. "You like Boston that much, huh?"

"Yes. I never want to leave. I could explore one street every day for the rest of my life and still never see it all." She thought of the arena, Grace's penthouse, the discovery of the dog park right down the street from her house. She had to have walked past it before and never noticed it until today. "It's a town that gets familiar fast, but remains kind of a mystery, too."

A grin was spreading across his face. "I . . . guess I never thought of it that way."

She smiled. "Well, now we both can."

Elton was seriously cute. Lanky. Six foot one, maybe? Sandy brown hair. Crow's-feet that extended from the corners of his wraparound sunglasses. But she'd meant what she'd said—Elton wasn't her type. What *was* her type, though?

Chloe envisioned a lineup of men, each one a various archetype. A cowboy. A preppy. A biker, even. But they were all just Sig dressed in different outfits.

Oh dear.

Who besides Sig could make her want to cry and cheer and laugh just by existing?

Would anyone else ever be able to make her knees feel like gelatin or her throat strain with the effort of keeping three words locked up inside? Make her hot, bothered, and wet with a smirk? Perhaps there was nobody in the world who could do that, except for Sig Gauthier. But she needed to try. She needed to separate her romantic life from her eventual stepbrother.

"So have you been playing baseball your whole life?" she

asked, hoping to distract herself from the fact that her belly was trapped in a free fall.

"Since I was ten," Elton answered. "My dad coached my Little League team—"

"Fascinating story, man," came a voice from behind Elton. One Chloe recognized, but couldn't quite place . . .

At least not until she turned around and found four fearsome Bearcats starters walking into the dog park the same way they skated onto the ice. Like they owned it.

Sig was leading the pack, but he wasn't the one who'd spoken. No, it had been one of the Orgasm Donors, as Sig liked to call them.

Sig.

Happiness went off like a confetti bomb inside of her. There was no use pretending otherwise. He was there. With her. That would forever and always make her happy.

Too happy, though?

From this high of a height, she could only plummet. And always did.

"Hey, Chlo," Sig drawled.

"Hi," she breathed, unable to modulate her voice or her heart. She couldn't look anywhere but right at him. "What are you doing here?"

"Just out for a walk."

"Oh." He'd moved his shoulder funny. "Are you sure?"

Sig moved in close and wrapped his right arm behind her back, pulling Chloe up onto her toes for a hug that arched her spine and made her feel weightless. "All right, fine," he said gruffly in her ear. "I wanted to see you."

"You just saw me this morning."

Ever so briefly, he squeezed her tighter. "It's never enough."

"Who *are* you guys?" Elton asked.

Oh yeah. Elton.

Chloe forced herself to wiggle out of Sig's perfect arms and observe the scene in front of her, which was straight out of a hockey horror flick. Sir Savage was leaning against a tree—which he almost matched for size—looking bored, but observant. Mailer and Corrigan were twinning as usual with matching expressions of blatant disrespect, pure and simple. They were focused on Elton, who looked nothing short of stunned at the arrival of four jacked professional athletes, all of whom looked like they needed a shower and some sleep, frankly.

"Who *are* we?" Mailer traded a booming laugh with Corrigan. "You don't watch hockey, bro?"

"That's Sir Savage, my guy," Corrigan blustered, indicating the legendary center behind him. "Show some goddamn respect."

Elton rolled a shoulder. "Might have heard of him. In passing."

"In pass—" Mailer was having a ministroke. "Okay, fine. I guess you have an excuse since baseball games last fourteen hours. You don't have time for anything else."

"It's America's game," Elton shot back.

"At best," Mailer drew out, "it's background noise during a nap."

"Wow." Still smarting from that insult, Elton turned his attention to Sig who was now standing in front of Chloe, all but blocking her view of the proceedings. Without seeing his face, she somehow knew he had his gametime expression locked in place. Forbidding. Murderous. Totally out of place in a peaceful dog park. "And who are you?"

"That's her . . ." Corrigan trailed off, scratching a red eyebrow. "It's complicated."

"Yeah," Mailer echoed. "It's complicated. More complicated than baseball, that's for fucking sure."

"Bottom line, she's a hockey girl. She's *our* hockey girl."

"Don't get carried away, Corrigan," Sig said.

Chloe poked him in the shoulder. "It's a little late for that, don't you think?"

He turned and winked at her. "Did you do your hair different this morning? God, you look beautiful."

Giddy pleasure shot straight down to her toes. "I used a beach waver . . ." *You're being had.* "Hey, you're just trying to distract me from the fact that you're ambushing this poor guy."

"Poor guy, Chloe?" Sig snorted. "That's a bichon frise."

"What is *that* supposed to mean?" half shouted Elton. "Whatever. You think baseball is so easy, why don't we have a little matchup?" Elton stepped toe-to-toe with Corrigan. "Your team versus mine."

Mailer and Corrigan fist-bumped. "Done, son. Name the place and time."

"Oh, my goodness," Chloe burst out, throwing up her hands. "This is exactly like the *Sandlot*, except you're full-grown men, so it's not a rite of passage, it's just toxic behavior." She shook her head at the man in front of her. "And in front of Pierre, too, Sig. You're setting a bad example."

Elton craned his neck to smile at Chloe. "You like the *Sandlot*?"

"You're finished speaking to her," Sig growled, sidestepping again to block Elton's view. "Consider yourself lucky you were allowed to do it once."

"Allowed?" Chloe sputtered.

"Yeah," Corrigan piped up. "We didn't even *get* one shot."

"Okay, I think I'm done here. Pierre!" She put two fingers in her mouth and whistled, but the bulldog only sunk deeper into the grass, forcing Chloe to march over to the grassy patch near the water fountain and hook the leash to Pierre's collar. "Seriously, Pierre? You barfed this morning when a pigeon landed on the fire escape, but you managed to keep your breakfast down around all this male posturing? That's called selective barfing."

She snapped the leash into place and the sound must have rattled something to life inside of the bulldog, because he rolled to his feet and snarfed, apparently as ready to go home as Chloe. She sent the group of men one final, disappointed look, then let herself out of the rear gate so she wouldn't have to wade through all their egos by leaving through the front.

They'd only made it about a block when she sensed Sig trailing behind her.

"Chloe."

She made sure he heard her gasp. "Don't say my name."

"Ah, come on. It's my favorite word." Silence fell as she walked faster, shocked when Pierre matched her speed. "I hate when you're mad at me."

"Good."

"*Chloe.*"

"No."

"What are you saying 'no' to?"

"Your presumed ownership over me. If I want to give a man my number, I'm allowed to do that. We agreed to see other people—"

"No, we didn't."

"—because *our* relationship is complicated and that's all it will ever be." Chloe's building was only a block away now and she couldn't wait to get inside, slam the door, and scream at the ceiling. On behalf of her confused heart, battered hormones, and womankind for having to exist in the same universe as hockey players. Who she actually *really* loved, but God. What gave them the right to swoop in like that and treat her like a piece of property? "I don't want to talk to you anymore, Sig!" she shouted over her shoulder.

Pierre yipped and she gave him a grateful look for being the goodest boy/hype man.

"*What?* You don't want to talk to me ever again?" Sig shouted back. "I just saved you from a baseball player."

"I don't need saving. And I didn't say I never wanted to talk to you again *forever*. I just meant, I don't know . . . until next week, at least."

He caught up with her at the door of the building, pressing his hand to the glass and nuzzling his mouth against her neck. "No. A week without you will *feel* like forever, Chlo."

Need slipped down the sides of her belly like hot oil. "What are we doing here, Sig? What are we *doing*?"

Several heavy seconds passed while he acknowledged the meaning behind her words. They were trapped in this crazy cycle of not being together, while also being totally committed—but not having him in all ways was not a sustainable place to be.

Couldn't he feel that?

Instead of answering Chloe's question—*what are we doing?*—Sig let them into the vestibule, taking his own set of keys out of the pocket of his sweatpants and unlocking the main building. He appeared to be chewing on leather as he escorted her up the stairs, Pierre clicking happily in front of them, probably hoping there would be food provided once they were inside.

Somehow, though, Chloe knew something else was going to happen.

Maybe it was the rough set of Sig's jaw.

Or the uneven sound of his breathing.

Whatever tipped her off, she still was not expecting to be

pressed up against the door as soon as they were inside the apartment, pinned there by Sig's body. She couldn't explain what happened inside of her at that sudden, hard press of tense muscle and the blast of intention from the man who usually held back so stubbornly. But her nervous system started to clamor, her pulse rocketing to a thousand miles an hour, the world's most telling moan sailing out of her mouth. Her fingers shook and snatched for an anchor, finding one in the thighs of his sweatpants, fisting in the soft material and pulling him closer.

"Is this what you want?" he asked, raggedly.

"Yes."

"Good. Take what I'm not supposed to give you." He vibrated with caged aggression, his need on a leash, but he was letting her have some of it and his erection elongating against her belly was like a feast after a famine. He raked his mouth up the side of her face, into her hair, and she almost dropped to the ground, it felt so divine. "Just don't be angry with me," he rasped. "I can't stand it."

Wait. She was angry with him?

Oh yeah.

She *was* angry with him.

"You aren't in charge of my love life."

"I *am* your love life, Chloe."

A two-handed shove didn't budge him an inch. "You're not," she said, frustration evident in her tone. "I want you to be, but you're not. You *can't*." Saying these things out loud caused her throat to ache, but they had to be said out loud at some point, right? "Eventually we have to admit this relationship is unhealthy and just . . . just let it change."

His head had been shaking the whole time. "No."

"Yes."

"You think we could feel like this with anyone else?"

"No," she whispered, still drawing him closer, her neck lacking its usual strength and all because that part of him, so heavy and thick, was sandwiched between them. "But I want things you won't give me."

His head lifted, eyes burning into hers. God, she'd never seen him this way. No, he'd never *let* her see him this way. So intense she was having trouble holding on to her thoughts. "Like what?"

Detailing the way she longed for physical contact felt wrong, because she'd only wanted that contact from him since the night they'd met. Saying that out loud wasn't going to support her point, though, was it? Only hurt her argument that their obsessive relationship wasn't serving either of them. "I want to be taken to dinner and kissed on my stoop afterward," she blurted. "I want to be told I'm pretty and feel your—a man's weight on top of me."

Slowly, his brows knit together, as if she'd spoken in a completely different language. "You want to be told you're *pretty?*" He repinned her so hard against the door, the hinges rattled and she sobbed, not even bothering to try and get free, because she didn't want to. His body against hers felt like being home for the first time in six months. "A man who calls you pretty, Chloe, is a fucking fool. You aren't pretty, you're brutally goddamn beautiful. You glow with life. You're crazy. You have heart. You have love pouring out of you. You're brilliant and creative. So gorgeous I've lost thousands of hours of sleep." His mouth melded to hers in a messy rub of lips. "You have a body that demands someone spoil it often and fuck it twice as often. Pretty?" He shook his head. "I'd spit on a man for calling you pretty. You're extraordinary. The first and last of your kind."

"Sig." Her throat felt heavy enough to drop into her stomach at any moment. *Oh my God. Oh my God.* Where had those words been hiding? Maybe their power is what she felt in her bones every time he looked at her. "How . . . I'm . . ."

"How many numbers do you have in your phone? For men."

"I don't like where this is going."

"Too bad. How many?"

"I'm going to kick you—"

He dipped his head and sucked the side of her throat, long and hard, while she gasped, his hands scrubbing up the outsides of her thighs, all the way to her rib cage, then higher into her hair, his fingers spearing in deep and holding her head while she tried to get her breath. "F-friends, too?"

"No." He stared hard at her mouth. "Men who are smart enough to be interested in you romantically. Past and present. Men who might show up and try to rekindle shit. Men who might lie about your dogs hanging out to get into your panties. How many of those you got?"

"I don't know. Seven?"

"*Seven?* Jesus fucking—"

"How many women do you have like that?" she half shouted.

"One. You." Leaving his left hand tangled in her hair, he dropped his right one and yanked her phone out of her purse, holding it up. "I'll kiss you once for every one of those seven contacts you delete, starting with the baseball player."

"He has a name."

"Not to you, he doesn't."

"You're pushing it, Sig. You're really pushing it."

"I know. You can be pissed as hell—just kiss me at the same time."

Fuses blew in her brain. *Pew. Pew.*

Because oh lord, he was even more magnetic up close, every inch of him sealed to every inch of her, the power inside of him on the verge of erupting. Lust and affection were joining forces in the depths of his eyes to turn her breathless and oh, oh, he very slightly dragged his sex an inch to the left against her belly and they both shuddered. "You only want to kiss me when you're jealous. Is that right?"

"I want to kiss you even when I'm asleep, Chlo." His open mouth feathered over hers and a melting sensation crept into her thighs, the muscles between them pulling taut, so taut she just barely caught a whimper. "I'm like this day and night."

"You don't always show me."

He tilted his head to the right, teased her lips open with a lick. "I'll show you now."

Who was she kidding trying to resist this?

The heartbeat between her thighs was pounding just as swiftly as the one in her chest. She was always starving for this man, but right now, she'd crawl on her hands and knees through the desert for another minute of being grinded into the door by his huge hockey body, for more time with his breath on her face, his fingers in her hair. And he must have read that truth in her eyes, because he shook the phone slightly. "Baseball guy first."

"Do I delete it n-now?"

"No, you'll do it later." He tucked the phone back into her purse, then removed the purse completely, letting it drop to the floor. "You're not going to be able to focus on anything else once I get started."

"You either."

"Facts."

They looked into each other's eyes for several seconds and it was like going to the top floor of a skyscraper in a glass elevator at a hundred miles an hour. She left her stomach on the ground, toppled into the bottomless well of feeling he had inside of him and flew, flew to the top, their lips locking and twisting, bodies pressing roughly on a mutual groan, the first kiss a precursor to madness—because that's exactly what ensued.

Their first kiss since the night they met was an *implosion*.

A whimper. A guttural groan. A damp slant of lips. Two bodies shaking.

Breath being denied. A refusal to give up the blessed suction. Texture. Friction.

"Miss me, dream girl?" he panted.

"Yes," she gasped, being drawn into round two. The ferociousness of it. How he opened their mouths wider than most people would consider appropriate, feeding her his tongue in an intimate lick that turned her fingernails to claws that she sunk into his buns—and to be clear, she had no idea when she'd grabbed his butt, only that his was firm and male and he was openly fucking her mouth now. No kiss count was being kept, even as they occasionally came up for breaths, loud gasps of air, before their mouths were attached once again, licking and suctioning and growing hungrier with every rasp of his stubble on her smooth chin.

"You're going to feel my weight on top of you, Chloe." His lips moved to her neck for a hard suck, followed by a cherishing lick. "You'll feel it behind you. Beneath you. You're going to feel the weight of me, of us, everywhere."

"I already do."

"I know, baby. God, me too." Another diving kiss, more frantic this time, his hands wedging between the door and her backside, gripping tight through her yoga pants, a shudder going through his big body when she rubbed her cheeks in those huge hands, savoring his touch there. "You're going to trust me to find a way for us, even though it's getting harder. You delete everyone else, but you don't ever delete me. *Ever*."

"I won't," she whimpered, writhing now between him and the door. "I won't."

"Good girl. *My* fucking girl."

"Yes."

"When I walk out of here," he said hoarsely against her mouth, his erection so full now, so close it felt like a part of her, "those contacts are gone. You don't know them anymore."

She was already nodding, wrapping her right leg around his waist, tilting her hips, begging without words for another kiss and he granted it, because he had no choice, neither one of them did and she could see that so easily. Feel it. The riotous pull that had anchored itself that first night at the country club and only grown heavier, unable to be pulled back up into the ship.

"If you do that for me, if you agree to knock this bullshit off about dating other people . . ." Unexpectedly, he rammed her into the door with his hips, pinning and grinding, mouth dropping open on a guttural sound. "I'll come back here tonight after practice and fuck you until your thighs melt. How does that sound?"

Huh. *What.*

Her blood turned to molten metal.

She couldn't respond. Couldn't speak or reason. She was too busy reeling. Trying to convince herself she'd heard him wrong. Had she? Or was he really, *finally*, giving in? "Really?" she whispered, holding her breath.

"I'm done being noble. I'm *not* losing you to another man. I'll die first. Do you understand me?" He pinned her roughly to the door, rolled his lower body. "It's going to feel so fucking good. I bet you're going to bite."

"Sig. *Please.*"

"You're not getting under anyone but me," he growled, lips moving against her ear, down her neck messily and back up. "I'd never waste my time with someone else. Neither will you. And, Chloe, listen to me good." He reached down and yanked both her knees up to his hips, sliding her up the door slowly, slowly, *slowly* like a prolonged thrust, all while watching her beneath his hooded eyelids, sweat forming on his upper lip. "My dick is well worth the wait. You feel that, don't you? You know I'm not lying."

Oh God, oh God, oh God. "You're not lying."

He crushed their chests together, hips moving in a slow rotation while he looked her right in the eye. "I wanted to wait until I was positive that I could make you my wife—and that is still the plan. That will always be the plan. If a single possibility exists that puts my ring on your finger, I'll find it. But I can see I'm losing you. I can see you need me inside you and that's what you're going to get. My dream girl gets her way with me every time."

Wife.

Had he said the word . . . "wife"?

Why was every corner of her heart lighting up like the Fourth of July?

Was that the outcome she'd wanted all along? Was it inevitable?

No. It wasn't inevitable.

That's what he was trying to tell her, wasn't it? *If* a single possibility exists . . .

"Delete those contacts the second I'm gone." He kissed her hard. Once, twice, three times. Lingering, while slowly letting her legs drop, her feet finding the floor. "And don't give your number to any more baseball players unless you'd like to see me in prison. Do we have a deal, Chloe?"

Perhaps threatening murder wasn't romantic, but her heart didn't seem to understand that, evidenced by its position lodged in her jugular. "I shouldn't make that deal."

"Make it, baby. I'll come back later and reward you with ride after ride on this dick."

"Deal," she whimpered. "I'm yours. You know I am."

A gruff, emotional sound left him. "I'm going while I still can," he slurred, rubbing his mouth on her cheek, against her temple.

And then, after a hard kiss of her forehead and a whispered *thank you*, he was gone.

CHAPTER FIFTEEN

The Bearcats had a pavilion-style viewing room that resembled a small movie theater, which is where they were conducting tonight's meeting. Players filed in wearing various forms of business casual, as the late-afternoon email had instructed. Some of them had apparently interpreted that dress code as a mere suggestion, others had made an effort to *at least* wear their nicest sweatpants. Their coaches sat at the front of the room, nodding at players as they passed—and Christ, they looked grim.

Sig was torn between wanting to know the reason for the meeting, as it pertained to his future as a Bearcat, and a desperate need to get back to Chloe.

I'm going to fuck her tonight.

I'm going to fuck Chloe.

Finally. Finally.

The lock on his cage door had been picked and he was out. And he had no idea if he'd be able to get back in that cage, now that he was free. That's what scared him. That was why he'd refrained from taking her to bed for six long, painful, frustrating months. Because once he let himself taste heaven, purgatory was going to be infinitely harder. And frankly, he couldn't get much harder than he was right now. Just the knowledge that he was going to be inside of that woman in a matter of hours had him throbbing in his briefs.

Kissing her that afternoon had been . . .

Lord.

He couldn't adequately describe the feeling of connecting with her like that. The first time he'd kissed her at the country club, he'd been in a state of suspended euphoria. Almost like he was having the best dream of his life. But nothing—nothing—compared to kissing Chloe after six months of learning her. Studying her, confiding in her, comforting her. Getting all those things in return. Falling in deep, rich, unbending love with her.

But they were on a countdown clock . . . and the stakes were going to be even higher after tonight. *What the hell am I going to do?*

"You seem preoccupied," Burgess said, beside him in a pair of pressed khakis and a black button-down. "Look alive. This is important."

Sig dragged his index finger around the inside of his dress shirt collar. "Coach McCarren looks like he's about to give a eulogy," Sig returned dryly. "Let's hope it isn't mine."

"They'd be out of their minds to trade you."

"Don't be so sure. They got me cheap, but I could be too expensive now."

"Could you see yourself leaving Boston?"

"If it meant being paid what I'm worth?" Sig sighed through the vulnerable feeling that came with the possibility of being on a new team, in a different city. Starting from scratch. "If it meant more security for Chloe, yeah. I'd take her and go . . ."

Those words were out of his mouth before his brain acknowledged them.

Sensing Burgess's knowing—and troubled—stare, Sig ran back through what he'd just said, weeding out the parts that made no sense. What reason would Chloe have to go with him if he got traded? What would that look like to the outside world? And she was now actively training to become first chair with the Boston Symphony Orchestra. Maybe . . .

Maybe she wouldn't *want* to come with him.

Sig's palms grew damp in an instant, the meeting taking on a new importance.

"All right, men," said McCarren, standing up slowly to address the room. "Thank you for coming in. Some of you even look half decent—"

Their coach was interrupted midsentence when Mailer and Corrigan swaggered into the room in T-shirts and bow ties, dapping up teammates as they passed.

"Spoke too soon. Congratulations, you both look ridiculous," drawled McCarren. "Now sit the hell down. This is important."

Too late, Sig realized Corrigan and Mailer were on their way to take the two empty front-row seats on his right, but there was nothing he could do about it now. They adjusted their bow ties with a flourish and took their seats, Corrigan sending Burgess a quick salute.

Burgess sighed.

"As I was saying," boomed the coach. "Thank you for coming in on your night off. A little bit of housekeeping, then we'll get to the point." He proceeded to talk strategy for their next two games, which would take place on the road. Chicago and Detroit. "Moving on, I know we all saw this coming, as he's been open with the staff, not to mention the press, about this being his final year with the Bearcats, but we're officially saying goodbye to Abraham at the end of this season." The staff started clapping, followed by the room full of players, the applause carrying on for a full thirty seconds. "He leaves behind a tremendous legacy . . ." McCarren's gaze flickered briefly in Sig's direction, but Sig couldn't read his expression. ". . . and some mighty deep skates to fill."

Some murmuring kicked up around the room.

Sig could feel eyes on the back of his head.

If McCarren was going to name Sig as the new captain, now would be the moment. But he didn't. Obviously. They hadn't even offered him a contract yet.

A bead of sweat rolled down Sig's spine.

"Now." The coach planted his knuckles on the table in front of him and leaned forward. "We have another announcement. And an introduction. For that, I'm going to hand it over to our general manager, Pete Bauer."

Everyone simultaneously sat up straighter, trading looks.

Since Sig didn't see the wealthy, somewhat notorious Bostonian in the front of the room, he turned and watched Bauer stomp his way down the aisle. Expectant silence fell as Bauer shook hands with McCarren and took his spot, front and center of the room, commanding attention with a curt nod. "Hello, gentlemen. Thank you for being here. I'm very pleased to be able to share some news with you tonight. I'm too excited to wait, so let's get to it." He clapped his hands together. "As you might have seen, so inelegantly reported in the press, I was recently married. For a fourth time, but who's counting?"

Some of the coaches huffed a laugh, as if they could relate.

And yeah, Sig had seen those headlines about Bauer and his new, much younger, wife. None of it had any bearing on hockey, however, so he'd mostly ignored the stories. Right about now, he wished he'd done more than skim.

"My wife is expecting twins now, if you can believe it. I haven't had any little ones running around in a while, but the news has made me realize how grueling the life of a GM can be. My health is more important now than ever and I need to focus on that, so I can be around for my twins." He added dryly, "Stress drinking while I analyze the league standings and playoff predictions isn't going to help me be present. For them. In fact, my cardiologist suggested I take a step back years ago. It's time to listen. And so, without further ado, I'd like to announce that my daughter, Reese Bauer, will be taking over operations as general manager of Bearcats."

You could have heard a pin drop.

Their hockey team was going to be managed by a woman.

One they'd never heard of.

Okay. Setting aside the fact that the league didn't have a single woman as general manager, only *assistant* GMs, her name was totally unfamiliar. What were her qualifications? If she knew how to work hard and make tough decisions, Sig welcomed her as much as he would a man, but at that moment, he only had one thing on his mind.

How was this going to affect his contract? His captainship?

Bauer continued, undeterred, the air of a man who didn't necessarily care how his news was received, only that he'd made the decision, everyone had to deal with it, and he was probably late for a dinner reservation. "Reese is a Princeton graduate. Top of her class. I've been quietly ushering her in under my wing for the last few months and I'm confident that she is exactly who this team needs to remain as one of the league's top competitors while I take some time to focus on my health. My family."

He cleared his throat, indicating the back of the room with a sweep of his hand.

"Reese."

Sig turned and watched a woman in a red pantsuit glide down the aisle, a gold watch winking on her wrist, chin held high. Reese was a child from Bauer's original marriage, pre-sumably, because he'd been married to a Black woman first and Reese appeared to be biracial. And if Sig hadn't spent six months analyzing Chloe for every little sign that might indicate what she was thinking, he probably wouldn't have noticed that this woman was nervous, but there was something about the way her fingertips dug into the folder at her side that told him she wasn't as confident as she came across.

Her voice, however, portrayed otherwise.

It was clear and firm.

"Hello. Thank you for the warm greeting. You can pick your jaws up off the floor now."

"I'm in love," Mailer whispered, reaching over to clutch Sig's forearm. "Son of a bitch."

"Daughter, actually," Reese said, without missing a beat—and that's the moment Sig decided he liked her. Which could change, depending on his status with the team now that the house of cards had been reshuffled, but for now, she seemed all right. "I know this news is a lot to digest, so I'm not going to go into specifics tonight." She flipped open the folder, scanned something, and closed it again. "Suffice it to say I'm committed to doing everything I can do on my end to put a Stanley Cup in the Bearcats' trophy case. Which could mean some restructuring. Reallocation of budget. A hard look at who is serving the best interests of the team."

For the second time that night, Sig was treated to a vague glance, this time from Reese.

What the hell did that mean?

Was he not serving their best interests?

Chloe's smile materialized in his mind and he struggled not to shift anxiously in his seat. If his time with the Bearcats was coming to an end, he couldn't serve her best interests, either. That was the true source of the pressure weighing down his shoulders.

"I've been watching hockey since the first day I opened my eyes. I know when a team is on the verge of greatness—again— and this one is. Lately, we're always second best. Runner-up. What's holding us back?" She nodded for a moment. "It's my job to figure that out. It's your job to trust me. Can you all get past the obvious fact that I'm a woman and do that?"

"Yes," Mailer rasped. "Implicitly."

Sig turned his head slowly to look at the rookie. "Are you okay, or what?"

Dude didn't even hear him. "I can be what you need," he said to Reese, before shaking himself. "I mean, I'm here to get results. For you. And show you around. Do you need to be shown around?"

"I'm all set, Bow Tie," Reese deadpanned.

That earned a chuckle from the room.

Mailer reached up and yanked off the bow tie, the scratching sound revealing it to be attached by Velcro.

"I'll leave you to enjoy your evening. Good luck on the road this week—you might not see me, but I will be there to cheer you on from the box," Reese said, pointing to her serene expression. "This is my cheering face. Don't take it personally." Another, warmer laugh from the team. "Good night."

Everyone shuffled to stand at once.

But the entire team simultaneously froze as Reese approached Sig. "Mr. Gauthier." She tipped her head in the direction of the exit—the one that led to the executive offices. "Might I have a word?"

SIG SAT DOWN in front of the white designer desk, numb straight to his fingertips.

Months of wondering where he stood with the team, praying they would offer him a worthwhile contract, came down to this moment. He could feel it. This woman didn't call people into her office unless she had something important to say.

His fate hung in the balance. As a Bearcat. Maybe as a hockey player. As the man who dreamed of providing for Chloe for the rest of his natural life. Longer, even.

Reese sat down in front of a picture window, Boston lit up behind her.

She folded her hands on the desk.

"Let's get right to it, Mr. Gauthier—"

"Sig."

She nodded hesitantly, as if not sure she wanted to be quite so casual. "Sig." She tapped a finger against her knuckle. "I won't beat around the bush. You're the best wing in the league. Your speed is unmatched. It goes unnoticed sometimes how many opportunities you create for other players to score, but it doesn't go unnoticed by me."

Unexpectantly winded, Sig coughed into his fist. "I thought you weren't going to beat around the bush."

Amusement briefly crossed her face. "Thank you is the response you're looking for."

"I'm not sure if I'm thanking you yet." Sig looked her dead in the eye. "Are you going to trade me or give me a better contract?"

The fact that she appeared to be conflicted did nothing to settle his stomach. "I'm sure you can appreciate my position. I'm new. I'm going to be under the microscope. And let's be honest, everyone will want me to fail, whether they say it out loud or not. Because of that, I have to be an exceptional general manager. I'm either the best or I'll be considered the worst."

"I hear you. I'm just not sure what this has to do with me."

"It was my intention to elevate you to captain and pay you the kind of eight-figure salary you deserve. That's what I *want* to do, because it's the best move for the team. And while I'm under a microscope . . ." She paused. "I'm not sure that's where *you* want to be."

Sig's blood rapidly started to drop in temperature.

His conversation with Burgess in the smoothie shop earlier that day came back to him in snippets. *What's the story with you and Chloe? Just get it out in the open so we can figure out how to keep it from biting you in the ass.*

He'd blown off his friend's concern. Was it being proven valid? Already?

"I'm sorry," Sig managed. "I'm not sure what you mean."

One of Reese's eyebrows ticked up. She didn't appreciate him playing dumb, but he didn't know what else to do. Not until he heard the extent of the problem.

"There has been a lot of chatter on the Bearcats message boards about the girl in the pink Gauthier jersey. She's in the front row at every game, sits with the fiancée of Burgess Abraham, so naturally fans are making assumptions that Pink Jersey is *your* girlfriend, since your name is on her back." He remained stone-faced, but his pulse was going a thousand miles an hour. Message boards? What the fuck? "Obviously, we had to do our due diligence on this. It was easy to find out her name, because the tickets have been left at the box office under Chloe Clifford every week since the start of the season. She's your stepsister."

"Not yet," he managed. "Not for two months."

"Forgive me, Sig, but I don't think people are going to make that distinction. Furthermore, they don't want to." He read the hint of sympathy on her face, but he didn't care for it. Didn't want to see it or acknowledge it. Sympathy wasn't called for. He hadn't lost Chloe. Hadn't ruined her. Not yet. "And after the article that came out this afternoon in the *Globe*'s late edition, I can only imagine how the gossip is going to proliferate. Because it doesn't appear to be gossip. Does it?"

Sig could barely hear Reese over the pounding in his skull. "What article?"

Reese didn't move right away, but when she did, she opened the laptop in front of her, tapped a few keys, and turned the device around.

The pictures drew his attention first. Him and Chloe walking Pierre that morning, before sunrise. Shoulder to shoulder, smiling at each other, like they were the only two people in the world, his hand resting on the small of her back. Beside that snapshot, there was another one of Chloe at a recent game, her palms pressed to the glass as he skated by.

The headline reached out and sucker punched him—"Stepsister Goes Above and Beyond?"—and . . . Christ, he couldn't read anymore. Not without getting sick.

"Right now, it's only a small clipping in the entertainment section, but I don't anticipate the story remaining quiet for long. Not after your agent demanded they remove your name as one of Boston's more eligible bachelors . . . and now? This secret relationship appears to be why. The chatter only gets worse if we name you as the next captain."

This was his future being discussed. Eight figures. The captainship of an NHL franchise.

Everything he'd ever dreamed of.

But Sig could only think about getting to Chloe. Fast. Did she know about the article? Worse, had her mother caught wind of it? Perhaps been informed by her lawyers? Was he simultaneously losing the income he'd need to provide for Chloe and sawing off her financial pipeline, as well? Jesus, he needed to get to Chloe's apartment. Now. Or . . .

Fuck. Was that going to make things worse?

"I can't have the public questioning whether our captain is in a romantic relationship with his stepsister. And looking at these pictures, I don't even think they *would* question it."

Sig opened his mouth to deny he and Chloe were . . . *more*.

But he couldn't.

Not when he would sell his soul to marry her.

Not when he'd kissed the face off her that afternoon.

"It's not some . . . sneaky affair. It's not like that. She's my best friend. She's . . ."

"They won't care, Sig."

He was terrified to ask his next question, but he needed to get out of there. Now. Needed to get to Chloe—and he wanted to get the full picture first so he knew what they were dealing with. "Give me the bottom line, please."

"I can't force you to do the right thing, especially in your personal life—"

"The right thing?"

"*Yes.*" Her voice raised slightly. "You've been caught in an improper relationship. The press could blow this up at any moment. And this organization *wants* to have your back. We'll deny it, spin it, laugh it off. Whatever it takes. But only if we're being *truthful.*"

"In other words . . ."

"Back off. Reset the boundaries of that relationship. No more Pink Jersey at the games. Live as though you're being watched, because you obviously are—and that scrutiny will only increase. You want to be the captain and make a fat salary? You must be above reproach."

Reset the boundaries.

No more Pink Jersey.

His world was eroding around him, the thing Sig loved most being dragged out of his reach. Her. There *was* no backing off from what they had. That would kill him.

"We have two weeks to offer you a formal contract, before you become a free agent." She nodded at the laptop screen. "I need to see what you're going to do about this before I can pull the trigger. We need to kill the story. I'm not sure how to do that if you continue to be seen with her. If you keep the status quo." A line formed between Reese's eyebrows and again, he caught a touch of sympathy in her tone. "I'm sorry, but you're going to have to make a choice. Hockey. Or her."

CHAPTER SIXTEEN

Chloe was on the floor of her bedroom rubbing Pierre's belly and repeatedly calling him a g'boy when her phone started ringing. When she saw it was Grace calling, she hopped to her feet and cleared her throat, wanting to be alert and professional for the conversation.

The one where she informed her mentor she was going to give her all to the harp.

No more getting by on natural talent. She was ready for the hard work—the kind it would take to step in and occupy first chair once it had been vacated by Grace. Honestly, Chloe had expected to be terrified knowing the grueling practice that lay ahead, but now that she'd made the decision to swing for the fences, something inside of her had settled. Locked into focus. The strong sense of purpose in her bones, her fingertips, made Chloe wonder if she'd been putting off something she secretly wanted for a long time.

Greatness on her own terms. Not just a showpiece or an object to gloat about . . . but a member of a company. This was her chance to find out what she could achieve on her own.

Well. Almost on her own. Her mentor was going to play a huge role.

"Hi, Grace," Chloe answered, standing in the middle of the living room now. "I'm so glad you called. I've made my decision—"

"Have you been getting busy with your stepbrother? Yes or no."

The room started to spin, black bleeding into the edges of her vision.

A weight pressed down on the center of her chest, growing heavier, heavier, until she had to struggle to breathe. "What?"

"Yes or no."

"No."

"I don't believe you."

Chloe melted down to the floor, ending in a cross-legged position, one arm strapped tightly over her middle to keep the contents from spilling out. "I-I . . . I'm sorry, I don't understand where this is coming from."

"Someone sent me a *Globe* article titled 'Stepsister Goes Above and Beyond?'" Wind started to rush in Chloe's ears, her mind flashing back to the most recent home game. The reporter. The way he'd questioned her about her relationship with Sig. How had she forgotten about him? "There is *a lot* of snark in that question mark, by the way. Not to mention meaning. And these two pictures of you giving him googly eyes? Goddamn it, Chloe. I can't be attached to this kind of thing."

The floor had dropped out from beneath her. She was free-falling. "It's not what it seems. We're not . . ." What? In love? Planning to spend the night in bed, finally giving in to the plague of constant lust? How could she deny something that was very clearly true? Outwardly *and* inwardly. Her attention locked on the door, begging Sig to walk through it. *Help me.* "Our parents are getting married in two months. We're realistic about what that means . . . for us."

"And in the meantime?" Grace sputtered.

"He's my best friend. He's . . ." Chloe dragged her knees up toward her chest. "I don't have a word to describe him."

"How about 'The most perfect human on earth.' That's how

you described him to me the day we met." Grace let out a long exhale. "You're in love with him?"

A call came in on the other line.

Sig.

Oh God, he must have seen the article.

What was he thinking? Had she been quoted? What pictures had been included?

Did she end the call with Grace and answer? So she and Sig could get their story straight? Did they *need* a story when they hadn't technically done anything wrong?

"That about answers my question," Grace said dryly.

Hot pinpricks speared the backs of Chloe's eyelids. "I haven't seen the article yet. I just need some time to figure out what's being said—"

"So you can figure out how to lie to me? Chloe, I'm sorry. You're megatalented and I like you, despite your manic pixie dream girl energy. But this is my career on the line, too. I have to dip before this gets worse."

"You're dropping me," Chloe breathed.

The line going dead was her answer.

Chloe covered her mouth with her hand, the silence in the apartment somehow ear-piercingly loud. She was still staring at the door, waiting for Sig, but the frame blurred now, her heart hammering in her chest.

The phone rang again in her hand.

She answered. "Sig."

"Chloe," he said thickly.

That was it. Enough to know they'd both been made aware of the article.

Made aware they'd been caught being in love.

"Are you coming over?"

"I don't think that would be wise." Her whole body sort of

heaved forward at the news she wouldn't see him imminently. She'd been dropped by Grace. Now Sig was going to abandon her too. "I think we should meet somewhere else," he finished, his truck door slamming in the background.

Relief bloomed in her chest like a wildflower and she cradled the phone more securely to her face, as if it was Sig's hand. How could she have doubted him for a second? "Oh. I thought you were going to say you couldn't see me anymore."

"That's not funny, Chloe."

"I wasn't making a joke."

"I'll be dead and buried before I stay away from you."

"Likewise," she whispered. "That's why we're in this mess."

A blown-out breath. "Yeah."

The fact that Sig didn't immediately reassure her that said mess could be fixed caused Chloe's stomach to turn inside out. This was bad. This was really, really bad.

"I'm going to send you an address. Have an Uber bring you there. It's a twenty-minute ride. I just think . . . I don't know. Let's get some distance from your place. If you think someone is following you, turn around and go back."

"Okay." She climbed to her feet and started toward her bedroom, alarmed by the lack of sensation in her legs. The way her apartment suddenly looked like a foreign land. "What is the address for?"

"A hotel." Those two gruff words caressed her ear. "There's a guaranteed chance I'm about to make this situation worse, but I decided this morning that I was going to fuck you tonight, Chloe. There's no going back. I need you underneath me so bad, my stomach is in knots right now. I need you more now that what we have is being threatened, okay? You walk into that hotel room, do it knowing you're going to end the night moaning my fucking name."

She paused out of necessity on the threshold of her bedroom, her whole body racked with a hot shiver. "I want that. I've wanted that for six months."

"Get here, then. *Get to me*." Traffic whirred on his end of the line, the revving engine of his truck. "I'm going to make sure you're okay first, baby. But I can't keep going like this. No more. Everything aches for you."

Had she ever heard him this raw and honest before?

Is this what he'd been holding back?

Sig had always been wildly potent, but *this* side of him?

Her Uber driver was going to wonder why she was sweating.

"I'll be out the door in five minutes." A snarfing noise almost caused Chloe to jump out of her skin. Pierre waded into her bedroom with a bored expression and plopped onto his hiney. "Oh! I'll have to bring Pierre."

"Jesus Christ."

"Sig, you're going to make him feel unwanted. Does the hotel allow dogs?"

"They're going to tonight, whether they like it or not. I'm not accepting any delays."

"See? Listen to you. You're going to be a great Bearcats captain."

He didn't speak for so long, she started to worry, but before she could ask why he'd gone quiet, he spoke. "I'll text you the room number."

"Okay." She rolled out a carry-on suitcase from her closet and heaved it one-handed onto the bed. "See you soon."

A few seconds passed. "Fuck. I don't want to get off the phone with you."

"I don't, either. But I'll move faster if you're not distracting me with your sexy voice."

"You think my voice is sexy?"

"Yes! Have I never told you that?"

"No." He paused. "What's sexy about it?"

"Everything. It's so deep and gruff. You make every word sound like its dripping in chocolate." Cradling the phone between her ear and shoulder, Chloe retrieved her sexiest underwear, a nightshirt, and a change of clothes from her dresser, throwing them unceremoniously into the suitcase. "Do you think *my* voice is sexy?"

"The sexiest. Especially when it's shouting obscenities at the refs." He made a low noise. "I'm going to make it sound even better, though."

Heat rolled slowly from her nipples to her core, tightening muscles along the way. "How are you going to do that?"

"By making you scream until it's hoarse."

"Off topic," she whispered, openly shaking now, her skin flushed. "I might have to spend some time with my vibrator before I call that Uber."

"Don't you *dare*, Chloe. Stay on the edge with me."

She bit her lip until it hurt. "I can't even see the edge anymore."

"Keep. Packing. If I hear any buzzing, you're in serious trouble. You wet? Good. Stay that way until I've got a good, rough stroke going and your legs kicking on the bed." She heard his fist rap against the steering wheel. "Goddamn it, Chloe. I'm so hot for you. I don't know how I'm going to walk through the lobby with my cock this hard." His exhale was rocky. "Come take care of me, dream girl. Come get taken care of."

"I'm coming."

"Not yet. I mean it."

She laughed, but it was a blustery sound. A desperate, yearning one. She tapped the screen to put the call on speakerphone, tossed it on the bed, and finished running around, adding toiletries and supplies for Pierre to her suitcase, zipping it shut, and ordering the Uber while listening to Sig's measured breaths on the other end of the line.

"I'm out the door," she said, leash in one hand, suitcase handle in the other.

"Okay." He sighed. "I guess I better hang up. I don't want you doing something inappropriate to yourself in the back of the Uber."

"Let me tell you, it's not that far-fetched." She walked out of her building, spotted the black sedan rounding the corner of her block. "My car is already here."

"Check the license plate, Chlo."

"I am." She swallowed hard. "I'll see you soon."

"Thank God."

They hung up—and after a brief argument with the driver over transporting Pierre—they were off. Ten minutes into the ride, a text from Sig came through.

Room 1125.

And somehow she knew she'd remember that number for the rest of her life.

Boston traffic must have known how badly she needed to reach Sig, because it cooperated for once, her ride taking her north toward Medford while Pierre dozed beside her in the back seat, blissfully unaware that his new owner was about to realize a dream six months in the making, even if one of her newer aspirations had just been moved outside of her reach. She didn't want to think about it now. She just wanted to get to him, lose herself, be absorbed. Absorb him in return. Finally. Finally. They were finally going to break the rules and her body knew it was coming, turning her flesh sensitive, her nipples to peaks, her inner thighs flexed. Ready.

As soon as she pulled up to the hotel, she knew it wasn't the type that allowed dogs.

It was way too nice.

She'd have to be creative.

"Would you happen to have a luggage cart?" she asked the bell-hop while the Uber driver removed her suitcase from the trunk.

"Yes, ma'am."

He wheeled over the cart, an eyebrow ticking up at her one, tiny piece of luggage.

"Oh, I'm so thirsty!" She tapped her throat, gave an exaggerated cough. "I think I'm . . . yes, I'm going to choke."

"There are bottles of water in the lobby, ma'am. I'll get one for you."

"Thank you," she said weakly.

When the bellhop disappeared through the automatic doors on his way into the lobby, Chloe hustled a resistant Pierre out of the Uber, groaning while lifting him onto the luggage cart and covering him quickly with her jacket while the driver shook his head in disapproval.

"There's a thirty percent tip in it for you to keep quiet."

"I ain't no snitch," he drawled, climbing back into the driver's side.

"Sit, Pierre. Stay." The bulldog remained perfectly stationary. "G'boy. Such a g'boy!"

The automatic doors opened and out flew the bellhop, holding a bottle of water out to Chloe, which she took and sipped while squeezing his forearm gratefully. "Thank you! Oh my goodness, that's so much better."

He nodded. "Would you like me to take the cart to your room?"

"Oh no, I always wheel my own luggage." She took a twenty-dollar bill out of her wallet and pushed it into his hands. "It's a habit of mine. I'll take it myself."

"Okay . . ." he said, nonplussed. "The elevators are to the right of reception."

"Thank you."

Chloe wheeled the luggage cart containing one, little suitcase—and a mysterious lump—through the upscale lobby, smiling at everyone she passed in the hopes of either distracting them from the twitching animal beneath her coat . . . or convincing them to keep their mouths shut. Luckily, she sailed into an empty elevator and tapped the button for floor eleven without incident, melting back against the wall once the doors were closed.

Two minutes later, she was standing in front of room 1125.

She knocked, her adrenaline spiking when she heard the footsteps approaching, her heart booming like cannon fire in her chest. Palms sweating. And then, there he was. Sig.

Gorgeous and stressed out. In dress clothes—a glorious rarity.

His hair was wrecked from his fingers, hands gripping the doorframe like he might rip it off at any given moment. Eyes *starved* as they roamed over her body. Her face.

Down to the lump on the luggage cart.

"That's the dog, isn't it?"

"I improvised."

His mouth ticked up into a roguish half smile, his hand dropping from the doorframe. He didn't take his eyes off Chloe as he wheeled the cart into the room and uncovered the dog with a flourish, shaking his head when he revealed the dog was fast asleep. "Kind of fitting, isn't it?" Sig said, pacing back toward Chloe slowly, taking her wrist and drawing her into a big, beautiful, half-lit suite. Firmly pushing her up against the wall and sandwiching her there. Hard. Taking her face in his hands and tilting it up. "The night we met, you snuck me into the country club." He settled his mouth on top of hers, inhaling deeply, both of them exhaling in an identical, savoring way. Savoring each other. The fact that they were together. Alone. No rules. Their problems were equally present and far away, but they tacitly agreed to ignore them. Ignore everything but each other for now. Just for now, while it was dark and no one knew where they were. "Now here you are, sneaking a dog into a hotel the night I make you mine. I'm detecting a pattern."

Chloe gave a slight headshake. "I've been yours for a long time."

"It'll never be long enough." He dragged his lips side to side against hers. "Ten thousand years wouldn't be enough." He searched her eyes. "Are you okay?"

In her haste to reach him, she'd managed somewhat to put the article out of her mind, but the worry in his expression brought it all back, reminding her they were under scrutiny now. "Yes." She wet her lips. "How did you find out about the article?"

"At the meeting tonight. There's a new general manager. She—"

"She?" Chloe's lips twitched. "Cool."

"Yeah."

When he didn't continue, she reached up to stroke the sides of his face, her chest nearly bursting when he turned into her palm, rubbing his cheek there. "What happened?"

He closed his eyes. Shook his head. Pressed closer to her, as if pinning her in place would keep her from disappearing. Stop what was happening to them.

"Sig," she prompted again, dread prodding her in the side.

"They won't offer me a contract because of this. Because of us. How it would look to the public. How it would reflect on the team. They want me to stay away from you, but I can't fucking do it. I won't." He opened his mouth against her neck, kissing her pulse, dragging his lips higher to her ear. "Sweden is sounding pretty good about now."

Devastation peeled like a bell inside of Chloe. Denial. "Sig. I . . . I'm so sorry. I can't believe this is happening." She gathered all her strength and pushed against his chest. "You want that contract, that captain spot more than anything."

"*Wrong.* I want you more."

"If getting it means staying away from me, that's what you have to do."

"Absolutely not," he growled.

"*Sig.*"

"What was it you said about wanting to feel a man's weight on top of you?" He dragged her into a kiss. A hot, thorough one, his tongue licking in and killing every single protest in its infancy, his hands on her bare legs now, yanking up the hem of her skirt while he worked her mouth in the perfect distraction. Those big, calloused hands slid up the backs of her thighs to clutch her backside roughly, kneading her cheeks in his hands and lifting her up, moaning into her mouth. "Get those pretty thighs around me. You're about to feel my weight."

Chloe's legs moved on command, circling his hips, gasping at the outline of his erection against the mound of her sex. "We're going to talk about . . . all of this . . . later," she managed.

"Not until I've come inside of you," he rasped, walking her into the suite. Through a dark living area and into a lamplit bedroom, downtown Boston a distant blue-and-white outline in the window. "Not until I know how you sound at the end. When my cock is getting so thick we can't take another stroke." Sig lay her down on the bed, following her, flattening her *hard* on the mattress—and she nearly screamed over the concentration of the ripple passing through her. "Oh fuck, I've wanted this so bad."

"Me too." She gasped as he shifted his hips, their clothing rasping in the silent room. "All of your weight. All of it."

"You want some more? Take it. Like I said, I'm not stopping until your thighs melt." He shoved her knees up toward her shoulders, shuddering into a rake of mouths, a grinding of flesh.

"Can I be rough with you tonight, Chloe?" he panted, sipping at the seam of her lips. "Gentle isn't how I feel about you."

Tingles were racing to the crown of her head. "How do you feel?"

"Choked up. Possessive. Like my goddamn blood is on fire." He wrapped her hair in a fist and tugged her head back, groaning against the length of her exposed throat, razing her sensitive skin with his bared teeth. "I need to fuck my girl. *Now.*"

Chloe abandoned any remaining thought or care or worry, exchanging them for immediate needs. Necessities. And Sig was her only one. She licked the line of his jaw and latched her teeth to his ear, satisfied when his breath caught, his shaft swelling against her sex.

"Rip off my panties and finally fuck me then."

CHAPTER SEVENTEEN

He'd dreamed of being dirty talked to by Chloe Clifford.

Dreamed it so many times. Hearing her sweet and refined Connecticut voice popping off with something filthy—but *goddamn*, as many times as he'd imagined Chloe saying the words *fuck me*, he wasn't prepared. As in, his body, his psyche, his dick . . . none of them were ready. Anticipation welled so deeply inside of Sig, he couldn't even tell where the overflow was happening. Only that it reached his throat, his chest, his fingertips, and he could barely form a cohesive plan to give her an orgasm. Also known as the only thing higher on his list of needs than hearing her talk dirty.

They were frantically making out in the middle of this king-sized bed, her fingers twisting in his clothes and pulling him closer, which was a mind-blowing feeling. One he'd underestimated. Being held tight to this person, *his* person, as if her world would end, too, if they had to be separated and obviously, he wanted to be buried between her thighs, but he couldn't stop kissing her. Couldn't. They hadn't kissed enough yet. They'd never reach a point where they'd kissed enough. God. God, she didn't mind being messy and he loved that. She didn't mind him humping her like he'd just been let out of prison. Didn't mind him licking her jaw, her neck, burying his tongue so deep in her mouth, he could feel the vibration of her moan in the center of his belly.

Yeah, Sig probably wouldn't have been able to break the chain of breathless kisses, probably would have been there until the next morning, just feeling her lips get more and more and more swollen between the legs, but she started to tilt her hips up beneath him, rubbing on his fly, her pupils like saucers—and he knew she needed to come. Soon.

"I'll get you there, Chlo. That's my fucking job."

"Do it, then," she said shakily. "Please. Please."

A growl broke from his mouth like a thunderclap, and he forced himself to sit up slightly, straddling her body while they worked together to undress her with frenzied hands, panting and tearing at clothes, their gazes colliding and heating. More, more. Chloe drew off her shirt with a characteristic wiggle that made his throat clench even as he flipped up her skirt and yanked a tight little pair of black panties down to her ankles, his cock stiffening that final painful and urgent degree the first time he saw that beautiful blond strip of curls. Saw that place where her thighs creased, bracketing her pussy, so slippery and ready and perfect.

"It doesn't seem possible that I've never seen you like this, you know?" His voice was thicker than mud. "How could I know you like the back of my hand and not know what's under your clothes—" Sig cut himself off with a gulp as her bra was shed, leaving her naked, save the skirt flipped up at her belly. "Jesus, Chloe. You are . . . *incredible.*" His restraint gave out along with his stabilizing arm and he fell forward onto his dream girl who absorbed his weight with a happy gasp, threading her fingertips through his hair while his mouth found her tits, her nipples, the juicy palm-sized glory of her breasts and made out with them.

"Yes, Sig. Yes. Oh my *God.*"

He couldn't keep his eyes from rolling back in his head, out of pure bliss. Over the way she yanked on his hair, over the way her nipples started small, but grew big and swollen as he licked them, sucked them gently, the heel of his hand skating down her shuddering belly and kneading that wet flesh rhythmically, playing her body like an instrument he'd never played before, but was born with the expertise to make sing.

Like a prodigy.

I'll tell her that later. That we're both prodigies. It'll make her laugh.

And the fact that he was already dying to talk to her again—when his cock was stiffer than a fucking sledgehammer—spoke volumes. *I love this girl. I love her so much.* So much that he moved instinctively in the name of her pleasure, his mouth releasing her stiff nipple with a stuttered sound, lips moving down, down, suctioning over the top of her slit, his middle finger teasing open her soaked cunt, gently twisting a knuckle at her entrance, the sound of her whimpers making him feel like an animal.

"Sig. I just want you inside of me. Inside of me. *Please.*"

"Patience, dream girl."

"*No.*"

Sig chuckled, but cut himself off with a hard swallow when the lips of her sex parted that remaining degree, that indecent final opening that allowed him to get his tongue where it needed to go—and he put it there. Groaning brokenly. Stroking that gorgeous bud with the tip of his tongue, tracing the smooth perimeter of it, before gently grinding down from above with the flat center of his tongue, slowly, slowly, all while massaging the undersides of her knees with his thumbs . . . and fuck, she got wetter. Mewled *louder.*

He'd never need another trophy as long as he lived.

Feeling Chloe get more and more aroused while he ate her pussy was peak victory.

"Sig. I need you."

"Not half as much as I need you," he rasped, the palm of his right hand traveling down the inside of her thigh, his middle and index finger teasing her breach, preparing to tuck inside all that warmth and make sure she was ready, but he wanted to be looking her in the eye the first time he fingered her, so he jiggled his tongue against her clit a few more times, until her thighs started to spasm, then licked up the center of her body, pressing their foreheads together. Looking at her with all the wild and powerful feelings inside his chest.

Then he pushed two fingers into that sweet, tight pussy, moaning the whole way.

Cursing over the way her muscles seized up around his digits, her eyes glazing over.

"Swear to God, I've spent my whole life wanting to get inside of you."

"A-and?"

His fingers retreated and advanced, retreated and advanced, milking her, getting her as ready as possible. "Now I'm going to spend my whole life making sure I get to stay here."

Christ, she was a masterpiece, all flushed and beginning to shine. Dewy. Covered in suck marks. Swollen. Perfection. "You're the only one that belongs inside me," she whispered, unfastening his dress pants and carefully lowering the zipper. Stroking him through the starchy material while he choked a sound into her neck, still eye to eye. Hiding nothing. "You can be rough with it. Rough as you want."

Motherfuck.

Sig didn't wait another breath. He couldn't. Neither of them could.

He reached down into his open fly, past the elastic of his briefs and fisted his cock, bringing it between her thighs and pumping home with a shattered call of her name.

Blind. He was fucking blinded by the sensation of . . . of suction and compression.

The contraction of her muscles.

"Fuck. You are just . . ." He ground down, cinched back and fucked forward, groaning over the way she whined and tightened up, knees rising. "Shit, Chloe. Jesus. *Christ.*"

"Don't stop." She clawed at his hips. "You feel so good."

"Say I'm the only one, again. Say it filthier."

She accepted another one of his pumps with a cry. "If I get filthy, will you be filthy?"

"I'm going to be filthy, either way, Chlo." He worked his lower body in a rough circle, listening to her breath catch. "But if you tell me my cock is your reason for living, I'll feel more justified working you over. The way I've been obsessing over you for six fucking months."

Chloe visibly let that honesty wash over her, crooking her finger at him a moment later—and he went, closing his eyes as she whispered against his ear. "What if I tell you that your cock is so big and thick, I can feel it rubbing my G-spot?" She sucked his earlobe into her mouth, drawing his balls up so tight, he had to bear down to prevent himself from spilling. "And I know exactly where that spot is because I think of you every time I play with it."

"Okay," he panted, beginning to thrust. Hard. *Hard hard hard.* "Oh fuck."

"Work me over." She ripped her nails down his ass. "Work me so good, honey. Please."

Honey?

The headboard was slamming into the wall at this point, her tightness accepting him with wet sounds he'd never get out of his head. "You can stop now," he growled.

She arched her back on a moan. "I want you to fuck me like this in your hockey pads."

His body lit itself on fire. "*Chloe.*" Balls strained with pressure, he couldn't help but buck his hips faster. Accept more of the heaven she was offering. "I'm warning you."

"What are you going to do? Pound me harder?" she asked, her breathing shallow, reedy. "Good." Slowly, she snuck her middle finger into the split of his ass, pressing the tip inside of him. And then she locked up her pussy muscles while his body, mind, and soul had a full-scale meltdown. Code red. Sig didn't even have a name for what he was feeling. It was a kind of out-of-control bliss below his waist, and a loss of coherence everywhere else.

The bedsprings were protesting beneath them.

At some point he'd hooked his arms beneath Chloe's knees and bent her in half so he could plow into her from above and shit, shit, shit, she had her finger in his asshole now, all the way to the knuckle, massaging in places he didn't know needed massaging, and he was panting like a dog, sweat making the half-buttoned dress shirt cling to his back . . . and he was losing control of himself. Completely. She was causing him to desert it when he was supposed to be focused on making her come. Toning down his roughness was easier said than done, though, when she was whimpering for it, her eyes searching the ceiling for God.

"How close are you, baby?" Whose voice was that? He sounded like the big, bad wolf. "We keep this pace . . . and you keep that up . . . I'm going to come soon."

"I'm close."

"How close. How close."

"I don't know." That finger sunk deeper. "I just know I love your cock and I want it inside me forever. I love it, I love it, I love it—"

"Chloe. *Please.*"

"I love that you treat me like a princess everywhere but in bed." She licked at his jawline, her blond hair in a tangled cloud around her head. "Here, you treat me like a—"

"Don't say it," he warned raggedly, his dick throbbing with a final warning shot.

"Say what?" she purred, her hips working up, up, up to meet his downward drives.

"Anything. Whatever you're going to say. I'm begging you."

She didn't have to say it. Something about the mischievous curl of her upper lip completed the sentence and Sig shouted a vile curse at the slapping headboard, forced to pull out or he was going to finish before her.

"No!" she screamed, as if this wasn't her fault.

"I've got you," he growled, levering up long enough to tear off his shirt, buttons flying every which way, then dropping down on his bare torso, tongue skating up her inner left thigh. "Keep your fucking legs spread."

She sucked in an eager breath at his first lap of her pussy, her belly hollowing, shuddering, fingers clutching the sheets. "Sig."

"Don't worry, you're close, beautiful," he praised, rubbing his mouth in her flesh. "It's dripping down your ass cheeks."

"Please."

"I wanted to be in extra deep when you came, but you had to be a bad girl, didn't you?" He pressed two fingers inside of her, rotating until he found that rough spot and rubbed, fast and firm. "You won't catch me complaining about getting to lick this pussy twice." He waited until she was squirming and crying out his name before he fastened his mouth gently over her clit and dragging loose lips side to side over the swollen pearl, then sucked with increasing pressure, pride blooming in his chest as her thighs started to shake uncontrollably, her screams of release bouncing off the walls, the insides of his skull, the chambers of his booming heart.

As soon as she was through the height of the orgasm, Sig was pinning down her heaving body and slamming his cock back inside of her to the hilt, driving into her like there was no tomorrow, no sun coming up, no reason to live but the woman beneath him—and at least one of those things were true. In that moment, there was nothing but Chloe and the beating boulder inside of his chest that existed only for her. And his body lost control in the same way he'd lost control over how much he loved her long ago.

He choked out her name and succumbed to the lust, feeding it into her with disorderly punches of his hips, the only one who could ever inspire it to the point of pain. The love of his life. His Chloe.

"My Chloe. You'll always be mine. *Always.*"

"Yes. I know. I know."

"We'll get through this," he said, mouth open and panting against the side of her neck, body still thrusting inside of her, their bodies sealed together by sweat, her thighs boneless and dropped open on the bed, but her arms wrapped around him like he was a port in a storm.

And in a sense, he was.

He just didn't know which direction the strongest gale winds were coming from.

Not yet.

CHAPTER EIGHTEEN

Sig was tracing his index finger up and down the curve of a sleeping Chloe's spine, marveling at the shape and softness of her, when room service arrived. Pierre yipped and—from the sound of it—rolled off the luggage cart on full alert, barking at the new arrival.

"Shit," Sig grunted, grabbing a pillow off the bed to hold in front of his dick when he answered the door. On the way to get the delivery, he snapped up a couple of twenties from his wallet and hushed the dog, to no avail. "You're going to get us thrown out, man," he hissed. "Have some chill."

Sig opened the door, pillow over his lap and clocked the pinched expression of the hotel employee. "I'm sorry, sir. Dogs are not allowed in this hotel—" Sig tucked the cash into the man's jacket pocket. "Let's keep this between us."

"Dog? What dog?" said the delivery guy without missing a beat, then nodding at the room beyond. "May I come in and set up your meal?"

With Chloe lying naked on the bed? "No, thanks. I'll take it from here."

"I'd hand you the tray, but there'd be nothing to keep your pillow in place."

"Right," Sig said dryly. "Just set down the tray and I'll slide it in."

"You've got it."

A few minutes later, Sig had fed Pierre a kid's menu cheese-burger and arranged the table settings for him and Chloe, complete with covered plates, a beer for him, wine for her. He set aside the small, brown paper bag containing the item he'd requested, smiling to himself in anticipation of Chloe's reaction to what was inside.

When he finally ventured into the dark bedroom of the suite to track down his pants and pull them on, leaving the button undone, Chloe rolled over onto her back and yawned, stretching her arms up over her head and pointing her toes in a combination of moves that he'd seen a few times before but that never failed to make his pulse play leapfrog. Although now, his body reacted with a lot less restraint than usual, his cock more than a little excited by the sight of his girl all naked and warm and inviting, thickening and pressing against his zipper. Wanting out. Wanting in.

Sex with Chloe . . . Jesus, he didn't have the words for how fucking hot it had been. Hell, he'd known they were going to be compatible. That their chemistry was fire. It had been since day one. But she'd blown his goddamn mind tonight. Obliterated his expectations . . . and ruined him forever. All orgasms were not created equal—and he could attest to that now. The one he'd had inside of Chloe had been so painfully thorough and intense, his lower back and abs were still tingling and sore.

"Did I hear Pierre barking?" she murmured, blissfully unaware that he was obsessing over the smooth, wet clutch of her pussy.

"Oh. Yeah." He cleared the gravel from his voice. "At the room service guy."

"There's food?" She sat straight up, tits swaying *gorgeously.*

Maybe they never had to leave this hotel room. Maybe they could live here forever and pretend the bullshit outside this room didn't exist.

Instead of making that fanciful suggestion, he said, "There's a surprise, too."

Chloe paused in the act of scooting to the edge of the bed. "Better than food?"

"Depends on how you look at it, I guess." He searched the floor for his shirt, hunkered down, and picked it up, before making his way over to Chloe, barely quelling the urge to drag her back down onto the mattress and kiss that beautiful mouth, get between her legs. "Here, you can wear this." They maintained eye contact while she stuck her arms through the holes, Sig slowly engaging the buttons of the garment, pausing every so often to stroke his knuckles down her cheek. "So, it turns out, you're an animal in bed, Chlo."

Her jaw dropped on a startled laugh. "Is that a complaint?"

"A complaint? I came so hard, I'm temporarily blind in my left eye."

"Stop it," she gasped. "Wait, really?"

He reached out and felt her features with his fingertips. "Chloe, is that you?"

Sides shaking with amusement, she pressed against him, going up on her toes and nuzzling the crook of his neck, which had to be the best feeling in the world. "You were perfect," she whispered beneath his ear. "The way you can be so rough while still thinking of me the whole time . . . it's very you. I'd expect nothing less." She trailed her fingertips down his pecs. "And for the record, I've never been like that before. I trust you. That's the difference." She kissed his shoulder. "You're my Sig."

"I need to do it again," he said hoarsely, attempting to back Chloe toward the bed, already hating himself for buttoning her into his shirt. What the hell had he been thinking? "Need you again."

"I need you again, too." Though her cheeks were flushed, her pupils dilated, she wiggled out of his grip and gave him a playful look over her shoulder on her way into the living area. *"After* food and my surprise."

They made quick work of the burgers, splitting an order of fries. Washing everything down with drinks while laughing at Pierre's exploration of the suite. The damn dog sniffed every inch of the carpet and plopped his butt down in various spots to leave his mark. The hotel would definitely be charging his credit card for the violation, but Sig couldn't have cared less. Not with Chloe sitting in his lap, feeding him french fries with the perfect amount of ketchup, as if she'd studied his habits.

There was a shroud of doom hanging in the air above their heads, but they were ignoring it. Smiling through the worry. Pretending tomorrow was a year away, instead of mere hours. For Sig's part, he knew exactly what he needed to do. Chloe was worth the sacrifices he was prepared to make, so he'd make them with a smile on his face.

"Is that my surprise?" Chloe asked, pointing at the brown paper bag.

"Yup. Open it."

He groaned as she leaned forward in his lap to retrieve the bag, that tush pressing down in just the right spot. *Fuck.* Fingers digging into the arm of the chair, he watched her open the top of the bag and peer inside, grinning when she started to laugh.

"A shaving kit!" She twisted around, oblivious to the stiff dick syndrome she was causing. "You remembered."

"Of course I did."

"You're going to shave for me? *Now?*"

Her excitement made him lighter than air. "That was the deal, right?"

"Yes!" She hopped off his lap and dashed for the bathroom.

"It's a good thing you didn't let me open the bag before we ate, because our food would have gone cold."

Sig pushed out of the chair and adjusted himself with a wince, before following in her wake. "What is it about this everyday ritual that has you so excited?"

"I don't know." When he entered the bathroom, he found the shaving cream and razor laid out neatly on the sink, Chloe sitting on the opposite side of the vanity, those graceful, bare legs swinging back and forth. Lord. With messy hair and smeared eye makeup, wearing his shirt . . . she stole his fucking breath. "I always wonder why you shave when so many guys on the team have beards. But it makes so much sense for you. You like tidy. You have your personal traditions, and you don't deviate from them. When your mind is made up over something, you never change it." There was a hint of something dark he couldn't name in her eyes, but she quickly blinked it away. "You aren't the type to wake up one morning and decide to grow a beard. And I guess . . . I don't know. I guess I want to watch you shave because it's part of your daily routine. Your dependability is one of my favorite things about you and I want to watch you . . . be you. In the quiet moments, too."

"The same way I wanted to watch you pick out an outfit."

"Yes."

"What other routines of mine are you interested in?"

A sparkle set off the blue of her eyes. "I wouldn't mind watching you put on your hockey pads. Do you think you'd be able to sneak me into the locker room?"

Sig squirted white shaving foam onto the flat surface of his four fingers and begun smearing it evenly over the lower half of his face, noting that Chloe watched this happen with grave fascination. "What is this apparent obsession with hockey pads and how have I been unaware of it for six months?"

"I love hockey pads," she whispered.

His throat hurt from holding in a laugh. "Because they make me look bigger?"

The suggestion seemed to surprise her. "No, because they keep you safe."

Now his throat hurt for a whole different reason. "Oh. Yeah, they do. Although Burgess pointed out recently that I used to be a lot more reckless. I didn't realize until I played a few games and noticed what he meant. I keep my guard up, I anticipate better. I keep . . . me safe, too, Chloe. For you. You did that."

She released a long exhale and scooted closer to him.

For several moments, she watched him shave in silence, the quiet scraping sound filling the scant space between them.

"Can I ask you a question?"

"Anything," he responded.

"What was it about me . . . that first night? What did you see?"

Sig's hand dropped to the counter like a stone, the importance of the question obvious. So important to her, he could feel the weight everywhere. "It was your voice, first. You sounded . . . essential. You turned everything alive and brought the present into focus. Made it bigger. More beautiful. And that was before I even turned around." Letting go of the razor, he reached up to cup her face, his heart turning over when her eyes took on a light sheen. "You talk about trusting *me*, Chlo? That night, I saw a person who made me want to trust the good in people. In life. Because you were the proof, standing right in front of me. I saw all of that in one night because you're not hidden. You're a fucking star that fell out of the sky and I was lucky enough to be standing in the right place."

"Sig." She took a big, heaving breath. "That's so much more than I expected."

I love you.

I'll love you until the sun goes dark.

Sig wasn't sure what made him put those words off for another time, maybe it was that elusive dread that continued to drift in and out of her eyes, so brief each time that he wondered if it was there at all. And all Sig could think to do was make her smile. Take away anything but the happiness they could share tonight. *Every* night. Together.

"You want to see how much I trust you?" He picked up the razor and handed it to her. "Take a stroke."

"You're not serious."

"Dead."

"That's what *you're* going to be."

Sig chuckled. "Nah, you got this." He guided her hand to his lathered jaw. "Easy. Easy. You're going to do fine."

She screamed in her mouth as the razor glided upward, letting out a shaky breath when nothing but a clean path was left behind. "I didn't cut you?"

"Hey. I'm looking into your eyes, Chlo. I'd die happy."

"What a beautiful thing to say," she said on a watery laugh, dropping the razor into the sink. "I'm still never doing this again."

"What? You're shaving my back next."

"Did I mention I have a doctor's appointment tonight?" She started to slide off the sink. "I should probably get moving."

Sig trapped her against the counter before her feet touched the ground. "You're not going anywhere," he growled against her mouth.

"I know," she whispered back, openly trembling at their contact.

"Listen." He rode his mouth over the top of hers, tangling her tongue in a kiss that could only be described as carnal. A precursor to sin. "While I have you here, I might as well tell you some bad news."

"Bad," she said, staring at his mouth as if hypnotized. "What could be bad?"

"I'm afraid sex in hockey pads isn't going to live up to the fantasy."

His playfulness registered and she smiled into their next kiss. "Oh no?"

"No. For one, I won't be able to feel your skin on mine and that's a crime. Two, I won't be able to move as easily. You like when I move, right?"

"Like isn't the right word. Revere?"

"We'll go with revere. Three, I'm going to get real hot, real fast fucking you with all that shit on." She was starting to breathe faster. So was he. "Finally, four—and probably most important—my dick is going to be buried under padding, a cup, and some annoying ass laces. Not very easy to access."

"I've considered this. A lot. I've considered this a lot."

"Have you?" He urged Chloe's thighs around his hips, snuck a forearm under her butt, and turned to carry her out of the bathroom. "What are your thoughts?"

"Unlace you, remove the cup from that pocket in front of your shorts, push down the elastic, get you inside me, hold on to those big shoulder pads, and ride." She blurted all of it without taking a single breath. "I'll be quick, I promise." She licked the underside of his chin. "You won't have enough time to get overheated."

His cock swelled into an ache, the length of him pulsing so insistently against her bare sex through the fly of his pants, getting inside of her became a matter of urgency. "How'd you know about the pocket for my cup?"

"Some people surf internet porn. I surf sporting goods websites."

They let out breathless laughs against each other's mouths for several stolen moments, there in the dimness of the hotel room, as Chloe lowered her feet to the ground. Standing in front of him with her face tilted up, eyes closed as if lost to the bliss as much as he was, she unzipped his pants and nudged him backward onto the couch, straddling him and lowering that tightness onto his cock, whimpering inch by whimpering inch. Hurriedly, before he could lose the ability to make mental commands, he unfastened the buttons of her borrowed shirt, yanking it down her arms, away, palming her tits, groaning as Chloe, fully and gloriously naked, rode his cock like she fucking owned it.

"Good girl, just like that. Take me in. Take me out. In now. *In in in.*"

"Oh my God," she whined through her teeth, hands tangling in his hair, twisting, thighs open wide, hips bucking. "It's so good."

"I'll wear the pads. I'll do whatever you want, just keep that up. Oh. *FUCK.*"

She rolled their foreheads together. "Did you like what I did to you last time?"

His thoughts were fragmenting, the clench of her cunt, her scent, the full body contact with her skin, everything was so much. Overwhelmingly perfect. Intimate. Real. Nothing would ever be this perfect again. "I love everything you do to me, baby. Be specific."

"I put that finger in back," she whispered, lapping at his tongue, as if his brain wasn't already on the verge of implosion. And this girl, she looked him right in the eye while implying she'd like him to finger her asshole. Part of him seriously questioned in that moment if she loved him or wanted to kill him, but he didn't care, either way. Not when he obliged her and she moaned, working that slippery pussy up and down his hard shaft. "Feels good."

"Tuck it in a little more?"

"Yes."

"Oh *Jesus*. She's even tighter back here."

"Sig. Stop. Keep going. *Sig.*"

They gasped into a kiss and her lower body went into test-his-stamina mode, grinding down on his root, throwing her hips back to partially free his flesh, then riding back down. Up and down, while their mouths moved in a frenzy, stealing each other's breath and giving it back, teeth sinking into neck tendons, fingers burying in muscle, grunts hitting the walls of the living space and echoing back, the couch springs growing louder with protest the longer and harder she rode, Sig holding on to his come with every ounce of willpower in his body, until she finally screamed into his sweaty neck and let go, allowing him to throw her down on the couch and deliver one final, shattering drive.

And afterward, the way they clung to each other was just as powerful as the act itself, her laboring breath baptizing his skin, their hearts making vows their lips weren't capable of speaking. Maybe theirs was the kind of love that didn't need to be spoken out loud. Later, though . . . he'd wish he had. Maybe it would have made a difference.

CHAPTER NINETEEN

Chloe stared up at the ceiling, sandwiched between the greatest high she'd ever experienced—and dread that multiplied by the second. It scaled the walls of her insides like the kind of black mold that couldn't be wiped out without total demolishment. She didn't quite have an explanation for the sense of impending doom yet, only that a turning point was coming . . . and no one was there to give her directions anymore.

For once, the man she depended on for directions was lost.

More lost than Chloe.

Looking across the pillow into his smiling face, one couldn't tell. He was wreathed in his usual confidence. His hand stroked her face like an artist framing a landscape—one he found breathtaking and worthy of staring at for decades. He was the picture of masculine beauty, casual in his nudity. Not in a rush to go anywhere. Content to hold her after the most incredible rounds of sex she could have imagined. Their physical chemistry was the final shred of proof they were made for each other, as far as Chloe was concerned. She'd never felt free to be so uninhibited before. So positive she could only do right in the arms of another person.

This man was her soulmate, through and through. But the dread only ran amuck now, spreading to her limbs, scraping the walls of her heart.

You want that contract, that captain spot more than anything.

Wrong. I want you more.

If getting it means staying away from me, that's what you have to do. Absolutely not.

A sharp twist started in her throat and rose higher, causing pain behind her eyes. "Sig—"

"Hey, sorry. I was distracted earlier by . . . you." That roguish grin on his mouth only grew. How could his face appear so content when they had monumental decisions in front of them? Didn't he sense what was on the horizon? "I'm always distracted by you, Chlo."

Her fingers curled into the pillow. "Same," she whispered.

Affection warmed his features. "But I should have asked . . ." He tucked hair behind her ear, his amusement dimming slowly. "How did you find out about the article? Did someone send it to you?"

Chloe kept her expression mild. Why she chose this exact moment to start lying to her best friend? She couldn't say. Only that there was an instinct inside of her—one she didn't have before moving to Boston and living on her own—and it was informing her that Sig would *not* react well to finding out their relationship had caused Grace to excuse her as a mentee. He'd raise hell. And he'd take it upon himself to fix the issue . . .

But she needed to fix her own problem this time.

She'd been dropped by Grace because of her own decisions. She'd allowed her relationship with Sig to become something indefinable and vague and questionable, at least to the outside world. Not to mention, she'd blabbed to the reporter. Now? Handing off the situation to someone else wasn't an option. Sig had his own mess to deal with—she'd handle her own side of it like a big girl.

"Tallulah sent it to me," Chloe said, tuning out the memory of the conversation she'd had with Grace. Refusing to let the truth show on her face. "I think she has a Google alert for anything Bearcats-related. I don't even know how to set one of those."

"Me either," he murmured, his expression turning serious. "I have to tell you something, Chlo." He opened his mouth, snapped it shut. "Damn, I know it must seem like I've been keeping a lot of important shit from you, but I swear . . . I was planning on telling you this when the time was right. Or if I managed to find a solution."

"A solution to what?" she managed, her throat thick. What was this?

"Us. A way for . . . us."

Afraid to hear the explanation, afraid not to hear it, too, she wet her lips. "Tell me."

Sig wrapped an arm around her waist and drew her closer, both of them sighing over the soft collision of bare muscle and flesh, the new lack of barriers between them. "Feels so good to hold you."

"I can't believe we made it so long without this," she said honestly, nuzzling his jaw.

He kissed her forehead hard. Lingered there. "I haven't really talked a lot about how I grew up. Haven't really talked about it with anyone. But, uh, . . ." He shifted against her. "Like I told you before, Harvey left us when I was young. After that, my mom . . . she wanted nothing to do with her family. The way she explained it to me, they didn't approve of Harvey. Thought he was after my mother's wealth. Called him a grifter—and they were right. Hell, he did exactly what her family said he would. Took off with my mother's money and never looked back. After that, my mother's pride wouldn't let her take another cent from her parents and we ended up struggling. Bad. My whole childhood."

This must be what love truly felt like.

Feeling a burning ache in her chest for everything Sig had experienced in the past.

Pain and frustration and sympathy and helplessness.

A fierce desire to go back and take his place.

"But he's changed since then, right?" Chloe asked. "Is that why you got back in touch with him?"

"That's the thing, Chloe, I don't know if he's changed. He was married to two other women after my mother and he climbed higher on the social ladder with each relationship. That's how it looks from the outside, I've just never been able to . . . be objective. I can't tell if I'm seeing the real Harvey or if I'm looking through the lens my mother created. Does that make sense?"

"Yes." Alarm prickled in her scalp, fingertips. "Should I be worried about my mother?"

He tipped her chin up to meet his eyes. "Your mother knows I'm suspicious of Harvey, Chlo. She knows what those suspicions are, too. I never would have let her fly blind."

She took that in, let it settle. "Why didn't you tell me?"

His throat worked with a swallow. "I was embarrassed. And that's a new feeling for me. I taught myself how to overcome shame out of necessity a long time ago, but suddenly . . . there you were and . . ." He traced her jawline with his thumb. "I was suddenly a lot more aware that I didn't have the kind of background I'd need to marry you. Or the kind of money. I guess I didn't want to draw attention to that."

"So . . . the same reason you didn't tell me about selling the memorabilia?"

"Yeah." He nodded for a moment, then rolled Chloe over onto her back, burying his face in her neck. Rubbing it there in such a raw and loving way, she could only anchor her fingers in his hair and survive it. "I just wanted to be good for you. I just wanted to give you everything."

At the cost of everything he *wants.*

No.

No.

She loved him too much for that.

"Did you tell my mother about Harvey's past hoping she would call off the wedding?"

"She overheard me making some accusations. They weren't enough." His body was fully on top of hers now, her thighs snuggling around his hips, their bodies shifting and conforming, shifting and conforming, two beings enjoying the various ways they could mold together. Luxuriating in what they'd denied themselves for so long. "I hired a private investigator," he said against her ear, catching her breath in her throat. "He hasn't had any luck yet. But if there is something my father did that might mean calling off this marriage, I'm going to find it, okay?"

A beat passed.

Two.

Sig seemed to be waiting, bracing for her reaction to the news.

But somehow, the revelation that Sig had hired someone to investigate Harvey didn't come as a total shock. Did it surprise her? Yes. Of course, it did. But somewhere deep down, she'd known Sig was working on the problem. Trying to find a way for them to be together. She'd known it in her bones. Still, despite her strained and complicated relationship with Sofia . . . did she *want* to ruin her mother's happiness? Did Sig want to do that to his father?

No.

Sig wouldn't be able to go through with hurting Harvey and Sofia. That wasn't an act of the man she'd fallen madly in love with. And she wouldn't be able to do it, either. Which only left one option—walk away from his skyrocketing career. Leave her

own aspirations behind. In other words, there *was* no good outcome if they stayed together. Didn't he see that? Any which way
they sliced it, someone lost. "What if the private investigator
finds . . . nothing?"

"I don't know." Slowly, he pinned her wrists above her head,
his breathing pattern beginning to change, along with hers, his
sex swelling against her inner thigh. "But I do know there is
nothing that could keep me away from you."

Chloe's growing appetite for Sig battled with that nagging
dread, which was transforming from a mere feeling to something concrete. A clear picture that she could see and read and
predict. Conversely, Sig wasn't thinking clearly. She'd known
that from the time she'd arrived at the hotel. As usual, he was
considering her first. *Them* first. He'd implied he would give up
playing hockey for the Bearcats because of her. Because of their
relationship.

Never.

She would never let him give up his dream.

Would never let him do something so destructive.

With a walnut-sized object stuck behind her windpipe, she
lifted her hips for him, their groans filling the room as he fit
himself home inside her and started to rock.

"Tell me about Sweden again," she whispered, blinking back
the tears in her eyes. Tears that turned to a warm glaze when the
headboard started to thump against the wall once more. "Are you
shirtless and chopping firewood in our yard?"

His chuckle turned into a groan. "Who am I to deny you that
view?" He leaned down and lapped at her nipples, one by one,
his eyes pitch-black as he sucked. Watching her. "There's a frozen pond in back. Where I'm teaching our kids to skate."

His mouth roamed back up her body and over her lips, seduc-
ing any thoughts straight out of her head, except for the ones that

228 · TESSA BAILEY

concerned him and the fantasy world he spun with his words. "Kids," she breathed. "You want kids."

He tilted his head, regarding her with an overwhelming amount of love. Adoration. "I want to watch you be a mother."

His weight bore down harder, more insistently, something a little animalistic and wicked flickering in his expression a split second before he flipped Chloe face down and pumped into her from behind, leaving her screaming into the pillow, nails clawing at the sheets.

"I want to make you one, too," he rasped in her ear, his calloused thumbs digging into her hips. "Keep this ass up like a good girl and let me practice."

THE FOLLOWING MORNING, Chloe cried the whole way to Grace's penthouse.

Pierre sensed something was wrong, keeping his sleepy head in her lap in the back of the Uber. Wordlessly, the driver passed her back a box of tissues over his shoulder, which made her cry all the harder. Okay. She'd give herself until the end of the ride. Then it would be time to suck it up and be a grown-up.

Nothing could keep images of last night and this morning from bombarding her brain, but she could control how she reacted to them. At least, on the outside. When she thought of Sig lifting Pierre onto the foot of the bed last night and covering him with a spare blanket, before flipping on the Home Shopping Network so she could fall asleep to her preferred soundtrack, she wouldn't sob and break down and faint dead away on the street.

She'd keep moving.

When she thought of the way Sig had kissed her so passionately when he left for the airport, making promises to call her as soon as he landed, she wouldn't unleash an unholy scream over the twist of guilt in her stomach. She would keep breathing. Keep living, even if her heart was in jagged, petrified pieces all over the floor.

"Are you okay back there?" asked the driver hesitantly, clearly hoping she wouldn't respond. Or that she would say fine and leave it at that.

Well, too bad.

She was cutting off the love of her life to keep them both from losing everything.

"No, I'm not okay." Moisture tracked down her cheeks and she mopped them up with a Kleenex. "This is my first time being the strong one."

"Ohhh. I see."

"So far, it's not all it's cracked up to be. I don't know if I'm going to be very good at it."

The driver seemed on the verge of answering, but Chloe's phone rang. Thinking it was Sig, her pulse skipped approximately eight beats. Was this going to be the first time she didn't answer one of his calls? But no. It wasn't Sig.

Sofia was calling.

"Hello, Mother," she answered, holding on tighter to Pierre.

"Chloe. You don't sound well. Has Boston finally gotten the better of you?"

Chloe dropped her head back against the seat. She wanted to say no. Wanted to lie and say things were better than ever, but she didn't have the energy to lie. "Maybe so."

"Aw, my poor dear. I hate to hear that."

"No, you don't," Chloe blurted. And it felt fantastic. Because unlike the evening she'd stood up to her mother at the dinner table, she didn't hesitate. Didn't feel guilty for calling out her mother's passive aggression, either. In fact, she felt capable of letting those words hang between them without qualifying or backpedaling. "You don't hate to hear I'm having a bad time. You've wanted me to fail in Boston since the beginning."

"Oh, Chloe," scoffed her mother. "That's not true."

"Yes it is. Own it. Just *own* it. Stop pretending to support my independence. You want me to depend on you. That's how it has always been."

Ice cubes clinked into a glass. "You were never this negative in the past. It's that man having this effect on you, Chloe."

It took the world's greatest effort to keep her voice even. "Don't talk about Sig like that." She thought of him packing memorabilia in his apartment and her throat grew crowded. "You have no idea what he's done, what he's sacrificed so I can learn to be on my own."

Several ticks passed. "Careful, Chloe. You're letting your feelings for him show."

Chloe's skin turned into a layer of ice. Sofia knew. Her mother *knew* she was in love with Sig. For how long? How could she know and not say anything?

"Come home now, Chloe, and we'll forget any of it ever happened. Preferably before any more articles find their way online, hmm?"

A part of Chloe really wanted to run home in that moment. Despite her mother's toxicity. Despite the resolutions she'd made this morning. She wanted to go back to Darien, put her blinders back on, and pretend she'd been studying in France for six months, instead of dwelling three hours south. But her new backbone wouldn't let her do it, nor would the heart that had grown ten sizes thanks to the love Sig had filled it with. "I'm never coming home, Mother. Not now. Not ever. I'd rather struggle with my own decisions than have someone else make them for me. Goodbye."

★   ★   ★

A FEW MINUTES later, Chloe stood in front of a very taken aback doorman who appeared more inclined to call the police than buzz Grace's intercom. And rightly so, because she couldn't imagine how she must look. Tearstained and exhausted and heartsick. A wreck with a bulldog.

"Is Ms. Shen expecting you?"

"Not exactly, but if you could just ring her and give her my name—"

The doorman cut her off by shaking his head. "She has asked me not to disturb her with any guests, because she's rehearsing."

"I respect that. I do."

"Have you tried calling her?" He mimicked a phone call.

Chloe had considered that. However, the last time she'd spoken to Grace, her mentor had hung up on her, so she'd figured an in-person approach was the best bet.

"I need to speak with her face-to-face." Her voice was beginning to split, the feeling of Sig's arms and the sound of his even breathing, layered beneath an announcer's voice selling silk makeup bags was playing on a loop in her head, choking her up. "It's complicated."

Sympathy rolled across his face. "Do you . . . maybe need a drink of water?"

"Do I look that bad?"

"Yes."

The culmination of emotion wrought by the last few hours resulted in Chloe grabbing the poor man's arm. What did she have to lose? "Please, I've just sent the love of my life off to the airport with no idea that I'm breaking things off. For his own good and mine, but I feel like a ghost, you know?" The inhale that followed felt like torture. "And I just need a break. A tiny break. *Please*."

The doorman hedged.

She could already hear him letting her down gently.

Thankfully, the elevator doors chose that moment to open and reveal Grace in a matching purple yoga outfit, a Stanley cup, and sunglasses that looked more like goggles.

She stopped short upon seeing Chloe. "Oh fuck. Seriously? I have the worst timing." Her head dropped back on her shoulders. "You better not be here to return the dog."

"What? No. I *love* him."

"Well. Your taste in men is highly questionable. We've established that."

A defensive shriek built in Chloe's chest, but she kept it at bay, because losing her cool wouldn't serve anyone. Not her and not Sig. "Can we talk privately?"

"Why? I'm not changing my mind."

Chloe wasn't sure how much more dread she could handle in a single day. "That thing you read about . . ." She glanced at the doorman with a swallow, grateful when he took a hint and whistled his way out onto the sidewalk. "I'm not going to lie, there was something there, but it's over now. It's over. Okay?" *Oh God.* Saying those words out loud made her legs want to collapse. "Our parents are getting married in two months. Technically, we haven't done anything wrong, but like I said . . . it's over. And you know what? I love him. I love him and I'm giving him up so he can have hockey. So I can have the harp. And if you think I was good before, just wait until you hear me with a broken heart, okay? Because I'm going to fucking shred and you're not going to get any credit when I waltz into that symphony and take your spot. That's what I'll do. Because people are going to pay money to see a child prodigy. That was always going to be true. But I want to be extraordinary. I better be fucking *extraordinary* if I'm giving him up for this. Are you going to help me get there or not? Because I'll play until my fingers bleed. I'll play until they are numb. Don't drop me, Grace. I'm here to work."

A stony—but perhaps, reluctantly impressed—Grace regarded her for several moments. "This thing between you and him is really over?"

Don't hesitate. Just get it out. "Yes."

Chloe pretended not to see the layer of sympathy flit across Grace's face, because she couldn't handle sympathy just then or she might wallow in self-pity forever. "Fine. I was looking for a reason to skip yoga, anyway." She sniffed, looking Chloe up and down. "I guess torturing you could pass for cardio."

Hope ballooned in Chloe's chest. "Definitely."

"Let's go. I guess the beast can come, too," Grace said, backing into the elevator and smacking her hand on the side of the metal door to keep it open while Chloe rushed forward with grateful tears in her eyes. "Don't expect me to console you."

"I won't."

"He's shit hot, I get it. But . . ."—she made a slashing motion—"there will be others."

There wouldn't. There would be no others like Sig. Not in a billion, trillion years.

But Chloe just smiled and nodded, beginning her life of keeping it to herself.

And hoping it wouldn't kill her.

CHAPTER TWENTY

Something was wrong.

The plane had landed five hours ago. They'd been transported to the hotel, eaten a team meal, and changed into business casual attire in which to arrive for the game.

During that time, Sig had called Chloe approximately fifteen times.

Without an answer.

As he sat in the eighth row of the charter bus, watching Detroit go by in the waning sunlight, he pulled nervously on the knot of his tie, leaving it skewed to the left. The organ in his chest was fluttering in a way that he hated. Not like it fluttered last night, in an I'm-so-crazily-in-love kind of way. This was anxiety. If Chloe wasn't answering his calls, something was up. She always answered, immediately catching him up to speed on everything that had taken place in her life since the last time they spoke, be it her lunch order or an itch she couldn't reach.

He lived for those details.

Had she lost her phone? Was she hurt? Kidnapped?

"You're not going to believe this motherfucker," Corrigan shouted, popping up a few rows ahead of Sig, holding up his phone. "He actually named a time and place for this game."

"Who? What game?" Burgess groused. "The one game you should be talking about is the one we're playing tonight."

"I hear you loud and clear, Captain," Mailer chimed in, standing up in the row across from Corrigan. "Normally, I would, anyway. But we're being challenged by a baseball player. Named Elton. The significance can't be ignored."

"Elton from the dog park?" Sig's attention had been caught. "Didn't we scare this guy off? Why is he still a thing?"

"He hit on your sister," Corrigan pointed out.

"She's not my sister. And by the way, you've hit on her, too."

Corrigan snorted, looked around for support. "Yeah, but I play hockey."

Sig looked back down at his phone, willing a text from Chloe to appear. "I fail to see your logic."

"The bottom line is," Mailer started, "he named a time and a place for this baseball game. Us versus them. We have to show."

"Have you ever played baseball?" Burgess asked the Rookies.

"How hard can it be?" Corrigan shrugged. "They don't even wear mouthguards."

Mailer was nodding along with his friend. "They wear hats, instead of helmets."

"No pads. Just a little cup over their dicks." Corrigan curved a hand over his junk to demonstrate, as if it was necessary. "It's not even a sport."

"Have fun embarrassing yourselves," Sig said. "You won't catch me out there learning a new sport on the spot. I need better odds."

"If we start losing, we just incite a brawl," Mailer said, as if that should be obvious.

"Something tells me the new GM won't like us brawling in public," commented someone in the back of the bus.

That gave Mailer pause. "So you don't think I should invite her then?"

"We're done with this conversation," Sig called. "Sit down and shut up."

"Next Saturday," Corrigan said while collapsing back into his seat. "Nine in the morning. That field near the dog park."

"Nope," Sig barked, agitated. No text from Chloe. No call back. What was going on?

"Hey," Burgess said from the row behind him. "What's going on with you?"

Sig shook his head. Wasn't going to answer, but the words just tumbled out, because he couldn't carry the abundance of nerves alone at this point, especially before a game. He'd get himself killed out there. "Chloe isn't answering her phone. It's been too long and I'm getting worried," he said, turning slightly in the seat. "I hate to ask, but do you think Tallulah could check on her?"

"Does she have a performance tonight?" asked Burgess, taking the phone out of his suit jacket pocket. "Something that might prevent her from answering?"

"No. She should be home."

The captain grunted. Dialed. "Hey, gorgeous. Have you spoken to Chloe today?" He listened for a second. "She hasn't talked to her since last week," he said to Sig. Then to Tallulah, "Could you give her a call? Go see if she's all right, if she doesn't answer? Sig can't get her on the phone . . ."

Sig had turned all the way around by now, a strange ripple passing through his chest on repeat. "She didn't speak to her yesterday?" He lowered his voice. "Chloe said Tallulah sent her the article."

Burgess raised an eyebrow, repeated the question to his fiancée—and shook his head. "Tallulah didn't send her anything."

Alarm pitched in Sig's stomach. What the fuck was he missing here? He whipped back around in his seat and dialed again. Why would Chloe lie about who'd sent her the article? It didn't make any sense. Yet. Something wasn't clicking. He just needed to speak to her and clear everything up. There had to be an explanation.

"Hello. Clifford residence."

Sig looked down at his phone to make sure he'd dialed the correct number. Chloe's name was on the screen, but the woman's voice on the other end belonged to someone else. "Who is this?"

"I need no introduction, but whatever. This is Grace."

Grace? Grace. He searched his jumbled thoughts for that name and why it sounded so familiar. When the answer came to him, it did absolutely nothing to calm him down. Chloe's mentor. "Where is Chloe? Why do you have her phone?"

Visions of beeping machines and hospital gowns were flashing in his head. "She's at my place. Well, physically she is here. Mentally, I'm not so sure." There were some footsteps, followed by the ethereal flow of notes that he instantly recognized as harp music. Not just any harp music, but the kind that came from Chloe. His heart recognized when something belonged to her. "When she showed up here this afternoon, she said she'd play until her fingers bled and I think she meant it. I can't get her to stop."

Sig's chest was trapped between two boulders. In one sense, he was relieved.

In another, he was more alarmed than he'd been ten minutes ago.

Until her fingers bled? That didn't sound like his girl at all.

"I don't understand." Sig's head started to pound. "Is she okay?"

"She's . . . incredible, actually. I think we hit a breakthrough around two hours ago. Dropping her might have been the best move I could have made."

"*Dropping* her?" he repeated, throat dry.

"After reading about her in the gossip section? Like a sack of potatoes, my guy." The woman sighed. "Then she showed up here with a speech that gave me chills—and I don't get those easily. I'm pretty sure the last time I got chills, I was at the Magic Mike show in Vegas. But I digress. She begged me to take her back, promised to work her tail off . . . and here we are."

Pieces of the story were locking into place. Tallulah hadn't sent Chloe the article.

Grace had.

And she'd let her go as a mentee over it.

Why the hell didn't Chloe tell him any of this?

Burgess smacked him on the shoulder. "What's up? You find her?"

"Uh. Yeah." Sweat was causing his dress shirt to cling and he couldn't swallow to save his life. "Yeah, I found her. You can tell Tallulah not to worry."

"What is a Tallulah?" Grace asked, followed by the sound of a martini shaker. "Listen, Sig. It is very apparent to me that you and Chloe are madly in love. The first time I met her, she called you 'the most perfect human on earth.' Which, barf." Liquid was poured into a glass, but he could barely hear anything over the crashing waves in his head. "Unfortunately, the fact that you love each other is also obvious to a reporter at the *Globe*. And more will follow, I'm sure. She had to make a choice."

"Put her on the phone," he rasped, moving beyond panic into a place he'd never been before. His entire body had gone numb. Was he in shock?

"Do you hear the magic she's making? I'm not interrupting that."

As soon as he talked to her, everything would make sense. "Please."

Grace let out a long breath. "Hold on."

The bus had pulled up at the team entrance of the arena. Players were filing off the bus, shoving each other and shouting as they passed his row. Somehow he knew Burgess hadn't budged. That he was still sitting behind him. But Sig couldn't move, couldn't turn around. Couldn't breathe. Finally, the music stopped and his hand flexed involuntarily around the phone, listening for her voice. Her footsteps. Anything.

Finally, "Hi, Sig."

That was all it took. Two words and he knew. She was ending things.

The regret in her voice told the whole story.

"Chloe," he started thickly, leaning forward in his seat. Subtly rocking side to side. Restless. Helpless. Oh God, what the fuck was happening here? "You should have told me about Grace. I'm sorry that happened—it's . . . this is all my fault—"

"No, it's my fault. I spoke to that reporter during the last home game and . . . I don't know, maybe by that point nothing I could have said to him would have made a difference. Even a denial. People can see what's between us, you know? We don't hide it very well."

His chest was on fire, along with his head, his blood. "We'll figure this out. Whatever you're doing, whatever you're going to say, don't. Chloe. Don't do this."

"You're the best player in the league, Sig," she continued, though he could hear the effort it was costing her to get the words out. "I've told you this for so long. You've worked hard and you've earned that captain patch and I'm not going to let you give it up. I'm not going to let myself give up the possibility of first chair, either. I've been coasting my whole life, but . . . you make me want to have purpose." Her voice wavered. "We both need to have purpose, because it can't be each other. Especially at the cost of hurting our parents."

"*Chloe.* Don't say anything else. I'll come home right now. Right now."

"No."

"Please, I fucking love you. I love you so much. Don't fuck me up like this."

He could hear her on the other end, attempting to catch her breath and failing. He'd never surmount the pain and frustration of not being there to hold her, kiss her, talk her out of breaking his heart. "Will you do something for me?"

"I'll do anything for you as long as I live."

"Go play the game of your life. For me. Show them they're nothing without you. Don't let this be for nothing, okay? *Please.*"

"Chloe—" he growled.

But she'd already hung up.

Sig sat on the bus with a smoking crater in his chest, staring into a void for an unknown length of time, begging himself to wake up from the nightmare of losing her. But daylight never came. The darkness stayed, sucking him in deeper by the second. In the end, it was Burgess who helped a devastated Sig off the bus, holding him up like a soldier from a battlefield. The only thing keeping him relatively sane was having a mission to complete. For her.

Go play the game of your life.

And even though doing as she asked would only drag them further apart, his heart gave him no choice but to fulfill her wishes. That's what he'd been built to do.

So he did.

CHAPTER TWENTY-ONE

Chloe blinked gritty eyes at the screen of her phone.

Doggie date?

The number was unknown . . . but she had an idea who it was. Elton. That baseball player with whom she'd exchanged numbers in the park. She'd deleted his number, but apparently, he had not done the same with hers. And she wasn't in the mood for this. Not remotely.

Every part of her body ached. Her lower back throbbed from sitting on a wooden stool in perfect posture for hours on end. Her arms hurt from being elevated without cease. Her fingers were stiff. Yet she would go back to Grace's today and do it all over again. What was her other option? Stay here and think? No. God, no. She couldn't do that.

A week had passed since she'd spoken to Sig.

This was the time of day she wanted to call him the most. He wasn't a morning person, either, and they would grumble together over the phone. Pep talk each other into moving, getting out of bed. His voice was so gruff in the mornings, his humor a little less sharp than usual, kind of like he was still in the process of waking up. He'd stay on the phone with her until her morning Pop-Tart was ready, then he'd promise to see her later.

Chloe made a hoarse sound and turned the phone upside down on the mattress.

The way she missed Sig was inhuman. She was pulverized.

An apparition haunting her own life.

There were positives and she tried to focus on those. For one, she's transcended her own God-given abilities on the harp. Grace's directives were beginning to click with ease. She'd begun anticipating her mentor's advice and implementing it without having to be asked. The music she made now was somehow more satisfying. Smoother. Like it had been languishing for years, waiting for her to come and do it justice. She was better than she'd thought—and that made her proud. Of herself. When she stopped and let herself feel it. Which wasn't often, because when she stopped to think, melancholy and heartbreak flooded in and carried her away on a tide she couldn't control. But she could control the harp. Her fingertips. So she'd get back on the stool today and bury everything under notes.

The second positive this week had been walking past newsstands while taking Pierre for his evening stroll and seeing Sig on the cover of the Sports section. "Hat Trick for Gauthier." He'd done it. Gone out and played not just the game of his life while on the road, but *games*. Pride overflowed her, made it hard to breathe. She'd done the right thing. For him. For them. For her.

Why did it have to feel so terrible?

A canine snarf forced Chloe's eyes open to find Pierre standing at the edge of the bed. She'd already taken him for his 5:30 a.m. jaunt—accompanied by her landlord, as she'd been doing every morning for the last week. "Mister Sig asked me to go with you on these early walks," Raymond had said, by way of explanation.

Of course Sig did that.

Of course he did.

Pierre sat down with a blustering sound, looking up at Chloe expectantly. She'd really been giving him the bare minimum this week, hadn't she? Walking him, feeding him, petting him when she could muster the energy. The poor pup deserved better.

"What kind of a dog mother am I?" she murmured, her voice muffled by the pillow. "You deserve to go on a doggie date, don't you, boy? Do you want to go see your friends at the dog park?"

Pierre's tongue lolled out, his butt scooting forward an inch on the carpet.

"That looks like a yes. Okay." Chloe turned the phone over again and punched out a stiff-fingered text to Elton. "I'm a little surprised he reached out, aren't you, Pierre? Considering I brought four hockey players down on his head the first time we met."

The afternoon Sig had kissed her up against the door.

His touch, his voice, his scent remained fresh in her head, like he'd just been there.

You're going to feel my weight on top of you, Chloe. You'll feel it behind you. Beneath you. You're going to feel the weight of me, of us, everywhere.

You're going to trust me to find a way for us, even though it's getting harder. You delete everyone else, but you don't ever delete me. Ever.

Chloe fairly dove out of bed and speed walked to the bathroom, as if those memories were hot on her heels. They found her and plagued her as she went through the motions of brushing her teeth, running a comb through her hair, sighing when it refused to cooperate, and fashioning her locks in a messy bun. She cleansed her face and did her best to conceal her lack of sleep with a quick, natural layer of makeup, but proceeded to look like hell.

"Oh well, Pierre," she said a few minutes later while pulling on yoga pants and a Bearcats sweatshirt. "It's a dog park, not a fashion show, right? And, anyway, you look good enough for the both of us, don't you?" She reached down to snap on his leash, scratching his head for good measure. "Yes, you do, goodest boy."

It was only a five-minute walk to the park, though it took ten because Pierre kept stopping to taste the air. Chloe let Saturday morning in the North End wash over her, trying to glean what comfort she could from the familiarity of locals meeting for brunch, crisscrossing with tourists on the Freedom Trail, the scent of coffee and bacon drifting down cobblestone streets. The sky was overcast and her sweatshirt was definitely warranted, but spring was beginning to kick in, the promise of warmer days giving the temperature a slight lift.

When she reached the dog park a few minutes later and found it empty, she frowned.

Elton had liked her text response. Had he changed his mind? Stood her up? Or was he just running late. Chloe had just slipped her phone out of her front pocket of her sweatshirt when she heard the commotion. Men's voices. A lot of them. *Loud* ones.

Coming from the neighboring baseball field.

Were some of those voices familiar?

She stepped into the gated area and started to close it behind her, her chin jerking up when she heard someone say, "Suck my balls." And that someone was Corrigan. Not a doubt in her mind. And where Corrigan went, so did Mailer. What were the Orgasm Donors doing at the baseball field at 9:30 a.m. on Saturday morning . . .

Chloe's mouth fell open.

They hadn't gone through with that ridiculous challenge, had they?

Certainly not.

But she found herself exiting the penned dog park and marching up and over the small rise, anyway, just to be sure. When the baseball field came into full view and she saw the parties assembled, she resolved to never again underestimate the competitive nature of professional athletes. Although they were being noticeably unprofessional this morning, if the "suck my balls" comment was any proof.

Corrigan and Mailer were shoulder to shoulder, facing off with Elton, who had a whole baseball team of men—and one young woman—standing behind him, attempting intimidation by crushing their fists into their leather gloves. Burgess was leaning against the chain-link fence, arms crossed, as if he'd just come in case an adult needed to step in. Several other members of the Bearcats team were also in attendance, and she couldn't help it, her eyes raced furiously from face to face, trying to locate Sig, but he wasn't there.

And that feeling in her chest was far from relief. It was crushing agony. A momentary spark of hope had lifted her and now she plummeted to the ground, her legs heavy enough to sink into the earth if she didn't move. Move.

But . . . wait.

Why had Elton texted her to meet him at the dog park if he'd planned on going through with this asinine matchup, instead?

Maybe Grace's take-no-prisoners personality was rubbing off on Chloe. Or maybe she was simply too heartbroken to be nice or too exhausted to second-guess herself. Whatever the reason, she marched with a building head of steam in the direction of the field, Pierre trotting beside her in the grass, not stalling for once. Did he sense the gravity of the situation?

"We win, you show up to our next home game in our jerseys," Mailer was saying.

"And *when* you lose?" Elton scoffed.

"How about this? Your prize is you don't get your asses kicked," Corrigan barked, before hesitating and leaning to look past Elton to his hoard of teammates, his voice softer when he said, "Obviously, the lady would not be included in an ass kicking of any kind."

The brunette ran a hand down her ponytail, which was cascading down from the opening of her cap. "Aw shucks, that's so sweet." She wrinkled her nose. "But I think I'll stick around and give you the junk punch you so clearly deserve."

Corrigan's eyebrows shot sky-high. "Fair enough."

The girl smiled back, sweetly. While grinding her fist into her glove.

Chloe liked her. A lot.

And that was the beginning and end of what she liked about this morning.

"Hey, *Elton*," Chloe said, slowing to a stop beside the rangy baseball player, the leather dog leash biting into the palm of her hand.

"Chloe!" seemingly every Bearcat shouted happily at once, many of them converging on her with open arms to give her a hug. She whipped up a hand to stop them in their tracks.

"Uh-oh," Mailer muttered, stepping back. Pausing. Frowning. "Hold up a second, what is Chloe doing here?"

"That's what I would like to know," Chloe said, squaring off with Elton, whose eyes were hidden behind a pair of wraparound Ray-Bans.

"I invited her," Elton responded to Mailer, grinning. "She's here to cheer the real baseball players on."

"Excuse me?" sputtered Chloe.

"Excuse her?" Corrigan echoed, rearing back with visible affront.

Chloe was vibrating, head to toe, a week's worth of frustration shooting upward from the soles of her feet to occupy her throat in a wreath of spikes. "Did you invite me here under the false pretense of a doggy date, just so you could piss off my friends?"

"I don't know, did I?" He shot the Bearcats a wink. "And did it work?"

Cue the eruption of the century.

Hockey players converged on baseball players, everyone arguing at the top of their lungs. Gloves were thrown down into the dirt. Off to the right, there was a heavy sigh and the rustle of chain-link, Burgess inserting himself in the middle of the fray with an air of exasperated patience. "Just a reminder that we're all adults here," said Sir Savage. "Let's take a second to locate our maturity."

"Some of us never had any to begin with," Elton said, taking a step closer to Chloe. "Obviously she figured that out and made a better choice."

"Get any closer to her and I will use your kneecaps for batting practice."

Chloe's world froze at the sound of Sig's voice behind her.

Her bruised heart climbed through her aching throat into her mouth, fingernails curling into her palms and possibly drawing blood. How could everything be right and wrong at the same time? Sig was there, the heat of his chest warming her back. She could see his shadow on the ground, those broad shoulders, the outline of his beloved head in a baseball cap, his dark hair doing that hockey flow flip at the back and sides. More than anything in this life or the next ten, she wanted to turn around and leap into his arms.

But she couldn't.

She'd cut him off, for one.

Severed the thing in their lives that brought them the most joy.

And . . . she didn't know if anyone present had seen the article. Almost certainly, Sig's teammates knew about the insinuation made by the reporter in the *Globe*. But hadn't they already been aware of the odd relationship between Sig and Chloe prior to that?

Hadn't everyone?

Did these baseball players know, though? Did Elton?

Chloe's brain told her not to turn around, because she wouldn't be able to diffuse or dampen the happiness she felt, just to be close to him, but her heart overruled her mind and she turned, anyway, letting the sight of him smooth the rough-edges inside of her created by their weeklong separation.

Sig's wild-eyed gaze, however, remained fastened over her head. On Elton.

His pupils blocked out every bit of brown, his thick chest rising, falling, his hockey body poised to throw down at a split second's notice.

"Did you fucking hear me, or not?" Sig's jaw popped. "Step away from her."

"Sig . . ." Burgess said, a wealth of meaning in his tone.

"You heard the man," Mailer chimed in. "She's ours."

"I didn't say ours," Sig corrected Mailer without taking his attention off Elton.

Mailer coughed. "You were thinking it."

"No, I wasn't." Finally—finally—Sig looked at Chloe, blinking several times, chest plummeting, before hitting Elton with another warning look. "You brought her here just to be a dick. You're going to delete her number now, because you don't deserve to have it."

"Whatever." Elton shrugged, sauntered the few steps that separated him and Sig, lowering his voice, so only Sig and Chloe could hear it. "I hear she's taken anyway."

Sig's eyes collided with Chloe's.

There were too many emotions to name in that look. Hunger, concern, apology, misery.

"I wasn't going to play," Sig said, shrugging off his jacket. "But the possibility of hitting you with a line drive between the eyes it too tempting."

Elton smirked. "My sister, Skylar, is pitching and she's D1 all-American. You're welcome to try."

Sig started to respond, but Skylar appeared out of nowhere, slapping her brother, apparently, in the chest with her glove. Hard. "Asshole. Can't believe you pulled something like that." She hit him again for good measure, before heading for the pitching mound and calling over her shoulder, "I'm telling Mom."

Frowning, Elton stomped after her. "You better not."

Everyone dispersed around Sig and Chloe, but they didn't move.

"Hey," Sig rasped, a muscle sliding up and down in his throat. He took his cap off and slapped it back on. Then he took a giant step away from Chloe, nearly causing her stomach to land in the grass, the distance between them—and the act of him putting it there so viscerally—nearly intolerable.

It's the right thing.

She'd done the right thing.

He obviously realized that, too.

Why was that so blindingly painful?

"I'm sorry that happened to you. For him to have the freedom to call you like that . . . and *squander* it?" He massaged the center of his forehead. "I'm sure you're dying to get out of here. Away from all this testosterone."

"And miss Elton's comeuppance? I don't think so." She lowered her voice to a stage whisper. "If they start to win, just incite a brawl."

Affection warmed his face. "Once a hockey girl, always a hockey girl, huh?"

Chloe swallowed a painful lump. "Yeah."

"Yeah," Sig said, sounding winded. "Stay where I can see you."

"Okay." *Hug me. I can't stand this. We'll try again tomorrow to stay away from each other. Please, everything hurts so bad. I need you.* "Sig—"

A shrill whistle came from the pitcher's mound. "Are we going to play baseball, or what, boys?"

Sig gave her a final, long look, his hand flexing at his side . . . nodded once, firm, and walked away. Chloe followed, dragging her broken heart behind her like a string of noisy tin cans that only she could hear.

CHAPTER TWENTY-TWO

Sig had learned to block out fear a long time ago. Fear that his mother wouldn't be able to make ends meet and they wouldn't have dinner on the table. Fear that he wouldn't get drafted, be able to provide for her. Fear of serious injury while playing hockey. Fear had ceased to be part of his emotional vocabulary— until Chloe.

Since meeting her he'd learned what it meant to be scared. Of something happening to her. Of losing her. But right then, as she stood at the end of the dugout, nervously playing with the end of Pierre's leash, he could admit to full-on terror. Because he'd been walking around with no pulse for the last week, and it had only started beating again when he saw her reading Elton the riot act. *Oh, thank God. There's my girl.*

She wasn't his girl now, though, and he was too scared to face the rest of his bleak existence in this new reality.

Pierre plopped down and rolled over at Chloe's feet, offering his belly to her with his tongue hanging out the side of his panting mouth . . . and she made this adorable *h'awww* sound, shooting Sig an amused look. And at the same time, a gust of wind slapped him across the face with her scent and he swore his lungs started to cry. To shut down out of self-preservation.

Was it possible for love to be so severe it caused organ failure?

"All right," Sig said, hoarse. "What's the lineup?"

Everyone looked at Burgess.

"You clowns think I'm risking another back injury for baseball?" Burgess spat. "I'm just here to break up the inevitable fight. Ask Sig for the lineup—he's your new captain."

"Not yet," Sig responded automatically, feeling Chloe's gaze on him. There hadn't been any communication with the front office since his initial meeting with Reese, but David had called this morning to inform Sig the Bearcats wanted another sit-down. Sig's agent even predicted that an offer was on the horizon. Sig definitely should be more excited about that, right? "Either way, I'm going to go ahead and take the lead on this. Since I'm here and everything."

"*Captain. Captain. Cap*—"

Sig shut down Mailer's chant with a glare. Then he scanned the rest of his assembled teammates. "Has anyone here ever played this godforsaken sport?"

Two hands went up near the rear of the pack. "All right, one of you lead off. The other goes second. Just get on base and I'll bat you in."

"Gauthier with the baseball lingo," someone said. "I think I just sprouted wood."

"Really?" Mailer adjusted himself. "Because I fucking lost mine."

Corrigan punched him in the shoulder. "There's a lady present, jackass."

"Sorry, Chloe," Mailer said automatically.

"What? No, Chloe is used to our bullshit." Corrigan rubbed the back of his neck, his attention glued on the field. "I was talking about the pitcher." He sniffed, rolled a shoulder. "She's obviously feeling me."

"No, I'm not," called Skylar, tossing up the baseball and catching it without looking.

"You will be," Corrigan shouted back, grinning.

"Only if I have to check for a pulse after the game. Because we're about to murder you."

"Trust me, I've got a pulse, sweetie. You're making it race."

Was the pitcher *blushing*? Unbelievable, but yeah. Appearing to be of Mexican descent, her skin tone was already a natural burnished brown, but the furious deepening of color had the young woman pulling down the brim of her cap to hide her face. Apparently, the bar was low these days when it came to pickup lines. "Are you just trying to psych me out?" asked the blushing pitcher. "You are, aren't you?"

"Holy shit," Corrigan muttered, frowning. "It's almost like . . . she doesn't know she's hot."

Sig clapped a hand down on his shoulder. "You better marry her before she finds out she could do way better."

Corrigan was already nodding. "I know, right?" Then to the pitcher, "Can't wait to tell the grandkids how we met, Skylar."

"Hey." Elton barked while striding to first base. "Stop talking to my sister."

Corrigan unleashed a groan toward the overcast sky. "Why does every attractive woman have to be somebody's sister?"

Sig and Chloe traded a sideways glance. "All right, let's get this over with." He jerked his thumb toward the batter's box. "Jorgenson, lead us off."

"There goes my boner again."

"Shut up."

Jorgenson swaggered out to the batter's box . . . without a bat. "Shit." He looked back over his shoulder. "I think we forgot something. Like . . . bats?"

Sig massaged the bridge of his nose. "Go borrow one from them. Jesus Christ."

"This is off to a fine start," offered Burgess, from his casual lean against the dugout wall.

Mailer came up beside Sig. "Speaking of gear we neglected to bring, I forgot to bring a cup. Do you happen to have a spare?"

"If I did, do you think I'd share it with you?"

"If my grapes get crushed, I could be out for weeks. I'd really hate to have that conversation with the new GM." He cleared his throat. "Not because my broken testicles would put me on the injured reserve list, but because I'd like her to know they're fully functioning."

"Please tell me you're not hot for the new GM."

"I won't. Because that would be an understatement." Mailer sighed, before giving Sig a subtle elbow in the side. "Look on the bright side. At least I won't hit on Chloe anymore."

Fire encompassed the back of Sig's neck.

He'd been fighting the urge to turn and look at Chloe for the last five minutes and he finally gave in now, finding her watching him, too, her expression open and vulnerable and . . . missing him. Yeah, she missed him. Maybe even half as much as he missed her. And that was going to make staying away infinitely harder. God, it might kill him, but he had to respect the decision she'd made. The hard one he didn't have the ability to make himself.

You okay, Chlo? Sig mouthed at her.

There was a long hesitation, followed by a series of too-quick nods.

She's not okay. We're not okay.

"Play ball," shouted someone from the opposing dugout, dragging Sig's attention back to the field, though his awareness never detached from her. Not for a second. Not even when the first pitch came whistling into the strike zone at what appeared to be at least eighty miles an hour.

"Son of a bitch," Corrigan intoned, looking dazed. "Did I just meet my future wife?"

"No," everyone shouted back, including Skylar and Elton.

Corrigan just grinned. "Can't wait to prove everyone wrong."

It came as no surprise that Jorgenson struck out.

The second batter managed to get on base, but only because Sig advised him to bunt—but it was not pretty. In fact, Sig wouldn't freely admit to anyone who listened that he did not want to try his hand against Skylar, because, yeah, she had an arm like a fucking cannon and she hadn't even broken a sweat. Outwardly, though, he kept his cool and approached the batter's box, taking a couple of practice swings along the way. And he reverted back to the fake mind bets he used to make with himself as a kid for motivation. Such as, *if you score today, you get to meet Sidney Crosby. If you practice for one more hour, you get drafted in the first round.*

Man, the stakes were a lot different as a twenty-nine-year-old man.

If you hit this ball, you get to marry Chloe.

It was a ridiculous bet to make with himself, since the outcome was impossible, but hell if he didn't lock in on the baseball as Skylar wound up and . . . threw a pitch that was slightly off—and he didn't swing. On instinct. "Ball," called the baseball player acting as the umpire.

Skylar rolled her eyes, accepting the ball her teammate threw back.

Rolled her shoulder, scuffed the dirt with her cleat.

Leaned forward.

Much later, Sig would admit he got lucky. Or maybe getting to pretend the impossible dream of marrying the love of his life could come true caused him to smack the ball out into the right outfield, over the heads of the players who were clearly not expecting him to connect. Dazed, Sig stood watching the ball sail into the trees, but Sir Savage shouted at him to run and his legs took over, instinctively following the directive of the man who'd been his captain since rookie year. But he only made it past first base when all hell broke loose.

Because of course, Pierre chose *that* moment to come alive.

To discover a resource of energy that perhaps he didn't know existed inside himself.

Yes.

The bulldog went sprinting through the field after the ball, like his very life depended on retrieving it. Which obviously meant Chloe went running after him in visible distress, her blonde hair coming loose from its bun, her squeals of the dog's name echoing across the park.

Sig didn't even hesitate—he ran after Chloe, envisioning all manner of heinous ankle breaks or violent murderers lurking in the woods, just waiting for a beautiful girl to come running straight into their trap. Nope. Not on his watch.

"Chloe!"

"Pierre! Stop!" When the dog officially vanished into the trees, his leash sailing out behind him, she made a desperate sound and ran faster. "Sig!"

Yeah, he'd be lying if Chloe reflexively calling out to him for help wasn't the balm he needed over his aching wounds, but he'd savor it later. He passed Chloe in the race to reach Pierre before he became unfindable, breaking into the trees, winded—

Only to find the bulldog rolling around in a puddle of mud. No, *sludge*.

With the baseball in his mouth.

Sig had never seen the dog look happier.

"Oh no, *Pierre!*" Chloe panted, jogging to a stop beside Sig, planting her hands on her head. "Look at you! You're all covered in filth. What am I going to do with you?"

The problem at hand sort of slipped to the wayside as Sig looked at Chloe, her face contoured in shadow and sunlight, her hair a windy mess, cheeks flushed. The most incredible sight he'd ever seen—at least, since the last time he'd looked at her. On top of the morning glow she was sporting, she was wearing a Bearcats sweatshirt he'd given her.

You can't have her anymore.

You shouldn't have taken her to begin with.

Chloe looked up at him, slumped a little. "You didn't even get credit for your home run, did you?"

If you hit this ball, you get to marry Chloe.

If only.

"No, it counts," he said, throat hurting. "I'll make sure it counts."

After a moment, she nodded. "How am I going to get him home like this?"

"In the back of my truck?" he suggested.

Their gazes collided. Heated. Tried to break free, but came right back. Fired up even more. Driving Chloe home was a Very Bad Idea. They both knew it.

"I'll just get him inside, then go," he said, adding, "It's been almost two weeks since those pictures were taken. I doubt they've been staking you out this long."

Chloe swallowed. "Okay."

His heart nearly leapt out of his chest at the news that he'd be spending time with her, no matter how short. "Yeah?"

"Yeah. I can't think of any other way to get him home without getting mud on everything and everyone he passes." She wet her lips. "Can you?"

"No," he said, way too quickly. "Let's go." *Before you change your mind.*

They walked out of the trees and back onto the field, stopping in their tracks when they saw the brawl taking place in the baseball diamond. Everyone was embroiled in the knock-down, drag-out fistfight, except for Burgess who was patiently peeling men off one another and tossing them down on the ground like yesterday's trash.

And Corrigan, who was marching away from the fray with a struggling Skylar over his shoulder. "Let me save you!" he growled at her, while she pounded on his back.

"Let's just pretend we never saw this," Chloe whispered.

Sig was already ushering her toward the parking lot. "Good idea."

CHAPTER TWENTY-THREE

Chloe was laughing so hard, she tripped over her own feet into the apartment and nearly went sprawling face down onto the hardwood floor. Somehow, she managed to balance herself without touching any of the furniture with her dirty hands, turning just in time to watch Sig saunter into the apartment with a sludge-caked bulldog cradled to his chest.

A twinkle lit his eyes, but he didn't smile.

He probably couldn't, because there was dried mud hardening on his face, due to the struggle he'd undergone putting Pierre into the bed of his truck. It was a miracle Chloe hadn't peed her pants on the way home, because though they'd secured Pierre to the truck with his leash and driven five miles per hour down busy Boston streets while horns wailed, Pierre still managed to lose his balance, plop, and roll several times, making Chloe cry out in concern and laugh her head off in equal measure.

"Come on, let's put him in the bathtub," she wheezed, staggering down the hallway of the apartment and falling to her knees in front of the tub, turning the tap to warm. "I'm not thinking about the mess this is going to leave behind. That's a later problem."

"I'll help you." Sig unhooked the removable showerhead and started rinsing mud and sludge from the bulldog right away. "Let's just get this behemoth clean."

The word "behemoth" spoken through gritted teeth caused

Chloe to shake with mirth. "If you think about it, he saved us from that brawl," she said over the sound of pelting water. "I think he knew exactly what he was doing. Didn't you, thoughtful boy?"

Pierre glared at her, one tooth poking up from his bottom lip.

"Hate to break it to you, but this dog doesn't have a single thought in his head, Chlo." He hunkered down beside her on the tile floor so he could spray Pierre's undercoat. "He eats and shits and causes trouble."

Chloe bumped him in the shoulder with her own. "Is this the kind of daddy you'd be? The kind who complains about having to hose dirt and Cheerios off a toddler?"

"Nah." He seemed to get distracted by her face, his attention falling to her mouth. "If we made a baby, I'd live for every second."

Her heart dropped to her knees. "You've been talking about making babies a lot lately."

Was it her imagination or had he leaned closer? Was that his breath on her lips? "I've been thinking about it a lot longer than I've been talking about it."

"Sig."

"You brought it up."

"Yes, I did. Sorry."

Chest rumbling, he tore his gaze off her. "How is practice going?"

"Good," Chloe said, feeling dazed from being blasted by so much intensity only to have it taken away . . . and struggling with the need to get it back. In an effort to distract herself, she looked down at her fingers, running the pad of her thumb across the blister that had formed yesterday on her middle finger. "I'm working as hard as I can. I'm grateful for the work, even if it's grueling. The harder the better, actually. When I get into the zone . . ."

"You don't have to think."

"Yes."

His throat worked. "I know, baby. I'm doing the same."

Chloe dug her nails into her palms to prevent herself from crawling into his lap, clinging to him, absorbing his heat. "Have they offered you a contract yet?"

"I have a meeting with Reese tomorrow. Could be it."

Her face lit up. "I hope so."

"Yeah? I don't feel a fucking thing anymore."

Pulses started clamoring in her neck, wrists, and chest. "Sig."

"I'm sorry," he rasped, his knuckles turning white around the shower nozzle. "It's painful to be this close to you."

Chloe didn't know what to say. What to do. On some level, she'd entertained the hope that they could stay friends. Authentic ones this time. But that obviously wouldn't be the case. Because she couldn't pretend, either, that she didn't ache to be held by him, feel his hands skim her flesh, while his mouth fastened to her lips, her breasts. She'd have to completely let him go, wouldn't she? They'd never had a chance to be anything but . . .

Apart.

"I'll go see if I can find you a big T-shirt to wear," she said, standing on legs made of gelatin. Trying and failing to ignore the way his eyes ran their full length, darkened when they reached the juncture of her thighs, his jaw popping. "Yours is covered in mud."

"It's okay."

"No, I'll find something," she breathed, nearly tripping over the threshold saddle to escape the tension in the bathroom. Her options were to get away from it or run headfirst into it. Once inside her bedroom, she stripped off her sweatshirt, which was streaked in brown and probably needed delousing, hurriedly searching through her drawers to locate a shirt for herself, as well as Sig. Her heartbeat was booming in her ears, hands clumsy. Of course, they were. She was separated by a wall from the man who ruled her senses.

The riot taking place throughout Chloe's body and the concerted effort she put toward ignoring it were a distraction. And probably why she only realized absently the water had been turned off in the bathroom. But when the hair raised on her arms and the back of her neck, she knew he was there. Standing in the doorway of her bedroom with his shoulder propped against the jamb, hunger running rampant across his features.

"Sorry, still trying to find you a shirt."

"It's probably a good idea if you find one for yourself first."

Heat clawed at her skin. "Okay. I just . . ." All the shirts looked the same. Nothing made sense. She couldn't recall what a single one of them looked like or ever having seen them in her life. There was nothing but the magnetism and frustration radiating from the man in her doorway. "Um. Hold on."

Sig pushed off the door and went to pace the hallway, arms crossed. And she hated herself for being swamped in disappointment by that. By the fact that he didn't charge into the bedroom, swipe her off the floor, and throw her down on the bed. Take her like an animal. Her body craved that rough treatment. Craved release. For both of them. God, she wanted his almost as much as she needed her own.

Finally, she found a black tank top for herself, pulling it on over her head.

Down toward the bottom of the folded stack was a Bearcats shirt she'd bought at the first game she attended. Before she'd ordered her custom pink jersey. The only size they'd had left in her favorite design was a men's XXL, so she'd resolved to sleep in it.

"Here," she murmured, holding out the shirt to him on her journey into the dark hallway. Yes, dark. The overcast day lent little light to the apartment and they hadn't bothered turning on any lights, apart from the one in the bathroom.

There was more than enough light, however, to see every muscle of Sig's body flex, ripple, and snap when he stripped off his ruined shirt and dropped it on the ground, his heavy-lidded eyes fastened on her. When he looked ready to spring for her, he merely held out his hand for the shirt.

She handed it over, shivering when their fingers brushed.

He hesitated to put on the garment, his chest rising and falling in an unsteady pattern.

"I'm trying to respect your decision, Chlo," he said thickly, his steps seeming to bring them closer involuntarily. Closer. Closer until his breath on her temple. "Quit looking at me like that."

Another step forward from Sig. A backward one from Chloe.

One by one, her back muscles melted into the wall, head falling back so her eyes could trace the perfection of his jawline, his throat, his sculpted mouth. "Like what?"

That breath—and the tiniest hint of his tongue—made contact with her ear. "Like you remember how hot we fuck. Like you want to do it again." He planted his left hand above her head on the wall, his right hand dropped to the front of his sweatpants. Gripped that thick ridge while he groaned. "Look what you do to me, Chloe."

"That's what you do to me, too," she whispered, head swimming. "The lady version."

His lips twitched, but he seemed almost pained by his own amusement. "Oh God, I miss you so much."

"I miss you, too. So much," she gasped, because he buried a handful of fingers in her hair, tilted her head back, and licked upward along the curve of her throat.

"You want some?" He latched his teeth to her jaw. "Give me a green light."

Don't do it. She'd only set herself back. But there was no putting the brakes on a runaway train. No talking sense into herself when she loved this man in ways that defied logic.

"One more time," she whispered, nodding, her arms sliding up around his neck.

"No one will know but us," he gritted out, backing her more firmly against the wall and smothering her face in kisses. He planted his lips frantically, but lovingly, on her cheeks, her nose, her forehead, her chin, her hair, her ears, before finding her mouth and growling into a kiss that communicated everything inside of them both. Everything they both knew to be true, so true they'd feel it for the rest of their lives. "Goddamn it. *Goddamn it.*"

"Don't think," she whispered, dropping her right hand from around his neck and stroking his erection through the soft material of his sweatpants. "Just enjoy me."

He moaned brokenly, dropping his face into the crook of her neck. "I do. I enjoy you more than anything else in this life."

"Sig, you're going to break me saying things like that."

She felt his teeth baring against the spot below her ear. "I hear you, Chlo. I'll keep it about fucking. That's how we're going to survive this, huh?"

"Yes."

"Fine." He tilted his hips, rolling them into her touch. "Touch me."

"I'd rather taste you, honey."

A shudder passed through his big frame. "You don't have to suck my cock, Chloe. But if you do, I'll reward you so well for it."

Her legs simply evaporated beneath her, knees landing on the floor, her eager hands tugging down his waistband. She'd wanted to give him a blow job in the hotel room last week, but every time she'd attempted one, he'd shaken his head, flipped her over, and gone down on her instead. A week without him had left her starving and if this was going to be the last time, the real last time they were together, then she planned to feast. Her grip circled him, tongue giving a long lap of that shiny dome, playing in the salty slit. And then she put as much of him in her mouth as she could stand, feeling herself choke, her eyes watering from the pressure but not caring. Only wanting more of his flavor, the satisfaction of his groans.

"Dream girl has a dream mouth, doesn't she? *Christ.*" He gripped the base of his shaft in his right hand, threading the fingers of his left into her head, urging her forward. Rocking into the warmth she eagerly offered. "Moan on it. Let me know how bad you want me in your wet fucking mouth. Good girl. Good. That's real deep. That's how I need it."

His obvious pleasure, which seemed to heighten by the second, worked like a drug in her bloodstream. She couldn't feel the hard floor beneath her knees or the stretch of her lips. Couldn't feel the moisture leaking from her eyes or coating her chin, she just knew she wanted to keep going and going, find out how high she could drive him. The way he'd done for her. The way he would do for her as soon as he got the chance.

"I'm getting too stiff now. That's enough. I need to last." He urged her head toward him faster, as if he couldn't help it. Couldn't stop. "I want to come inside you."

Chloe made eye contact while raking her hands up his bare chest, nails scraping gently downward over his nipples, the fullness of him jerking in her mouth, salt trickling down her throat. "Mmmm."

"Enough. It's too good. *Enough.*" Panting, he tugged himself free of her mouth with a gritted curse, then scooped Chloe onto her feet, walking her backward toward the bedroom, his mouth sealed and sliding on top of hers, their hands colliding in an effort to pull down her yoga pants, a feat she finished off by wiggling and using her toes as hooks to pull them the remaining distance to the floor, kicking away, leaving her in a bra and panties. So much of his warm skin touching hers, her mouth fell open on a shaky breath, hands reaching, stroking.

Just before they reached the doorway, he cupped his hand on the back of her head—and when she realized he was protecting her skull from bumping the frame, her heart flipped upside down. Her entire world went with it. Along with any remaining filter she possessed.

"I love you, too. I love you, too," she said, fingers in his hair, bringing his forehead down to meet hers, his breath catching against her mouth. "Maybe I shouldn't tell you that, maybe it's terrible timing, but I can't live without saying it."

He seemed incapable of speaking, but while searching her face, right to left, up and down, he let the words out in a gruff rush. "I know you love me, Chloe," he said. "You've made sure I feel it every single day." He squeezed his eyes closed. "Did I do that for you?"

"Yes."

Tangible relief made him shudder and then his lips were back on hers, his tongue stroking the interior of her mouth, deeply, adoringly, fingers tangling in her hair. And the effect of him was so potent, she stumbled slightly, her hip connecting with her dresser. With a groove of concern forming between his brows, Sig broke the kiss and rubbed the spot where she'd hit the furniture. Seeing his big hand massaging her hip, the length of him hanging free of his sweatpants, she couldn't wait. Neither could he, said his glazed eyes, his flushed face.

They moved at the same time, boosting her up onto the dresser.

"This is good. This is . . . good. I'm afraid to get into your bed," he said in between shallow breaths, his throat bobbing. "I'm afraid I won't be able to leave it."

"I wish you didn't have to," she whispered.

He slammed his fist down on top of the dresser, as if that statement had wounded him. "Get these fucking panties off," he growled, lifting her with the crook of his arm, divesting her of the underwear in one long yank. Gone. "I got your reward right here."

Sig fell to his knees like a thankful man in prayer, parting her flesh with an undulating tongue. Watching her. Prodding her clit a little, teasing, then bathing it with the flattened surface, raking it side to side, side to side, stealing her ability to think or breathe.

Upon her first shudder, he hooked his grip beneath her knees, squeaking her backside closer to the edge, then found her butt with both hands, clutching, pulling, grinding her sex against his face, pressing his tongue deep, deep, *deep* into her entrance until she screamed, her body quaking reflexively, throat already sore from whimpering, straining.

"Sig. Oh. Oh my God. Sig, that's good. *That's so good.*"

The orgasm was like sinking into a hot bath, all the way to the crown of her head. Her body sort of just melted, the human form of candle wax, while her core clenched and tightened around his still-thrusting tongue, those hands still on her cheeks, urging her as close as possible to his mouth, his mouth, his *perfect, beloved mouth.*

She was still gasping from the intensity of the release when Sig stood, drawing her body up against his roughly, his brown gaze wild as he looked down at her from above, holding that blistering, soul-crushing eye contact while entering her. Hard. One thick, hot pump and he was seated, swallowing her scream with an open mouth and starting to thrust. Holding nothing back, neither one of them caring as the dresser drawers rattled, perfume bottles toppled over, the back of the furniture slammed into the wall.

"You're going to feel me in ways you won't forget, Chloe," he rasped.

"Yes. *Yes*. I am."

He bore down on her, his hips moving like the pistons of an engine, his smooth inches finding their home inside of her again, again, again, her knees jostling on either side of his waist, more screams building in her throat. "I won't spend a minute the rest of my life without you in my head and I don't want it any other way. I don't care if it hurts, you're going to stay there," he said hoarsely, kissing her in a way that was somehow rough and sweet at the same time. "Always my dream girl. *Always* mine."

"Always, Sig."

He dragged her upright and off the dresser, bouncing her on his stiffness once, twice, before shouting her name like an epithet, his fingers bruising as they pressed, pressed, grinded her onto his spurting sex, both of them crying out when he lunged forward, giving her a final series of gloriously violent drives against the dresser, which she encouraged with whimpers of his name, rakes of her nails down the powerful breadth of his back.

Then, like two beings that had lost animation, they dropped to the floor, Sig cradling Chloe in his lap, his mouth dropping furious kisses on her hairline, even while he struggled to catch his breath.

"Chloe, please—"

She never found out what Sig was going to say, because both of their phones rang at once.

CHAPTER TWENTY-FOUR

Sig's instincts were telling him to pin Chloe to the floor to prevent her from answering the phone. Drag her into bed, pull the covers down over their heads, and never leave this bedroom. There couldn't be anything good on the other end of that call. He couldn't say what made him so positive of that fact. Maybe trepidation had become his default because the world was trying to take this woman away from him. Or maybe he just wanted to stay cocooned in this moment with Chloe forever, their scents on each other's sweaty skin.

"The phones . . ." she said, trying to lift her head, but losing power in her neck and sagging more firmly against him, her cheek in between his pecs.

"Ignore them. Do you have anywhere to be today?" he asked, stroking her hair.

"Practice with Grace in a couple of hours." She yawned against his chest and he saw the life he wanted flash before his eyes. Waking up with her every day. Forever. Watching her shake the drowsiness. "Not a long one, though. She has a performance tonight."

"And I have my meeting." He tightened his arms around her, raising his voice to drown out the incessant chimes coming from the bathroom. "But we have a couple of hours."

The phones stopped ringing.

Almost immediately, they started again.

"Ignore the world with me a little longer, Chlo," he begged.

"But who would be calling us both? Continually?" Her focus was drifting. He was losing her. "Something could be wrong."

"Please. I don't give a fuck."

She looked up at him with a smirk that slowly started to flatten. "Do you think . . . there's another article?"

"What would it be about? We haven't seen each other in a week."

"I don't know." With a visible effort, she peeled herself off his chest, though she eyed it with regret, as if she wanted to stay there a lot longer. "I'll go answer mine."

"No."

"Sig."

She started to get up, but he pulled her back down, arms wrapping around her tightly, like she was a life preserver in a storm. And she didn't struggle, she simply let him squeeze her, stroking the parts of his forearms she could reach, tilting her face to the side so he could plant hard kisses on her cheeks and eyelids and forehead. "Tell me you love me again."

"I love you." No hesitation. "It'll always be that way."

His arms wouldn't work after that, so he couldn't prevent her from crawling out of his lap and standing up. He watched through bleary eyes as she found her panties on the floor and tugged them on, leaving the bedroom in underwear and a bra. The phones were still ringing in the bathroom and he didn't want to know why. But he found out a second later when Chloe answered, her voice reaching him clear as a bell from the other room.

"Hi, Mom. What's up?" She paused. "I'm sorry we argued, too, but—" Chloe stopped. "You have news? Okay. What is it? Did the dresses arrive from Paris?"

Chloe must have tapped the icon for speakerphone, because

a tinny, muffled voice was echoing in the bathroom, joining Chloe's. Momentarily, anyway. Both voices grew closer as Chloe moved back into view, propping her hip on the bedroom doorway, her gaze fastening on Sig, phone aloft. A line between her brows. As if she'd just now started to sense the impending doom, along with him. As if she wished they'd just climbed into bed and shut out the world.

Too late.

Something told him it was way too late.

"Well. Harvey and I . . ." Sofia paused to laugh, a male baritone chuckle joining her in the background. One belonging to his father. "We're just a couple of impulsive kids these days. And the wedding planning was becoming so tedious, dear. I was stressed and Harvey *hates* seeing me stressed, so we decided to cut our losses . . . and *own it*. Just like you suggested, dear."

Chloe was starting to breathe faster. "I don't . . . I'm not following . . ."

"Are you sitting down?" Sofia didn't bother waiting for an answer. "We got married last night. In Las *Vegas*. I mean, it's so not my style, but I think that's why it was so *wonderful* . . ."

Sofia continued to chatter on without stopping for breath, but Sig couldn't hear anything else over the sound of his bones buckling. Loud booms in his head that might have been his pulse or maybe the world was really ending, but reality grew distorted and muffled, his stomach roiling to the point he thought he might get sick on the floor.

Their parents had gotten married.

It had happened.

He hadn't stopped the marriage from taking place.

Done deal. It was a done deal.

Meaning . . . Chloe was now his stepsister. She'd been his stepsister since last night.

Her fingers were white around the phone, her expression hollow. Dazed.

He needed to get up and comfort her, but his limbs weren't working.

"You got married in Vegas?" Chloe wheezed. "You're . . . married now. To Harvey."

"Yes! And oh dear, we really wanted to include you and Sig, but sometimes you have to go where the wind takes you. After your big, impulsive move to Boston, I knew you would understand." A prolonged pause. "Are you upset?"

Chloe's eyes were rapidly turning glassy. "Only that I forgot to see something like this coming," she muttered, swiping at her moist eyes. But she wasn't giving her mother the satisfaction of hearing it, even after the barb about being impulsive—and Sig had the presence of mind to be proud of Chloe for that. He wouldn't have been able to accomplish shit in his current state of destroyed. But Chloe? She squared her shoulders and forced a brave expression, even though he could see the positivity cost her a great deal. "We'll just have to throw a fabulous party so we can wear those dresses at least once."

"Now that is the spirit. Maybe we'll just have a second wedding! Though the planning will be a lot less nerve-racking this time, because I'm already married to the love of my life."

There was a loud kiss on the other end of the line—and the bomb that dropped in his stomach as a result propelled Sig off the floor. He dressed without feeling the fabric of the clothes in his hands, only bothering with his briefs and sweatpants. Who gave a fuck about a shirt?

"We certainly hope we can celebrate together in person soon! When will you have time to make a trip to Darien? Of course, we're in Vegas for a stint, but maybe next week?"

"I don't know," Chloe responded, beginning to lose that

tightly leashed control of her voice with just the slightest wobble. "I've hit a breakthrough in training and don't want to lose any ground."

"Oh." Now Sofia was the one trying to mask her emotions. "Well, we'll work something out. Harvey is trying to get a hold of Sig. You wouldn't happen to know how to track him down on a Saturday morning, would you?"

She closed her eyes, instead of meeting the look he sent her. Would she no longer make eye contact? Out of shame? The possibility caused an ice pick to lodge in his jugular. "No. He's been on the road. I haven't seen him."

"Ah, very well. Maybe he's just sleeping in with his ringer off." Then, quieter, "Don't worry, dear, we'll get in touch with him before the day is over."

Chloe shifted right to left, still with her eyes squeezed shut. "I need to get off the phone now. But . . . congratulations. Enjoy Vegas and we'll speak when you come back."

"Thank you, dear! Kisses! Bye!"

When the call ended, the silence that followed was thicker than anything he'd ever heard. No sound. No horns, no doors opening and closing in the hallway, no floorboards creaking overhead. Nothing. Maybe his senses could only handle the abundance of shock and nothing else.

I failed.

It's over.

Chloe was lost to him. Gone.

Had he done everything in his power to sway the outcome of this? Without committing a felony? He had, right? Maybe this moment had always been inevitable. But it was also in this moment that he realized how deep his feelings ran for Chloe, because he still wanted to physically drag her into bed and throw up his middle finger at the universe.

He also loved her way too much to ruin her life.

To cost her that first chair with the symphony.

To drag her into a worse tabloid scandal than he already had.

Furthermore, being her provider was no longer an option and she'd need her mother going forward. She'd need the safety net of Darien now more than ever.

And so, when she made a choked sound, ran into the bathroom, and slammed the door behind her, Sig strode blindly out of the apartment, down the stairs and out of the building, his heart deadening a little more in his chest with every step he took.

CHLOE EXISTED IN a disturbing state of calm.

If she moved too quickly or allowed what-ifs to start pouring in, she would crumble. So she didn't. She didn't walk too fast or slow, she stayed at a medium pace, one foot in front of the other. She nodded when necessary. Gave appropriate responses to the barista at the coffee shop, said hello to Raymond on her way out of the building, while heading to Grace's.

Being in a funnel of people sounded like the worst possible scenario when she was more fragile than a glass figurine, but she took the train, nonetheless. Maybe she was hoping to be distracted or get sucked into a cacophony of motion. Whatever the reason, she went. And she held it together, dammit. Even when a tourist asked Chloe for directions and she realized, *holy shit, I'm officially a Bostonian* and immediately she reached for her phone to text Sig her amusement over that fact, she managed to keep her cool.

No more tears.

They wouldn't solve anything.

But it was impossible to ignore the fact that something inside of her was irrevocably broken. A light had gone out inside of her and she knew in her bones, the electrical lines had been cut. In other words, that light would never shine again. Not this particular one.

The one that had lit the corner of the world she shared only with Sig.

Something must come of this. Something good has to happen now.

If one tragedy begets another, she would abandon her calm and start burning down cities, one by one. There had to be a purpose here. There had to be a reason she'd met her soulmate only to have him taken away. This had to mean something, right?

She raised her hand to knock on Grace's door with no memory of the journey to reach it. Nor did she remember speaking to the doorman downstairs. Wouldn't he have buzzed Grace to let her know Chloe had arrived?

Yes.

That's why the door is already open.

Ordering herself to get it together, Chloe pushed into the penthouse, looking around for her mentor while hanging up her coat, a movement that taxed her in ways it shouldn't. It strained her arms, her neck, her insides. *Just keep moving. Slow and steady.*

The sound of footsteps approached from the rear hallway— and they were accompanied by the rolling of wheels. A second later, Chloe caught sight of the source. Grace strode into view wheeling a Louis Vuitton suitcase, a metallic gold neck pillow hanging from the handle.

Grace raised an eyebrow. "Why aren't you practicing? Time is in short supply."

"Why do you have luggage? Where are you going?"

"Right now? Nowhere." She lowered the handle of the suitcase, dusting her hands off against each other. "Tonight, I might head to Amsterdam, though."

"*What?*"

"After my final performance, that is."

"*Final?*"

Grace sighed long and loud. "You're especially blonde today, Chloe."

"Oh, excuse me for being caught off guard." She gestured at the suitcase. "Is this your way of saying you're giving up on me? Because no. I don't accept that. I've been here every day playing my heart out. I've improved. I'm . . . *formidable*. You didn't even have notes for me yesterday and now you're just going to walk? So you can go live your European love triangle fantasy? No. I'm not leaving."

"European love triangle fantasy. That has a ring to it." Grace's eyes twinkled ever so slightly in a rare slip of humor. "But alas, I plan on shoving the cellist's bow up her ass and getting my girlfriend back. Which means, you're taking over my shift. So to speak."

Chloe's blood stopped flowing. "What do you mean?"

"I *mean* . . ." Grace drew out the word while rolling her eyes. "There's a reason I had no notes for you yesterday. Chloe, you are . . . indeed formidable. And you have more mettle than I originally gave you credit for. Because of that, I met with the board of advisers and head of conducting late last night. They'd already been informed of my impending departure and sent a flood of our session videos taken over the last two weeks. To say they are eager to add someone with your talent to the ensemble is an understatement." She took a pleased breath. "As of Monday, you're the new first chair harpist for BSO. Don't fuck it up. And for the love of God, do *not* fuck your stepbrother, either. Or I'll come back here and shove the *harp* up your butt. Don't assume it can't be done."

Chloe almost collapsed to the floor, but she couldn't name the emotion that made her feel weak everywhere at once. Relief that she'd found the silver lining to her heartbreak that she'd so desperately needed. Or sadness that it wasn't even close to enough to make her happy. Proud of herself, yes. Determined to do justice to the first chair position. Yes.

Happiness remained elusive, though. Maybe it always would.

"Thank you."

"You're welcome." Grace's brow furrowed slightly as she studied Chloe. "Are you okay?"

There was no simple answer to that, so Chloe went with an answer that she desperately hoped had some truth to it. "No. But I will be."

CHAPTER TWENTY-FIVE

Sig looked down at the contract in front of him and had the strangest urge to laugh. One of those ugly, high-pitched hysterical laughs that would make everyone around him uncomfortable. One he wouldn't be able to stop once he started. David, his agent, currently sat to his right, with dollar signs in his eyes. Reese, who'd just slid the contract in his direction, had her usual pin-straight spine and a satisfied expression on her face. She no doubt believed she'd just given him everything he'd ever wanted.

An eight-figure contract. Five more years on the team that had become his family.

A way to support himself. Ensure his mother continued to live comfortably.

It might as well be a plate of worms.

The irony of it all was like brass knuckles digging into his jugular. The thing that had been driving him to re-sign a hefty contract with the Bearcats . . . was now out of his reach. Chloe.

Chloe.

Goddamn it.

Any urge he'd had to laugh, humorless or not, sunk in his throat like a rusted anchor.

She was officially his stepsister. No more playing house, no more hope. No more . . . her.

That phone call from their parents in Vegas marked the last time he'd felt coherent. Since then he'd been sitting in his living room staring at a television he didn't bother turning on. Drinking more than was responsible, damn the upcoming meeting with Reese.

Burgess had come over at some point to speak with him, but Sig couldn't remember if he'd even formulated responses to his friend's questions. Everything was a blur.

This moment, though, was becoming crystal clear.

Like a diamond with edges sharp enough to score his skin.

"Until I sign this, I'm still a free agent," he heard himself say—and God, he sounded like death. "Isn't that right?"

David leaned back in his chair, cleared his throat. Steepling his fingers. As if he was reading Sig's energy, interpreting his desire to negotiate. But the dude wasn't interpreting shit. He didn't have any inkling of the hell in Sig's mind. No one did. No one knew he was on the verge of self-destructing. A walking time bomb.

Chloe.

"Yes, that's correct," said his agent. "We've had several organizations reach out to us."

Reese narrowed her eyes at Sig. "You told my father once upon a time that you never want to play anywhere but Boston. That you wanted to start and end your career as a Bearcat."

"I don't feel that strongly about it anymore."

I don't feel anything except pain.

"What changed?" Reese asked, though he could tell she already knew. Or, at the very least, who had caused his change of heart. "I knew approaching you about . . . the situation with Ms. Clifford was going to be delicate, but I hope you understand that I had no choice. And the issue has been resolved, as much as possible. The press appears to have dropped the story and we've blocked any mention of her on the message boards—"

"What issue are we discussing, exactly?" asked his agent. "Is there something I should be made aware of?"

Reese and Sig ignored him.

"How can you be so sure it has resolved itself in the space of two weeks?" Sig asked. Reese didn't have an answer for that. "More than likely, I've just been playing so well, you no longer have a choice but to lock me down, skeletons and all."

"There is a certain risk involved," Reese said, her words clipped.

"Not anymore." His vocal cords were charred. "Not anymore."

Reese knew his father had married Chloe's mother. He could see that knowledge in the tilt of her head, the wringing of her hands. She'd been keeping tabs on him—and really, he couldn't blame her. She had a lot to prove and didn't want to make a bad investment. *Was* he a good investment, though? A hockey player needed heart to sustain greatness and his had been ransacked.

David smoothed his tie, laughed a little uncomfortably. "Can someone fill me in on the subtext here?"

"I want to play somewhere else." He dropped the words like a bomb, but he was too numb to feel any of the reverberations. "Anywhere but Boston. I need to get out of here."

"Sig," Reese began, panic beginning to creep around the edges of her cool exterior. "We do not underestimate your incredible value to this organization and that *is* reflected in what we're offering—"

"Yeah? It's two weeks too late."

His agent was already on his feet, moving swiftly out of the room. "I'm going to make some calls."

"Get me out of the division, too. I don't want to come back here. I don't want any fucking reminders of . . . this place."

"Don't throw away what you've built here," Reese said quietly, closing her eyes, as if she knew she'd already lost, but didn't know how to quit. "We're offering you a uniform with a C on the shoulder. You're not going to waltz onto a new team and automatically get the patch."

"I probably *shouldn't* be anyone's captain right now."

She allowed some incredulity to bleed into her expression. "Don't you think some time is going to make it easier? Being without . . . her."

"Not a fucking chance." Reese couldn't fathom the devastation inside him. That was obvious. "I hope you never have to feel anything like this."

"I won't." She opened her mouth, closed it, sputtering slightly. "I wouldn't let myself."

Now, Sig did laugh. And it was as ugly as he'd imagined. "Good luck with that, Reese." There was nothing left to say, so he stood on sore legs. More so than usual, because he'd been pushing himself in practice like a demon, almost hoping for an injury. Some pain to distract him from the agony. But now, he was thankful to be healthy and uninjured. That was going to be his ticket out of here. Out of Boston.

Away from the only girl he'd ever love.

"You'll hear from my agent, I guess."

"Don't do this, Sig. With Burgess retiring . . ." She held her hands up, palms out, in an imploring gesture. "Don't gut the team."

He was already walking out the door, nothing but the howling of wind in his ears.

CHLOE DROPPED HER fingers from the harp, accepting murmurs of welcome and congratulations from the musicians exiting the stage around her. Her very first practice sessions had just ended, but there would be three more over the course of two days to prepare Chloe for her first performance with the orchestra. Yes, in two days' time, she would debut as the first chair harpist, right there on the stage in Symphony Hall.

Her mother would be there. With her new husband.

Front row, of course.

Truthfully, Chloe wasn't sure she wanted Sofia and Harvey there at all, but she didn't currently have the energy to stop them. Or construct the boundaries that had been a long time coming with her mother. She would be erecting them soon, though. Oh yes, that day had arrived. It arrived as soon as the realization sunk in that her mother had eloped to keep her from Sig. Because while Chloe had abhorred the idea of hurting Sofia, her mother hadn't given her the same consideration, had she? No.

So, yes. As soon as Chloe could think straight, she'd put some sturdy walls in place and keep them clearly marked.

Grace had gone to Amsterdam, leaving Chloe the keys to her penthouse, so she could continue to practice on the Harp of Destiny, which she'd come to think of as her own. Not that she'd be mentioning that to her mentor, who'd sent her a picture in the middle of the night of a cello case propped against her bedroom wall, a bra hanging from the neck. Had she reconciled with her girlfriend? It appeared so. And Chloe was happy for her, in a my-chest-is-hemorrhaging kind of way.

She was the last remaining musician on the stage now, silence settling over the rows of black leather seats. Her gaze tracked up to the chandeliers glittering above, the statues of angels and saints tucked into the ceiling's perimeter. It was a glorious place. The hall where she'd always dreamed of performing—and she'd gotten there through sheer force of will. She'd stopped ignoring the possibilities in front of her and reached. Taken hold.

For the life of her, though, she couldn't imagine her first performance without Sig watching from the audience. She couldn't really imagine any performance without him present, first, tenth, or five hundredth. As much as she sharpened her craft since beginning her mentorship with Grace, she couldn't deny there was something missing.

She played perfectly. Didn't miss a note.

But she played without a soul.

It had been sucked clean out of her body.

Living without it—without Sig—grew more difficult by the second. And she was coming very close to slipping. Taking the train to his neighborhood and showing up at his door. *One more time. I need you one more time.* Or . . . asking him to his face if he'd been serious about Sweden. Although wouldn't their reputations and identities follow them there? Wasn't Sweden more of a placeholder for the concept of running away together?

"I can't ask him to do that," she whispered.

And she couldn't. No more than she could disappoint Grace, the orchestra that had welcomed her with open arms. Herself. She'd earned this, hadn't she?

Chloe rose from the stool and wandered backstage, not registering a single step. She found her purse in her assigned cubby, smiling at a group of string musicians who were congregated nearby. One of them waved her over and she held up a finger, indicating she'd join them in a moment—a moment she used to scroll through her camera roll, tapping on her favorite picture of her and Sig together. She'd taken it the first time he showed her how to use the train. He was holding on to a pole, arms crossed, quizzing her on how to make transfers, which stop would take her to the conservatory. He looked so serious, so worried, yet also . . . confident in her, too. Determined to help.

This love was going to break her.

Maybe it already had. And she desperately needed to feel whole again.

So she slipped.

She texted him in a rush of heartbeats and lack of breath, unable to go cold turkey.

Would the world end if she just saw him in person from a safe distance?

> My first performance is Saturday night. I wouldn't be here without you. I don't want to be here without you. Will you come?

She hit Send and her knees almost buckled.

Just the act of reaching out to him was like being revived.

Would he answer? Would he come to the performance?

When her text hung there for a full two minutes without a response, she hurriedly tucked her phone into her purse, took a deep breath, and went to go join the group.

SIG COULDN'T BREATHE.

He cradled the phone in his hands like a glass slipper, reading and rereading the text from Chloe. Christ. She'd broken first, in terms of contacting each other, anyway. He'd driven past her apartment building a dozen times since the day of the bombshell phone call from Sofia. Not to mention, he'd called the landlord every morning to make sure she'd come home safely after walking Pierre. He'd barely managed not to call or text or show up at her door, as if he needed any more proof he should leave Boston ASAP.

His instinct was to reply to her text immediately.

To say, *I'll be there. Of course, I'll be there.*

But he had a meeting in Los Angeles on Saturday. With a potential new team.

Sig set the phone aside on his coffee table and started to pace.

Dug his knuckles into his eye sockets as deeply as they would go without blinding him.

What the fuck am I going to do?

Go to Los Angeles. Save himself. Save her. She'd been strong enough to start the process of separating them, now she needed him to take the baton. Do what needed to be done. He couldn't live this close to her and not be with her. His heart was a constant eruption of pain the longer this went on. Being in the same town as her only made it harder.

Sig snatched up his phone and typed the words.

I'll be in LA meeting with a new team. I'm sorry.

He sent the message, felt his chest rip open, and immediately tried to unsend the text, no idea why or what it would accomplish. Only that he was going to die if he didn't give Chloe what she needed. Knowing the news would gut her, as much as it gutted him, was like a recurring blow to his solar plexus. But the deal was sealed. No unsending.

Sig fell onto his couch, head in his hands. Fingers ripping at his hair.

Go. He needed to go now before he went to see Chloe.

Get to LA. Sign a fucking contract. Play hockey until his body gave out.

That was all he could do now.

When an email alert popped up on the screen of his phone, signaling that he had a new message from his private investigator, he deleted the notification without looking, deciding he'd had more than enough irony for one lifetime.

CHAPTER TWENTY-SIX

Sig stood at the bottom of the narrow metal stairs, looking up into the interior of the private plane. He couldn't feel the duffel bag thrown over his shoulder or the nighttime breeze tousling his hair. His reflection in the hand railing was his only clue he'd made it to the airfield where LA had sent the VIP treatment. He'd slowly lost feeling everywhere. But he needed to get up the stairs, into the plane, so it could take off and fly him to the other side of the country. That's what was happening. No stopping now. *Go.*

Grinding his molars together, Sig forced himself to ascend, one step at a time, ignoring the phone that vibrated nonstop in the front pocket of his jeans. Burgess had been calling him all day, no doubt wanting to talk him out of the decision he intended to make. Reese had called, as well, asking him once again to reconsider. Hell, even Mailer and Corrigan were on his ass, but they didn't understand what it was like to love someone to the point of pain and give her up. God willing, they never would.

Sig collapsed into the first seat, staring blankly ahead.

His phone continued to buzz, carrying on for several minutes until he sighed, leaned back, and extricated the device from his pocket. Instead of Burgess, Reese, or one of the Rookies calling him, however, it was the private investigator.

"Jesus. What the . . ." Sig shook his head. Why was the guy still calling? He'd sent the final payment. What more did the man want from him? At this point, the fact that he'd hired a PI felt ridiculous. He'd never really had a chance of success, had he?

Maybe he owed the man a verbal goodbye. At the very least.

It hurt to think, to talk, so he'd avoided speaking to virtually everyone for the last few days, but he cursed and answered now, hoping to get the conversation over in under a minute. "Hey, Niko. Sorry I've been MIA, but I'm just about to take off on a flight—"

"Shit, man. You had me worried."

Sig frowned. That was a little extreme, wasn't it?

Maybe not. Maybe everyone in his life should be concerned about him, considering he felt like a bleeding chunk was missing from his chest. "I'm good," he lied. "Thanks for—"

"I shouldn't have sent that file over without preparing you first. Some people don't take that kind of news very well. It's upsetting, you know?"

What in God's name was Niko talking about?

"To be honest, I didn't bother looking at the file. My father ended up marrying Sofia Clifford in Vegas last week, so . . . not much point in trying to fight it now."

There was an extended silence on the other end. "You didn't look at the file?"

Beneath Sig, the plane engine started with a brief growl that settled into a hum.

"Nah, didn't look. And it's not that I don't appreciate your hard work. I do—"

"I think you should look."

Irritation crawled up the back of Sig's neck. Why wasn't the private investigator taking the hint? Hope had withered and died on the floor of Chloe's apartment and reigniting that flame was fucking cruel. "There's nothing it could say that would make a difference."

"Don't be so sure," Niko said, with a humorless laugh. "Look, I'm not going to force you to do anything you don't want to do. If this is where we part ways, so be it. I appreciate the prompt payment. Good luck."

"Thanks," Sig muttered, watching the screen as the call disengaged.

"We'll begin taxiing in five minutes," called the pilot from the front of the plane.

Distracted, Sig nodded . . . and looked back down at his phone, his curiosity multiplying by the second. What important revelation could possibly be in that file?

After another few seconds of hesitation, he tapped his email icon and scrolled down, down, past all the correspondence with LA, ads, subscription renewal alerts, until he landed on the message from Niko. He opened it, went to the attached PDF, and started reading.

While attempting to access marriage and divorce records with the county clerk of Hennepin County, a paternity test was discovered. At the behest of the Gauthier family, Harvey Lerner was asked, via the courts, to take the test that ultimately resulted in a false result.

It was determined that Harvey Lerner is not the paternal father of Sig Gauthier.

The words bled together. His pulse pumped in his ears.

That couldn't be right. That couldn't be . . .

But it made so much sense. His mother's resentment, her lack of communication with her family, Harvey leaving them so abruptly. *My God. Oh my God.*

If he wasn't Harvey's son, wasn't his blood relative . . .

Then the man married to Chloe's mother wasn't his real father. Not even his stepfather. Nothing.

There was no relation whatsoever.

Meaning . . .

Chloe wasn't his stepsister.

They weren't related at all. Not by marriage. Not in any way.

The revelation was too good to be true, though. He needed more than one source to confirm, before he ran with it. Otherwise he'd open up himself and Chloe to another disappointment. One that might very well kill them this time around.

Hands shaking, he called his mother, barely able to speak when she answered. "Rosie? Mom." Until she made a sound at his use of the word "mom," until that very moment, the implication of this news where his mother was concerned didn't occur to him. Now, the shock jolted him almost violently in his seat, his head shaking no of its own volition. She'd known. She'd held the key to his prison cell this entire time and hadn't offered it to him. "Rosie."

"Yes, Sig?" Silence passed. "Is something the matter?"

"He's not my father," Sig managed, lips parched. "Harvey. He's not my dad. Is that the truth? Yes or no?"

He held his breath.

"Sig, I . . ." Something toppled over in the background. "Why would you a-ask—"

Anger and something else—betrayal, possibly, yes—locked around his windpipe, causing the breath he'd been holding to burst out of him. "Don't lie to me, please. Give me a straight answer, just this once. This . . . God, if this is true, if Harvey isn't my father, not knowing the truth could have kept me from her. I could have left her for no reason, don't you *see* that?"

Her confusion was palpable even through the phone. "Who, Sig? Who are you talking about?"

"*Chloe.*" Sure, he'd never told his mother about Chloe. He'd locked the magic of her up tight, refusing to share until he knew for sure they were forever. But wanting to know the truth about his parentage should have been enough. No, it *was* enough.

"Who is my father, Rosie? I want the truth now. Now, okay? No more games."

Several moments swam past, each of them a blur. "Bobby Prince." Her exhale spoke of relief tinged with a telling dose of shame. "The man I was seeing before Harvey swooped back in . . . I— Oh my God. I'm very sorry, Sig. I should have told you. Old habits die hard and I was brought up to keep secrets, avoid anything that could poison the family name. And there was . . . more. There's more." Her voice fell to a whisper. "I just wanted to prove we didn't need any of them. We didn't."

Sig struggled to locate his compassion—and miraculously, he did, though it was buried deep beneath a wealth of anger and relief and urgency. Maybe because his mother's quest to make it alone reminded him of Chloe's journey. Or maybe staying mad wasn't possible when life had just become worth living again.

He and Chloe could be together. There wasn't anything stopping them.

Nothing but this flight to Los Angeles. Signing with another team.

He gulped in a shuddering breath, filling his lungs completely for the first time in a full minute. Maybe days. "Thank you for finally telling me the truth, Rosie. But right now, I have somewhere to be. I'll call you another time." He swallowed hard. "And I'll tell you about her."

"I'll look forward to it," she said in a weepy voice.

Sig hung up and stood on shaky legs, lurching forward to catch himself on the partition in front of him, the relief so wild and potent, it was hitting him in startling waves, knocking the air out of him over and over and over again. "Stop." He raised his thousand-pound arm, waving at the young woman who was in the process of closing the airplane door. "Stop, I'm getting off. I have to go. Now."

"I . . . what?" she sputtered. "Is something wrong?"

No. Something was finally right.

Christ. Chloe's performance was tonight and he wasn't there. But he'd get there. He'd fucking be there, like she'd asked. And afterward, he'd hold her and inform her he'd never let her go. Not ever. The misery and madness were over.

It seemed to take a million years for the steps to be lowered once again, but as soon as they touched the tarmac, Sig raced to the bottom and sprinted for the charter office, phone in one hand, bag in the other. He didn't bother calling an Uber, wasn't even sure he could manage to think critically enough for that, because the joy was an explosion inside of him, sending his muscles into bouts of weakness, followed by bursts of strength. And he couldn't think, he just ran, throwing himself into the back of a waiting cab once he exited the building.

"Symphony Hall, please," he said raggedly.

Satisfied that the driver was picking up on the urgency in his tone, based on the way the man hit the gas, Sig looked down at his phone once again and dialed, not even bothering to catch his breath.

"Reese?" Sig slumped back against the leather seat, unashamed of the moisture blurring his vision. "Reese, it's Sig. I'm going to forward you an email. It's from a private investigator. Read the attachment." He could barely operate his phone, his hands were shaking so violently, so he blew a heavy breath up at the ceiling, tried again and finally succeeded. "If that's enough for you, if the organization will accept this information and use it to have my back if anyone comes for me or Chloe, then I'll stay in Boston."

Sig didn't waste time exhaling with relief when the white pillars of Symphony Hall came into view. The taxi hadn't even reached a full stop before he dove onto the sidewalk, taking the concrete steps two at a time. Whether or not he'd planned on attending tonight, Chloe would have left him a ticket at the box office. He didn't even question that—their loyalty to each other was an unwavering fact—and the small ticket window was where he headed as soon as he cleared the entrance . . .

But he stopped in his tracks before he could reach it.

Harvey and Sofia stood between Sig and will call.

They were in a small group of people, Sofia holding out her diamond-bedecked hand for everyone to admire. An hour ago, that sight might have gutted Sig. Not now. Right there, in that moment, he could only think *I'm going to buy one twice as big for my girl.*

As if he'd made that declaration out loud, Harvey turned partially and locked eyes with Sig over the heads of the milling crowd. The older man didn't appear surprised to see him, but whatever he read in Sig's expression caused Harvey's eyes to narrow. With a gentle pat of his new wife's shoulder, he began cutting through the crowd toward Sig.

Sig waited, not willing to take a single step to meet the other man halfway.

Not now. Maybe not ever again.

At the moment, he didn't feel forgiving, but something in the back of his mind told him he was on the verge of so much happiness that holding grudges wasn't in his future.

"Son," Harvey said, by way of greeting, flicking a glance at Sig's attire. "Did you just come from practice—"

"Son?" Sig could feel his pulse hammering in his neck. "Care to rephrase that?"

Harvey rocked back on his heels. Took a long pull of the champagne in his hand. "Your mother finally told you the truth."

They'd both known. Son of a bitch. It took everything inside of Sig to suppress the fresh wave of rage. "I had to find out for myself first," Sig snapped.

"The private investigator?" Harvey made a sound. "He must be good."

"Answer my questions, please. Don't draw this out any more than you already have." Chloe was in the building. He just needed to get to where she was. The delay burned. "Did you find out you weren't my real father? Is that why you really left?"

"It was a complicated time—"

"Answers. Now."

"Christ. Fine." Harvey lost some of the starch in his spine, a hint of the bravado in his expression and for a handful of seconds, Sig could almost picture the man thirty years younger. "I was going to stick around, Sig. I was going to be your dad. You have to believe me on that. I spent that entire pregnancy at your mother's side. I was there in the delivery room. And believe me, her parents didn't want me there. I was not of their ilk, you see. But I was determined to raise you." He paused to take the final swallow of his champagne. "They couldn't have been more gleeful when the paternity test determined you belonged to your mother's on again, off again boyfriend, Bobby Prince, the rich kid they'd handpicked for her."

Sig forced his features to remain schooled at the utterance of his real father's name for the second time in an hour. Someday, with Chloe at his side, he'd track down Bobby Prince. He wouldn't get his hopes up for a tearful meeting or a meaningful relationship. At the very least he'd hope for clarity, closure. A chance to set the record straight. But he had a long way to go before he crossed that bridge. Knowing he'd cross it with Chloe as his wife made it a lot less daunting.

"Once those test results came back," Harvey continued, "they

294 • TESSA BAILEY

assumed your mother would drop me, go back to Bobby so you could be raised by your rightful father, but . . ." A fond smile danced reluctantly across his mouth. "Your mother was too stubborn for that. I'd forgiven her and we were determined to make it on our own. The three of us."

Sig could feel it. He was about to find the missing piece he'd been searching for since he'd been old enough to wonder why he didn't have a father. "What happened?"

Harvey's collar moved with the force of his swallow. "Her parents offered me money. A lot of it, Sig. Enough to support me my entire life." He looked Sig in the eye. "All I had to do was leave."

Sig's chest dipped with an inhale. "They bribed you."

"And I took it. I'm sorry, but I took it. I left."

"So you didn't steal anything. It was *given* to you."

Harvey nodded. "Again, they incorrectly assumed that your mother would return home like an obedient daughter, marry the right man, live the life they were organizing for her. But . . . she didn't. I only found out later through mutual friends that she'd given her parents the proverbial finger and left to raise you as a single mother. I was proud of her. And I was ashamed that I'd been the weak one. I regret it every day."

Sig stood stock-still, absorbing the events that had shaped his young life. He wanted to be angry at these adults for being selfish, rash. But again, he couldn't help but admire his mother for striking out on her own. Not giving anyone power over her. Hanging on to her free will with both hands, even though it was hard.

"Rosie's got her pride, that woman. You get that from her." The lights were dimming in the lobby, signaling that the performance was about to start. Briefly, Harvey looked down at the carpeted floor, then back at Sig. "When you reached out to me eleven years ago, I wanted to tell you everything. The truth. You deserved that. I'd signed a nondisclosure in order to receive the funds . . . but if I'm being totally honest, the guilt was still with me. I thought I could make up for leaving. I'm sorry I allowed the lie to continue, Sig."

Sig didn't know how to respond, so he didn't.

He needed time to sit with the news, the truth.

And he wanted to do all of that with Chloe.

"Does Sofia know you're not my father?"

Harvey hung his head. "No, but I'll tell her."

"Good. Do it soon. I'm not hiding what I have with Chloe anymore," Sig said, his voice rusted. "I need to be in there when the show starts. Excuse me—"

"I hope we can still . . . have some kind of relationship. Maybe that's unrealistic, considering it was tentative *before* I met Sofia and now—"

"You were going to let me lose Chloe so you wouldn't have to expose your shame. So you wouldn't have to admit you'd been lying to me for over a decade."

Harvey reddened slightly. "What do you want me to say? What *can* I say?"

"Say you and Sofia won't get in the way of what I have with Chloe anymore. Believe me, I don't care if I speak to either of you for the foreseeable future, possibly ever, but Chloe is a better person than me. And a lot more forgiving."

"I won't stand in your way." Perhaps symbolically, Harvey stepped aside, no longer blocking Sig's path to the will call window. "I'll do what I can with my wife."

Those two words, "my wife," and the possibility of using them in reference to Chloe someday soon, made it impossible for Sig to say anything else. Only move toward the window at a fast clip while the rest of the crowd filed into the auditorium, his heart locked in his throat.

I'm coming, Chlo.
I'm coming.

"GOOD LUCK TONIGHT," whispered one of the violinists as she passed, getting in position a few yards away, one face among a sea of talented bodies, poised to play their instruments.

"Thank you," Chloe said softly, going back to looking blindly at her harp.

Static snapped in her fingertips, urging her to touch the strings, but the crushing weight on her chest kept both arms stationary at her side. She'd play. She'd get through this. He wouldn't be there, but she'd live through the night and that was the best she could hope for.

On the other side of the velvet curtain, voices blended together and silenced, followed by a pleasant voice introducing the symphony—and then the curtain was gone and Chloe moved on autopilot, pushing her posture one notch higher into perfection, fingers lifting to the strings, head turning to face the conductor. To wait for the cues that would guide them all through the performance, though they knew it by heart.

She'd been reckless, given her fragile mental state, to leave that ticket at will call for Sig. Her heart wouldn't let her do anything different, however. She'd been compelled by some deep reserve of hope that hadn't quite been erased yet. And now, despite the fact that she'd been told not to look out at the audience, to never take her attention off the instrument and her conductor, Chloe's gaze ticked left, seeking out the seat she'd reserved.

Just in case.

Just . . .

Sig slid into the open spot.

Chloe's heart barreled up into her throat, beating, beating. Bright splotches of light temporarily blinded her. There he was. He'd come. A broad-shouldered badass among regular citizens. He was wearing jeans and a Bearcats hoodie and for some reason that made her want to burst into noisy, appreciative tears. Sig looked at her hard, his chest inflating, releasing, before cupping a hand over his mouth, like he was overcome.

Of course, he was. They both were, just being in the same room together.

Chloe gulped down a breath and tried to focus.

Focus.

And she did, because her soul had returned. He was right there, in the room.

Throughout the course of the next ninety minutes, she played every note for him, delivering them with imaginary kisses, closing her eyes, and reliving, relishing, memorizing every moment of their acquaintance from start to finish, even the hard parts. She let them bleed into her performance, her fingers moving over the strings unbidden.

When it ended, she stood up and bowed with the rest of her company, her skin turning clammy and cold when she found Sig's chair empty. Had he left? When?

As soon as the curtain came down, she walked offstage in a trance, surrounded by her fellow musicians, but not absorbing any of their praise or congratulations, barely aware of her own voice as she returned those compliments. She just needed to get somewhere quiet so she could think and cry and bolster herself for the next day. And the day after that.

There was a costuming room in the depths of the backstage area that no member of the ensemble used, because musicians came and went in the same clothing—and she moved toward it now, closing herself inside the cool darkness, falling back against the door and pressing her palms to the surface. Leaning her head back and inhaling, exhaling.

A knock sounded behind Chloe and her inclination was to ignore it.

To take her moment.

But the knock grew more insistent. Had someone left their purse in the room and needed to retrieve it? Why was this the one time someone needed access?

"Sorry," she said, forcing her wobbly voice to firm, while turning around and opening the door. "I was just taking a second . . ."

Sig.

Sig was there. Holding a bouquet of lipstick pink roses.

Her heart went into a sprint.

"Hi," she whispered.

"Hi." His gaze covered every inch of her face. "I couldn't stand the idea of not having flowers after watching you be so incredible up there."

"Thank you."

He shook his head slowly. "I wish I could watch you do it another ten thousand times."

"But you can't," she finished for him. "I know."

"I can, actually. And I will. Do you think they'll give me the same seat every time? It's the perfect angle to watch your lips move with the notes."

Confusion clashed with her joyfulness over seeing him. "I don't understand."

Briefly, Sig looked over his shoulder to find the crowd thinning backstage. Then he let the roses drop to his side and shuffled her forward, into the room, clicking it shut behind them. The sudden muffling of sound, the dimness of the room was so intimate, she felt a sob well in her chest. "We can't keep doing this." She was already twisting her fingers in the collar of his hoodie. "We're setting ourselves back—"

"Chloe." Without looking, he set the roses on a nearby vanity, quickly taking her face in his hands. "The private investigator I hired . . . he sent me a report days ago and I didn't think there was any point in looking at it, but, Jesus, there was. He caught me right before I took off for LA. I almost . . . oh God, I almost signed with another team. Away from you."

It took him several moments to keep going.

"Remember I told you my mother's family never approved of Harvey? It turns out, they paid him off to leave us. They bribed him. He took it because he wanted the money, yeah, but there was more. A paternity test done when I was born. I guess this is why it has been so hard for my mother to talk about what happened back then, but . . ." He choked on a laugh, before sobering. Stroking her cheekbones with his thumbs. "Chloe, Harvey isn't my father. He isn't even related to me by marriage, Chlo. We can be together."

"But . . ." The world had turned into a choppy ocean beneath her feet, wind whooshing in her ears. No. No . . . what? Was she imagining this? "Really? *Really?*"

"Cleared it with the team. I can't imagine you'll have any problems with the symphony . . ." A line formed between his brows. "If you want to wait until you speak to them, until you know for sure they won't—"

"No waiting. No." She was already midlaunch, her body colliding with Sig's so hard, his back slammed into the door. He was laughing, though. They were both laughing as they embraced, his powerful arms lifting her off the floor and squeezing tight as a vise, and it was the most beautiful sound she'd ever heard in her life. There were no reservations, their joy totally unfettered. And when his mouth found hers and the hunger came roaring in, they did nothing to stop it. They couldn't.

Sig reversed their positions, flattening Chloe to the door, his hands already rucking up her dress to her waist, unzipping his jeans while he looked her right in the eye, letting her see the love that ran wild there. Love that was no longer hesitant or worried or penned in. It would grow until it took up every corner of the universe.

His eyes slid closed and squeezed, squeezed so tight, his mouth slanting over Chloe's in a slow, thorough kiss that communicated promises and lifetimes together. "We could wait until I get you home," he rasped, pressing his hard flesh to the swath of cotton between her legs, finding her entrance through the thin barrier and rubbing. "We have forever now."

"I told you," she murmured, kissing his cheeks, his jaw, his lips, encircling his hips with her thighs. "No more waiting. No more. I love you too much. I love you *so much*."

"I love you, too. *I love you*," he said hoarsely, his mouth open and panting against hers as he jerked her panties aside and thrust home, his hand raising and cupping over her lips to trap the ensuing gasp and whimper. "Shh. Everything is okay now, Chlo." His voice vibrated with intensity. "We found a way. The bad is behind us."

Her neck lost power as he rocked into her roughly, tenderly, her chest almost in pain from the sheer amount of bliss that had been unlocked. "Wake up with me tomorrow morning. Wake up with me every morning."

He rolled their foreheads together, holding himself deep. So deep, she could feel him, and the fervent promise that followed, everywhere. All over. "Until my last sunrise, dream girl."

EPILOGUE

Five Years Later

Sig walked into the house he shared with Chloe in Jamaica Plain, a green suburb of Boston, and set down his equipment bag with a thud. His eyes closed automatically when he heard the harp notes drifting down the stairs, taking a moment to savor the fact that he was coming home to his best friend. And knowing without an iota of uncertainty that she would be equally eager to see him. There was something about a man believing his soulmate was out of reach forever that made him profoundly and eternally grateful to marry her. That gratitude seemed to triple every time he went on the road and returned to her arms.

With a knot in his throat, Sig started up the stairs, looking at the pictures that hung on the wall as he went. Their wedding day, which had taken place in Sofia's backyard, overlooking the Sound, the country club where they met in the distance. After he'd uncovered the truth about his paternity, there had been a few months of friction between the two couples. Not to mention, the tension between Sig and his mother. After all, either one of them could have put Sig and Chloe out of their misery with a single revelation about his paternity. And Sofia . . . well, she was Sofia and wasn't changing any time soon. Ultimately, Sig was too fucking happy to be with Chloe to hold a grudge and his wife felt the same, although she'd created some healthy boundaries with

Sofia and didn't feel guilty about redefining them when necessary. Just one of the million reasons Sig was the proudest husband on the planet.

They chose the dates they visited Darien.

Chloe refused to let her mother so much as pay for a muffin.

And when Sofia referred to Chloe as impulsive now, she responded with *thank you, that impulsiveness has served me well.*

Watching Chloe thrive so drastically that Sofia had no choice but to grudgingly embrace her daughter's independence and new strength of spirit? Priceless.

Sig would never be close with Harvey, but the reconciliation between him and the man he'd once believed to be his father had allowed for visits to Darien, so Chloe could see her mother—and being able to fulfill her wishes made swallowing his pride a no-brainer. He'd even let Harvey drag him to the country club for a round of golf once or twice.

Golf. It wasn't so bad, after all. As an added bonus, he got to think back to the night he'd met the love of his life on that very same grass. A night he'd remember in vivid detail until his very last breath.

Beside the picture of him lifting Chloe's veil and kissing her, there was one of him standing shoulder to shoulder with Bobby Prince, his unsuspecting real father, a carpenter who now lived in Maine and ran an Adirondack chair design company with his two boisterous brothers. Meaning, Sig had uncles, cousins. Loud ones. A family that wanted to know him. Fortunately or unfortunately, they also fucking loved hockey and were constantly hitting him up for Bearcats tickets so they could come cheer him on beside Chloe . . . who'd gone back to wearing her pink jersey with pride, of course.

In another picture, Sig held the Stanley Cup over his head, roaring over the victory in front of a sold-out crowd—including

Bobby, who applauded from the family section. A dream fulfilled in a way that was better than he could have imagined. For both of them. He'd gained a father, and Bobby, who'd never been made aware of the paternity test results thirty years earlier, was proud to call Sig his son. And give him unsolicited hockey advice.

Rosie still came to her one annual game, though she made sure it was not a game Bobby would be attending, and both of his parents seemed comfortable leaving their acquaintance in the past where it belonged. Sig thought they were being dramatic and stubborn, but Chloe liked to point out that Sig's stubbornness had come from somewhere—and if he hadn't been stubborn, he never would have hired that private investigator.

To her, that trait was something to be thankful for.

Sig? He was just thankful for Chloe.

Beside the treasured snapshot of him lifting the Cup was a photo of Chloe the morning she'd handcuffed herself to his truck after catching him on the phone with a dealership. And finally, a snap of their annual baseball game in the park, organized by Corrigan and Skylar, whose story was nearly as fraught as Sig and Chloe's.

Nearly.

Perhaps it depended on who you asked.

A soft sigh wove its way through the gentle harp notes and Sig took the stairs faster, needing badly to see his wife. Hold her in his arms. He knew from experience that the aches and pains leftover from the games he'd just played on the road would melt away as soon as he was kissing her. She was the ultimate adrenaline hit and she only got more potent, more extraordinary over time. God, the world would have been a dark place without her.

Quietly, Sig turned the corner into their bedroom, a grin spreading wide across his mouth when he saw Chloe was engaging in her favorite pastime.

Naked harp playing.

The sunlight poured in through the window and highlighted the gilded instrument, the leafy design inlaid along the polished wood. It had taken a full year of negotiations, but he'd finally convinced Grace to sell him Chloe's favorite harp. He'd paid dearly for the thing—and damn, it was worth every single penny to watch the enjoyment wash over Chloe's features every time she sat down in front of the instrument.

"It reminds me of our story," she'd said to him once. "It reminds me I was without you once. As I play the songs, you come back to me. Over and over. It's like joy on repeat."

How could Sig *not* buy the harp after hearing that?

Although, unlike Chloe, he did not like to think of a time when they weren't together. A time when he'd almost left Boston to avoid perpetual heartbreak. He was more than happy to leave that pain in the past . . . and focus on the present.

And the future.

The curve of Chloe's pregnant stomach came into view and he swallowed hard, winded by the sudden acceleration of his heart. What on earth had he done to deserve coming home to an angel playing the harp in his bedroom, their future son sleeping in her belly?

Unable to stand another minute without touching her, Sig kicked off the boots he'd forgotten to take off downstairs and padded across the carpet in his socks, approaching from the side so he wouldn't startle her. To his surprise, though, she didn't jolt or gasp when he came into view. She simply looked up at him and smiled.

"I knew you were there."

His heart boomed being this close to his soft, sexy wife, all covered in sunshine. Lord. It was impossible to prepare himself for this level of perfection. "Did you?" he asked, thickly.

"I always know." She graced the air with a few languid notes. "The house is happier when you're in it. It turns into a home."

"What about you? Are you happier when I'm home?" Sig asked, already knowing the answer, but craving the feeling of hearing Chloe say it out loud.

"Infinitely. I'm happy when I know you're out doing what you love." A few wistful notes, before she dropped her fingers from the strings and turned on the padded stool. "But I always want you here with me afterward. And every moment in between."

He knelt in front of her, resting the side of his face in her lap. Inhaling her unique scent. "I'm here now, thank God."

"I know." There was a smile in her voice as she ran her talented fingers through his hair. "Your son knows, too. He's kicking."

Sig's head came up so fast, he felt dizzy. "He's . . . what?"

Chloe's laugh rang out. "Feel for yourself."

Two hundred and thirteen career goals, a Stanley Cup, and the captain patch on his jersey . . . and none of it compared to gently placing his palms on his wife's belly and feeling life moving on the other side.

What *did* compare?

Looking up into the damp eyes of the woman he loved beyond reason and knowing they had a million more adventures to come. To share. Together, always.

ABOUT THE AUTHOR

#1 *New York Times* bestselling author **Tessa Bailey** can solve all problems except for her own, so she focuses those efforts on stubborn, fictional blue-collar men and loyal, lovable heroines. She lives on Long Island avoiding the sun and social interactions, then wonders why no one has called. Dubbed the "Michelangelo of dirty talk" by *Entertainment Weekly*, Tessa writes with spice, spirit, swoon, and a guaranteed happily ever after.

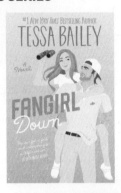

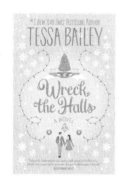  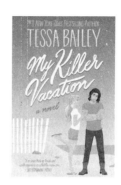
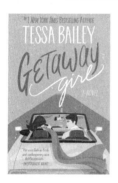 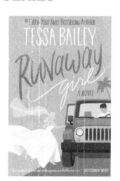
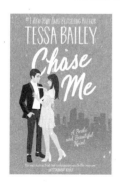  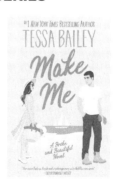